I0722648

The Soul's Awakening

THE SOUL'S AWAKENING

The Q'Zam'Ta Trilogy, Book One

Shireen Anne Jeejeebhoy

Copyright © 2024 Shireen Anne Jeejeebhoy

All rights reserved.

No part of this publication may be reproduced, stored in a retrieval system or transmitted, in any form or by any means, electronic, mechanical, recording or otherwise (except brief passages for purposes of review) without the prior permission of the author or a licence from The Canadian Copyright Licensing Agency (Access Copyright). For an Access Copyright licence, visit www.accesscopyright.ca or call toll free to 1-800-893-5777.

Cover Art by RLSather on SelfPubCovers.com at https://selfpubbookcovers.com/RLSather

Cover Text Design by Shireen Anne Jeejeebhoy

Cover, design elements, and text fonts Scriptina under Apostrophic Laboratories Freeware License and NovaSquare and Cormorant under SIL Open Font License.

WC Rhesus Dingbats by WC Fonts under Creative Commons Attribution-No Derivative Works v3.00.

Licence Notes, Print Edition:

This book is licenced for your personal enjoyment only. This book may not be resold or given away to other people. If you would like to share this book with another person, please purchase an additional copy for each recipient. If you're reading this book and did not purchase it, or it was not purchased for your use only, then please return and purchase your own copy. Do not use or reproduce any part of this book to train artificial intelligence (AI) technology and systems. Thank you for respecting the hard work of this author.

Paperback First Edition 2024.

ISBN-13: 978-1-7386788-4-6

ADDITIONAL TITLES BY SHIREEN (ANNE) JEEJEEBHOY

Lifeliner: The Judy Taylor Story

The Job Sessions: Why Do The Innocent Suffer?

She

Eleven Shorts +1

Concussion Is Brain Injury

Aban's Accension

Time and Space

Concussion Is Brain Injury:
Treating the Neurons and Me

Louise and The Men of Transit

Brain Injury, Trauma, and Grief:
How to Heal When You Are Alone

ONLINE PRESENCE

Bluesky: bsky.app/profile/shireenj.bsky.social

Website: jeejeebhoy.ca

Psychology Today **Blog**: psychologytoday.com/ca/blog/concussion-is-brain-injury

Brain Injury Information: concussionisbraininjury.com

My Books: concussionisbraininjury.ca

Books2Read Profile:
https://books2read.com/ap/RJ6305/Shireen-Jeejeebhoy

Mind Explorer on Substack:
https://shireenjeejeebhoy.substack.com

Flickr: flickr.com/photos/pario/

LinkedIn: Shireen Jeejeebhoy

Patreon: Shireen Jeejeebhoy

PRAISE

"Executed with grace, compassion, wit, and vulnerability, this is an innovative and potentially life-changing read."
– *SPR on **Brain Injury, Trauma, and Grief***

"Jeejeebhoy is a passionate advocate for patients, and a sympathetic narrator."
– *SPR on **Concussion Is Brain Injury: Treating the Neurons and Me***

"Put simply this is the best urban fantasy story that I have ever read period."
– *Shane Porteous, Writer, gives **She** 5 stars on Smashwords*

"A compelling story....Reading [**Lifeliner**] will make you laugh, smile, cringe, cry and most importantly, think."
– *Diana Rohini LaVigne, Online Editor, Indian Life & Style Magazine*

"What an amazing journey into the future!"
– *Ana on **Time and Space** on Goodreads*

"An amazing read, I think it's one of those stories that come to you when u need most! Thank you 😊 "
– *LeihaLeFae on **Aban's Accension** on Wattpad*

"A transformative and inspiring story. Thank you."
– *highker on **Aban's Accension** on Wattpad*

*For Ann and Frank Benoit, who encouraged and believed
in me and my books.*

Chapter One

DEATH

At the moment of my death, my life began.

I was upset. Angry. Horrified.

And confused.

Looking back to that moment in the Solar Age, I found the voices the most unsettling, certain my dying brain had created them and not daring to ask who they were.

I ran an accounting firm, my own one-woman office. I interacted with clients only when needed, saw my one-year-older sister as little as possible, attended my cardiologist appointments when required, and knew no one else. I didn't need anyone else. My existence had ended because I'd met a doctor who understood me. *Why then, voices?*

"Why is she surprised?"

Chimes, like tiny silver bells, slivered the air.

"You know why, Blair."

"I know, I know, Bailey. I'm frustrated with her decision."

"We're not here to decide for her."

"I know, I know."

I regained consciousness on the ceiling, hearing these two voices intermingled with chimes, as I spied below me my physical self lying in the bed under the blanket and sheet, the blanket's mounds outlining my legs lying straight together, my hands clasped over each other on my stomach while my head stuck out, denting the pillow, eyes closed, reminding me of a guillotined head. The face, my face, reflected peace. So still. I'd never seen such an unmoving face before. I squinted. *That's what death looks like.*

I smiled.

My last memory was peace.

The peace of drifting away into the perfect sleep.

Dr. Veritas had promised me that the sleep he prescribed his patients brought them only peace. It ended change's upheaval. It stopped having to explore a different way of living.

I'd liked my life the way I'd arranged it. I wanted it to continue in the familiar, predictable pattern of breakfast, work, news, dinner, and TV dramas. Toast, jam, orange juice, and breakfast tea to start my morning; followed by three hours of concentrated working on my clients' accounts; a lunch of tomato soup, omelette, and Red Rose tea to refuel; finishing my work day with four hours of client calls, emails, and resolving problems that had festered; suppertime news while I heated dinner—each night of the week had its standard fare—and, with dishes washed, three hours of television dramas and bedtime at 11 PM.

My diagnosis and the cardiologist's prescription had upended my meal routines and threw my work hours into chaos with the requirement to exercise. I didn't want to explore new recipes or a different way of living. Dr. V's prescription had filled me with relief, and his promise was true. He'd promised me I'd feel no more pain.

I didn't feel pain.

I frowned.

Why was I up here, pressed against the ceiling?

I thought about it. No answer presented itself as I played his last promise to me: "I will end your suffering. I will give you an end," he'd said.

But I was not at an end! I was here! On the ceiling looking down upon him and his nurse pulling a sheet over my head. Something interrupted her movement. Her eyes fastened on my peaceful face. Her brows drew down. She jerked her hands away. The sheet floated down, half covering my chin as she stared down at my face, eyes closed. The form of my body under the blanket lay there like an ugly sack of nothing.

Blonde hair—that dyed blonde hair Mom insisted I had to have, and I'd adopted. Dyeing it controlled my hair, except my bangs that waved over the faint lines on my forehead. My eldest sister Sally had mocked those faint lines. She'd pushed me to go for collagen injections or Botox. I'd covered them with bangs instead.

My skin waxed under the lamp's glow on the nightstand; across the bed, the nurse stood, scowling down at me. She'd been efficient, guiding me gently from the moment she'd met me at the Dying with Dignity reception desk. I'd recognized long experience in her practiced movements and soothing words. The receptionist had reassured me when she'd shared the nurse and doctor had started the Suite together as soon as the law had permitted it.

The nurse's small smile had comforted me, so why was she scowling now?

All of us in the Suite had wanted me dead, including her. Did she see I wasn't?

The nurse snapped herself upright and wheeled around to face Dr. V.

Why am I here? I yelled in my thoughts towards them. I reached up to feel my head. Energy surged in a magnetic force between my hands and my head. My hand flew back; I tried to breathe. But I felt...I didn't know what I'd touched. Atoms? Photons? My high school physics didn't explain this...this...peculiar sensation.

Lights appeared beside me; one of them chimed like the silver bells I'd heard earlier. I jumped away from them and gaped, frozen.

Three orbs hovered near me, blue energy encircling them like flowing jet streams around a transparent earth. Pink highlighted the flowing streamers on one orb, yellow the ones on the second orb in the middle, and silver that tinkled like bells on the third. The first one spoke, and my thoughts whirled inside my frozen form. *What's happening? I'm supposed to be dead! This is supposed to be the end! Dr. V didn't complete the job. He didn't put me at rest as he'd promised me!*

"It's okay," hushed into my brain. Except not a brain. Yet here I am conscious, on the ceiling, gazing at my blood-drained skin and dyed blonde hair and brown eyes hidden by closed lids. *That must be it. Dr. V thinks I'm dead because my eyes are closed.*

"Get a grip. We're here for you," said the orb with the yellow highlights.

"Hush!" commanded the pink-highlighted orb. "She's new. She doesn't understand we're here for her. We chose her."

No one chose me! I clamped down on the rising tide of panic. Dr. V had promised no more pain, and here panic came. My least favourite form of pain when my heart would thud against my ribs, my lungs solidified against inhaling, and every muscle tightened me into immobility.

"Dr. V, I'm not dead!" I yelled down at him as I shifted away from the three orbs beside me. Somehow, they remained locked in proximity to me. My heart raced, except I had no heart, I realized as I raised my hand to comfort it in long practice. Instead, energy magnetically responded out from where my heart should be towards my hand. I gulped. But I couldn't gulp. No throat contracted to meet my swallowing action. I whisper-shouted, "Dr. Veritas! Help me!"

"What we do here is important," he was snapping at the nurse.

I raised my voice to a louder whisper-shout. "Dr. Veritas, help!" They both ignored me.

"Oh, get off your high horse," she responded. "What we do here is save the health system a buck."

He drew himself up and stared down his beaked nose at her. "We started this Suite together because we both believed in this treatment. I," he pronounced, "am saving my patients from their pain."

"Are you? Why do you lie? You know as well as I do that the government gave us licence to kill so they could save a buck. Those progressive pantsy types are being taken in by blind greed."

"How dare you! What's wrong with you? Our patients are in real pain. There's no solution, no better health care than releasing them from their pain. I end their pain."

"End?! Is that what you call death?!" the nurse roared with laughter. "You've gotta be kidding me. You no more care about your patients than this…," she gestured to the machine that had delivered sweet medicine to my pain, the three tubes of drugs with their plungers standing at attention.

One drug to relax me, and it had. As I'd watched him push plunger one down, his eyes upon my own, relief had flooded my muscles. The second drug to put me to sleep. I smiled into his eyes as he'd pushed that plunger down. The last one to end my pain. I hadn't seen him push plunger three down. *That's why I awoke on the ceiling!* But I wasn't supposed to. Somehow, I must tell him.

The yellow-highlighted orb remarked into my ear, "You're dead."

"Hush Blair, she isn't ready."

"Okay," she replied. "You take the lead."

The pink-highlighted orb seemed to nod. I ignored them as I worried about how to tell Dr. V he hadn't ended my pain, how my life had survived because I'm still here! I tried to lower myself to his level, but I couldn't move. *Why am I on the ceiling, anyway?* I concentrated on that question. It made no sense to simultaneously exist on the ceiling and my body lie on the bed. I was supposed to be dead. *How could I still be existing unless Dr. V had failed to put me into my permanent rest?*

"After I administer the last medication, there is no more pain," Dr. V had assured me. "Because there's no more consciousness. Your consciousness is in your brain."

I'd nodded. I'd done some homework on the brain to verify his words. Stuff that made no sense, stuff about spirit and spirituality—

what Mom had called nonsense. "You don't need to fill your head with nonsense," she'd glared at me. I'd agreed with her and, remembering that agreement during my search, had skipped past those results. Nonsense didn't deserve my time.

"Look. You and I are supposed to be partners in our patients' final moments. We need to provide a unified front to them. Can you still do that?" Dr. V grilled his nurse.

"Sure I can. Didn't I do that for this woman there? I've had enough, but I'll keep going. This woman didn't know she's the second one today, and you have ten more lined up. You really do know how to kill them faster than a hornet stings a human."

Dr. V growled. I wanted to retreat, but the ceiling wouldn't let me. "Listen up. I'm not a hornet! I do this to save my patients' dignity—"

"Dignity," the nurse scoffed. "What's so dignified about being executed? You think because she's not a criminal, that you killing her is dignified? Only if she was a criminal, then her execution wouldn't be dignified? Do you hear yourself, Doctor? I'm in this because I've crossed the killing line. I'm honest enough to know that when I see a patient coming in once again with the same old, same old chronic illness requiring vats of empathy I don't have, my first thought is: 'They're better off dead.' I'm honest enough to know what I really mean is I'm better off if they're dead. I don't have to deal with their complaints, their pain, their mental pain.

"We're controlling their physical pain, but there's nothing we can do about a society that leaves them to fend for themselves with too little money. Uh-uh, Doc-tor Ver-i-tas, we're not saving them pain and giving them dignity. We're making it easier on ourselves, and we can do that because the Supreme Court and Trudeau government gave us a licence to kill. Stop being so high and mighty. You and me, we've crossed the killing barrier. And we're never going back." With that, she turned back to the bed, grabbed the sheet and blanket, and yanked them over my head. "And I suddenly hate myself for it," she rasped.

Dr. V glared at her bent back. I'd never seen him like that before. Neither of them paid attention to my body. *How did they know I was dead? Because I wasn't dead. I couldn't be. I was still conscious. Feel my pulse!* I thought with all my might. My whisper-shout had gone unheard. *Maybe he'll hear my thoughts?*

"I have to check her pulse," he said. Relief flooded me. Somehow he'd heard my pleas. The nurse stepped back. He stepped forwards, lifted the sheet up near my right wrist, grasped my arm, and hauled it out. *Why is he so rough with me? He was always so gentle, reassuring me with a soft touch that I'd finally be at rest.* He held my wrist in his left hand as he watched the second hand tick around on his magnificent watch. Its gold band glinted in the soft lamplight. I held my breath; I refused to contemplate there was no breath in me. I couldn't deal with that. Now he'd know he hadn't completed the job.

Dr. V dropped my arm. It bounced off the bed's side and hung down like meat. "I've cured another one. She has her dignity back. That's what they pay me for," Dr. V stated.

The nurse brushed past him and lifted my arm up to push it under the sheet. "Some dignity," she said sardonically.

The silvery-highlighted orb morphed and a hand shape emerged. Two fingers angled to the left, the other two fingers angled away from them, shaping a "V." I sensed the orb smirking with amusement. I didn't understand. Fear convulsed my shape.

"We're sorry," the pink-highlighted orb said.

"Forget them," the silvery-highlighted orb tinkled. "They don't understand."

I didn't understand, I thought. I sagged. *I wanted an end to everything. What had happened? Why had his fingers failed to feel my pulse?*

Doctors know how to take pulses, right? I asked myself. He hadn't ordered me hooked up to an ECG machine because he'd wanted to create a home atmosphere, a comforting one for my last minutes. I appreciated that. A doctor who understood me. A physician who'd grasped my desire—to die—and was willing to offer it.

Not like my cardiologist, who'd said that my heart disease was well controlled and all I needed was therapy for my suicidal thoughts. I could live a long, happy life with therapy. *I was sixty-one years old. What long and happy life? It'd been too long.* I disagreed with that arrogant man that I was suicidal. I knew what I wanted. The three-step medication prescription to pass me into the rest that Dr. V had promised me when we'd gotten talking at the Second Cup in the hospital cafe. That wasn't suicidal; that was me facing my reality of heart disease and choosing medication that worked for me instead of what the cardiologist had prescribed.

I remembered taking the pills the first time I'd received the cardiologist's prescription. I'd struggled to fight my way out of bed. Fatigue had transformed accounting from pleasurable flow to a persistent battle to focus on numbers instead of collapsing back into bed. I'd told the cardiologist that I needed to be alert and awake to calculate my long-time clients' budgets, to whip through theirs and occasional clients's taxes, to keep up with CRA's tax code changes. I shuddered at this year's sudden trust reversal a day before reports were due. *Typical Canada Revenue Agency move.* If I'd still been on the cardiologist's drug regimen, I wouldn't have been able to pivot to amend my last remaining client's tax return and email her before I closed down my practice.

"Your heart rate is down. Your blood pressure is under control. That's what matters," my cardiologist had said. I hadn't known what to do. *How could I work with that much fatigue? But he'd said I had to manage my heart.* I shook my head. His prescription wasn't the medication I'd needed.

I'd wandered out of the elevator on that thought and had spotted the mini-cafe near the hospital exit. I'd found the only available table after I'd bought my coffee. A few minutes later, a resonant male voice had asked me if he could sit at my table. I'd swivelled my eyes towards his voice, had nodded, and said nothing as he sat and placed his coffee cup on the round table with intense attention. Keeping his head lowered, he'd raised his eyes to mine, smiled, and gestured to my coffee, asking if it healed what ailed me. I heard myself talking. I never talked. None of my doctors, especially the cardiologist, had the time to listen. Years earlier, when I'd tried to talk, I'd discovered they were like Mom. They listened to the facts with one eye on the clock. My questions, and expressing the pain that camped in my head, led to being told off. Best to do what they say.

But Dr. Veritas had been different. He'd listened as I'd clutched my paper coffee cup with both hands, my black coffee cooling in the busy, echoing air. When I'd run out of words, he'd leaned forward and softly touched my arm. I remembered his gentle touch now, how it startled, because doctors didn't touch anymore and because it'd soothed. I'd grown used to not being touched to the point I retreated when someone leaned towards me. But his touch had been kind. He'd told me of another option. He'd told me about MAiD. I didn't know what MAiD was. Medical Assistance in Dying, or MAiD for short, he'd explained.

"Euphemisms are fun!" the silver-highlighted orb sung like chimes.

"Hush," the pink-highlighted orb remonstrated.

I barely registered either as the memory played in my head like a favourite film. Wonder had lit me up as I'd absorbed this new method to end my life-haunting pain. That's what I'd asked all my doctors for; all they'd done was tell me to go to therapy. But Dr. V hadn't. He'd offered me real health care. I'd snatched at it.

I blinked back into my present circumstances, except I had no eyelids to blink, yet for a moment black had obscured my vision. I glanced down. My body remained underneath me.

I existed in defiance of his promises.

Memories popped into my mind. Pop, pop, pop, like exploding bubbles. Empty promises doctors had uttered of controlling my heart disease as it worsened despite the visits and fatiguing prescriptions. *Dr. V's promises cannot also be empty!*

The pink-highlighted orb floated forwards. "We're here for you. We're your soul family. We came to help you."

Help me? The sole person able to help me had his profile to me, his face suffusing red while he and the nurse glared at one another. I didn't understand how Dr. V didn't know how to take a pulse, for I was alive, and my heart must be beating. No heartbeat, no life. I knew that.

"How can you help me?" I replied with no mouth or tongue to speak, confusing me even more. "How can you hear me when Dr. V can't hear me? How can I speak with no means to speak?"

A vacuum sucked at my back. Every atom of my being blew backwards, and the hospital's Dying with Dignity Suite where Dr. V and his nurse continued to argue disappeared like a car accelerating away from me.

Chapter Two

DARK

The vacuum let go. Darkness enveloped me. The absence of light pressed on me on all sides. I stood rooted. The air was so hot, it abraded my skin like sandpaper. No, not skin. My outer self felt magnetized, like a forcefield I dimly remembered hearing about from a client during one of those inane chattering moments before they'd left. Sandpaper air rubbed shards of electricity down into my thoughts and ignited my body, yet as I surveyed myself from my head down to my feet, I sensed heat leaching out as I scanned lower. I didn't want to understand what was going on with my feet. They were cold, so cold.

A strange force snaked around them. The force turned clammy as it inched up my ankles, then sloshed back down.

Water.

Water so cold it stuck to my skin as it swirled around my feet and ankles, clockwise and counter-clockwise, randomly switching direction around my motionless ankles and feet.

"Why are you here?" A voice boomed from in front of me, around me, behind me. It flung itself through me, assaulting my thoughts.

Buzzing filled my head. The familiar sign heralded a faint. *That* therapist's words thrust themselves into my consciousness. I shook them out. *Oh why, oh why was I still conscious? Why was I still alive?* The buzzing in my head normally winked out the light when I'd grow faint. *That* therapist's words bellowed past my resistance. "You faint because the world frightens you so much you retreat inside yourself where it's safe."

I'd heard Mom laugh and laugh at such nonsense. Upon the advice of my first cardiologist, my GP had referred me to *that* therapist when I'd first begun having heart palpitations. After six sessions with him, *that* therapist had suggested he meet Mom to explain my fainting reaction to her. "It's important to explain this to your mom so she can help you understand. Since she knows you best, she can explain it better than I can," he'd said. I'd complied and had brought Mom. When she'd stopped laughing at him, she'd gotten up and told me to "come along," snickering as I followed her out of the therapist's office. I never returned, although I'd felt uncomfortable at not fulfilling the ten sessions like the cardiologist had prescribed. My GP had sent me to a new cardiologist. The discomfort had vanished.

Somehow, in this dark place, with its hot sandpaper air and cold swirling water, the buzzing didn't lead to unconsciousness. I longed to hide somewhere. But I couldn't crouch in the water with its hidden alien forms. I hugged myself. Tighter and tighter, I wrapped my invisible arms around the forcefield of my body.

The voice boomed again. "Why are you here?"

I had to answer.

That frightening voice demanded an answer.

Fear like molten lava flooded my chest. I didn't feel my heart's familiar thudding nor hear its pulsing whooshing in my ears. Instead, the molten lava rhythmically thrust up and down inside my torso's forcefield as the air sanded it outside. *Where was I?*

"I'm Dark!" the voice boomed. I cringed. I tucked myself down into myself.

"You're not alone," said another voice, tinged with pink, like the harmony of a pink noise machine I'd used for a while, the one my second cardiologist had recommended to help me fall asleep.

"Who's there?" I whispered, liking the harmonious resonance the pink voice elicited in my body, but doubting its implied safety.

Danger.

The word floated up into my mind.

"I am Dark!" The first voice boomed like a crashing wave over the pink voice, yet not drowning it.

The pink voice said, "This is Bailey. I'm part of your soul family. We're all here."

A yellow-tinged voice said, "Blair here." A voice like silver chimed without words. I didn't understand how in this lightless vacuum, their voices sounded like colours. All three, pink, yellow, silver, sent wave fields that received answers from deep within me, from a place I'd long ago shut up and locked away. *Danger.* The word breathed out from that locked-away place, reminding me to doubt, to be wary when people speak, to seek shelter within myself as I ferret out what they want so as to give it to them.

"We're your soul family," the pink voice soothed.

Soul family?

"Yes," said the pink voice. "We're your soul family. You're not alone."

Vigilance shot me up straight. *I'm always alone. Those words are a lie!*

I shoved the idea of a soul family down as far away from my consciousness as it could go. It never paid to listen to that kind of talk. *I'm hallucinating*, I told myself. Long ago, I'd learnt how to shut out voices and be inside myself, safe from yelling, safe from others' demands. One part of me remained vigilant to know what to do; the rest stayed protected inside a locked-up part of my mind where no one could get at me. I tried to use the same tactics with these voices.

"I am Dark!" The words plowed through my defences. "I am not a hallucination. Answer my question. Why are you here?" The voice shot into my safe place, right into my thoughts.

How?! How did that voice get into my thoughts? Alarm shivered my being. The molten lava burned inside me, rising against the sandpaper on my outer side. Water surged, shooting chills up my calves. Something was swimming towards me. *What was there? What was coming at me?* I looked around, straining to find light to see. Those orbs were products of my oxygen deprivation, I decided. As such, they should provide me light like they had when they'd first showed up over Dr. V and the nurse.

Doctor V! He should be able to help me stop hallucinating! Where am I that I'm hallucinating this? Am I in bed? How much time has passed?

"No time has passed as you know it—"

"Hush. Don't try to explain time to her yet."

A loud sigh waffled my forcefield skin.

I remembered suddenly that he'd taken my pulse and had declared me dead. *But I'm not! I'm still alive. My thoughts are out of my control! I'm hallucinating voices, giving them personalities. I must stop this. Resume control, Charlotte Elisabeth.*

A snout struck my right calf.

I leapt.

I swallowed my scream.

The last time I'd screamed was when I was three years old, when my father had left us. Screaming and crying brought on worse. *What was attached to the snout?* The thought snuck in and froze me. Coarse fur brushed against my forcefield skin. It vanished. I counted seconds; after thirty, I exhaled.

Two teeth, appearing to lack any containing mouth, sank into my flesh, which quivered like waving energy fields. I staggered backwards—into a lumpen snout. I stumbled forwards and flung out my hands, involuntarily unwrapping my safety hug. I wrenched myself to a halt near a mass that appeared as if out of nowhere.

"Nothing can hurt you, you know," the yellow voice said. "Only yourself. You just need to answer the question."

"You're not real," I spoke out loud except it wasn't out loud. My voice sounded like my thoughts, felt like my thoughts. *This is not happening! Where is Dr. V? Why won't he kill me properly like he promised? Why has he left his job half done? Why is he wrapping up while I'm still alive?* I remembered him dropping my arm. It had fallen flaccidly like life had left it. *But I'm conscious! I must be hallucinating*, I assured myself. "This cannot be reality!"

"Oh, I'm real!" the booming voice said. "Call me Dark. Call me by my name."

I hugged myself again and clamped my lips. They, too, felt magnetized, both pushing away from each other and holding together. I compelled them to keep closed.

"Now!"

"Dark," I blurted out loud yet to myself.

"It's okay," said the pink voice. "This is reality. I know it's hard, but you're not alone."

"I can't see you," I babbled. "You're not real. You're oxygen deprivation, like Dr. V explained when I asked him about near-death experiences. He explained they're just hallucinations brought on by people losing oxygen to their brains. Or anesthetic-type dreams. Nothing more. This is not real. You're not real. I will deep breathe like he showed me."

I set my mind to inhale, and nothing happened.

The voice roared, its laughter thumping like the deepest, loudest bass against my core. I thrust my right hand out to steady myself against a wall. *That mass must be a wall near me.* I sensed another mass appear, opposite to the first one, pulsing magnetic energy against my hand, and I began to fall sideways. Those two teeth with no body punctured my heel, and I jerked. The jerk stopped my falling. I wanted to freeze against my strange flesh and against this wall that my hand repulsed. But the teeth were streaking electricity up me. I flung myself forwards, and magnetic masses enclosed me.

"Why are you here?" Dark demanded.

I had to answer. But I didn't know how to answer. *What kind of answer did it want?* It's always best to give people the answers they want, but I had no idea what kind of answer this place, this being wanted. I refused to think about where I was. But I needed to give it what it wanted. Then maybe it would stop. Something unidentifiable and new slipped itself around my right ankle, rippling icy tongues up my right leg forcefield. My throat constricted. My legs tensed. I didn't dare move. It unwound itself from my right ankle, and its surface licked my left as it wound its way around it. I fought the desire to ponder its nature. Prickles raced up my calves, my thighs, my chest and whirred around my neck. It left. I counted the seconds and relaxed when I reached thirty.

It returned. A soft texture like furry scales rubbed my right ankle and reminded me of the neighbourhood cats who'd meow hello and brush up against me as I walked to the post box. *Please stop. Please stop. Please stop.*

"It's okay," the pink voice said. "You're not alone. You can leave this place."

How? What is the right answer?

"Answer me! Why are you here?"

"I don't know," I whispered and instantly knew it wasn't the right answer. *Had I whispered it, or had I thought it?* If it's only thoughts, some logical part of my mind suggested, then this isn't real. *Repeat after me,* I instructed myself. *It's only oxygen deprivation. Say it. Repeat it. Dr. V knew about this. Believe him, not your hallucinations!*

"I am Dark!" My atoms whooshed backwards and forwards, within a confining magnetic force, under Dark's exploding voice, like a wind had disturbed them. Pops of energy panicked me all over. "I don't know is not an answer! Why are you here?"

The pink voice spoke at the same time, but I didn't understand.

I repeated to myself, "Oxygen deprivation. Oxygen deprivation. Oxygen deprivation." The space around me boiled like pitch from those medieval stories I used to read when hiding in bed away from Mom and my older sister Sally. Bad people drowned in pitch, screaming their guilty agony.

"I'm not a bad person," I wailed.

"You're not," the pink voice said. I stumbled away from that voice, and Dark constricted me like a python.

Dark chortled. "Good you're calling me by name."

I hadn't spoken. I'd only thought its name. *How can it say I called it by its name?* Dark mocked, "You know nothing, you puny human. Why are you here?"

"We speak through thought here, in reality," the pink voice susurrated.

Of course, I realized. *I'm hallucinating, so my thoughts are speech and vice versa. It's okay.*

Dark shoved me forwards as walls hidden from my senses thrust against me. *A cupboard?* Dark had squeezed me into a cupboard. It held me immobile. I was shut up. The cupboard was my punishment. I wanted out. Memory merged with my hallucination. *This cupboard is memory*, I told myself. *I only need to deep breathe.* The walls pressed against me, smashing the energy waves of my flesh into chaos. A snout slammed into my knees. A massive second snout hit my heels, my ankles, my calves so hard that my face smacked into the wall in front of me. The wall pushed itself against me.

"Answer me! Why are you here?" Dark roared.

Something like jelly touched my face. My head buzzed. The jelly caressed my cheek towards my left ear. It smoothed itself as it stroked my neck towards my upper back, splaying and flattening its membrane against me as it went. A gelatinous arm enwrapped me, spreading itself around my back until it covered the whole of my back. It yanked me forwards into the hidden wall that resisted its forward force. Blinded by fear and darkness, I panted against an irresistible rising scream.

"It's okay," the pink voice shouted as my atoms squeezed through the wall under the momentum of the gelatinous creature. The wall strained against my forced momentum, but it couldn't repel the force of the creature. I merged with the wall. I fainted at last.

Chapter Three

DESIRE

Fainting had been an illusion. I was conscious and sitting on a chrome stool with a black leather top that wasn't chrome and leather but faux, as only humans can mimic nature. A white counter machined into glossy faux marble faced me. When I raised a tentative hand to stroke it, expecting marble's soft feel, rough energy buzzed my hand. My hand fisted, and I saw it for the first time. I inhaled, but my breath made no sound, and my torso didn't expand. Fear clutched me, and I scattered my thoughts away from these non-sensations.

"I didn't see you go to Earth. I see you now. Where are you going?" A voice dripped like goo into my ears.

My head shot up. The gelatinous mass that had wrapped its extending, widening arm around me was bending over me, filling my vision. A childhood memory flew up into my consciousness. Mom mixing green Jell-O with boiling water, refrigerating it in a baking tin, taking it out, and cutting it with a ruler into 2 cm by 2 cm by 2 cm cubes. She'd count 12 cubes into a bowl and hand me a small, slightly bent stainless steel spoon. Under her watchful eye, I'd scoop them up one by one, dropping the wobblier ones, feeling her frown, trying again slower to lift one on a spoon to my mouth. I'd noiselessly suck it into my mouth and let its wiggly smoothness melt on my tongue's heat.

"Where are you going?" the purring voice asked. I reared back. I straightened my spine and sent my senses around. The abrading heat was gone; in its place, fresh air smelling faintly of sugar.

"There is no air here," said the gelatinous being. "And I'm not gelatinous. I'm Desire. You are in me, and I'm in you. You will call me by my name. Desire."

I gulped. I averted my eyes as I whispered, "Desire." That's when I noticed where I was. An ice cream parlour! All white and faux chrome and reflections of cleanliness. My favourite place. A mirror lined the wall behind the gelatinous—no, behind Desire—and the faux marble counter supported candy glass jars, filled with the kind of candies that top ice cream sundaes or top-heavy waffle cones. The mirror reflected cartons of freshly churned ice cream hidden underneath the counter. I leaned over the counter to gorge on the view. Smarties riotously filled one jar; next to it, chocolate chips waited to be scooped; in the next glass jar, mini peanut butter cups beckoned me; and in the one at the end of the row, cute marshmallows in white, pink, and green: a softer green than the green Jell-O that morphed as it moved in front of me. I felt it waiting. I hoped it'd forget its question. I hungered for an ice cream. *Maybe if I ask for a scoop of ice cream*, I thought, *it'll forget its question.*

"You haven't said my name yet."

My eyes flew to where its head should be in its amorphous blobby shape. *I had!*

"You whispered it, as quietly as you could. You thought you could sneak by me. You can't. Say my name!"

Desire, I thought.

"Louder."

"Desire!" I shouted, or maybe I thought it and didn't speak it. *I can't tell the difference!*

Desire wobbled its shape so that a dent appeared near its top, a dent like a smile. I crunched into myself, my stomach sinking into my back, and skirted my vision away from that smile. *I only wanted some ice cream,* I whimpered to myself.

"Who will you share it with?"

No-one, I thought. I have no-one to share it with because this is a hallucination.

A movement caught my eye to my right and turned my head. Two ceiling-to-floor plate-glass windows flanked either side of an old-fashioned glass door with an angled metal handle crossing its middle from side to side. The floor was black-and-white. Marble yet not marble. Artificial like the counter and stools, I somehow knew. People walked past the door on the other side of the plate-glass windows. Lots and lots of people. I froze, fearing they'd change direction and enter. But none did. Not one glanced my way or even paused to look inside Desire's ice cream parlour as they hurried by to the right or the left.

Then I saw them.

The three transparent orbs with their blue energy streams weaving around them like jet streams on a TV news weather map, one with pink highlights, one with yellow, one silvery. I didn't hear their voices or chimes yet sensed they were speaking. I rotated my stool to set my right shoulder against them.

"Where are you going?" Desire asked.

"I'd like some ice cream, please." I pondered what ice cream I'd like the most and tumbled into fantasizing about the flavours that had brought me joy. *Maybe chocolate? No, salted chocolate with caramel through it. No, lemon banana, with its tart citrusy ribbons cutting through the delicious rich roasted banana. Or maybe fresh strawberries, sliced and churned into fresh vanilla whipped cream?*

Desire leaned until their wobbling presence rippled my magnetic skin—or atoms?—I didn't understand which—and halted my sweet thoughts. I saw right through Desire's transparent artificial green to the mirror and froze at sight of the reflections. I didn't like what I saw. Energy like insect feet crawled up my back.

"Where are you going?" Desire asked me, so closely their smoothness caressed my lips.

"Um, death," I replied.

"Why do you lie?" they demanded.

"I'm not lying," I squeaked. Agitated movement on my right tried to claim my attention. I inadvertently glanced over; the orbs were bouncing up and down, trying to come in. I didn't want them in. If I couldn't hear them, then I could turn my back to them, and they'd disappear. I did. They did.

Desire leaned right into me. "Why do you lie?"

"I'm not, I swear it. I'm not. I want death. Dr. V promised me an end. He promised me endless peace. He promised me my pain would be over. You can ask him. Please," I pleaded.

"I don't know your Doctor V. I'm Desire. This is my domain, where I exist. You're alive in me, and I'm reflecting you. I didn't see you go down to Earth. Why do I see you now? Where are you going?"

I'd thought I was going to my end.

I'd thought when I'd lain down willingly on the Dying with Dignity Suite bed, its soft pillow cushioning my head, Egyptian cotton sheets stroking my neck, and blanket comforting my heart, that the end was only minutes away.

The intake worker had suggested bringing my quilt to cover myself in my final moments, but I'd wanted to have no part of my life in that room. They'd asked me to list my favourite scenes to play on the enormous LCD screen across from the bed as a balm, the last images I'd ever see, unless I desired to watch Dr. V push down the plungers. I'd desired seeing him act out my end, to ensure it was really happening, not a figment of my longed-for dream. I'd skipped the question on the intake form, but after reviewing my answers, the intake worker had pointed to the blank line with a polished red nail. "You can choose," I'd said, trying to push back the form on its clipboard.

"It's not for us to decide. This is your death," I'd cringed as she'd continued speaking, "...your desire."

"No, you know what's best."

She'd blinked up at me, picked up the phone, murmured a few words into it, and footsteps sounded behind me after a couple of minutes. The Dying with Dignity Suite manager sidled up on the right. She'd touched my right arm and smiled when I turned my head. "This is your death, Charlotte Elisabeth. Remember how we spoke about your death, your way?"

I'd nodded.

"This is part of that. Tell us what you like. Flowers? Meadows? The ocean?" She kept listing natural landscapes as I stared at her. "We like to think of these scenes as a balm for your soul as you transition out of your pain." After a silence that dragged on for a minute, she'd said in firm tones, "You must tell us your preferences Charlotte Elisabeth."

I'd turned back to the form and listed three. I didn't know what I desired, except one more ice cream treat. Ice cream, waffle cone, and ice cream parlour. When I'd walked into the Dying with Dignity Suite, a chrome and white ice cream parlour with a wall of windows reflected in the mirror behind the counter, greeted my eyes. Through the windows I'd seen a meadow and had grimaced. *How trite.*

This must be it! This hallucination is my brain remembering that image on the screen! Relief ran through me like sweet ice cream melting in my mouth and sluiced coldness into my stomach. *I'm remembering that photograph and making it part of my hallucination!*

"Why do you lie?"

The question again. *Why do they ask questions? Can't they stop interrogating me?* I conjured up my appeasing stock phrase, "Whatever you say, Desire."

The green blob jiggled. Wobbly laughter emerged from within its semi-transparent core. I leaned back from it and lowered my head, while lifting my eyes to track this strange part of my hallucination. *What are they going to do next? I've controlled my thoughts with an iron rod for decades. Why are they spinning out of my control now?*

Desire and I regarded each other.

It must be the relaxation drug Dr. V gave me. That was it! Desire and this ice cream parlour are a drug-induced hallucination. I have no control over such brain chaos. But it'll wear off, and when it does, Dr. V will know I'm still alive and will finish the job. I slumped in satisfaction.

Desire erupted. Cubes of green flew out of its front near its top as if a mouth had opened up and regurgitated its contents. They splattered all over me. My magnetic skin dented and bounced back as Desire screamed, "You lie! Why do you lie?"

"Please, I'm not lying. Tell me what to say!" Maybe if I appeased my hallucination, it'd go away. Then I could eat ice cream in peace. Being alone, not fearing anyone would walk in on me, was all I wanted right now. Guilt stabbed me as my sister Sincerity's face rose into memory. The last time I'd seen her was in our ice cream parlour. Shaking my head as if shaking her off me like water, I automatically pushed the emotion and memory back into their locked box. *I don't miss her; I desire death. This place is second best, if this is what my hallucination gives me, where no one can bother or berate me.*

An attractive force pulled me from behind. It willed me to turn around. Desire stopped spitting cubes at me and expanded itself into the entire area between the counters, the plate-glass windows, and behind me. The attractive force increased its drag on my back. I half turned to the right and spotted the orbs. *They're still here?* I frowned. *Why?* No longer bouncing, they were watching like they were with me, not spying or scrutinizing, waiting to pounce. Since that couldn't be true, I ignored them. People watched you to spy out an advantage over you or catch you in a weak moment or show you up.

The force strengthened; it added a rising screaming wind to its magnetic attraction. I dragged myself forward to grab the front edge of the counter.

Desire yelled, "Why do you lie?"

Was Desire asking me or the force? Easier to decide the force was their target. I swivelled all the way around to face the back wall, expecting the same hard white material as the floor's white diamonds, and seeing instead both that artificial material and infinity bordered by moulded baseboard stretching along its lower length with a matching old-fashioned cornice moulding. I gaped at this conundrum. Usually, these architectural features I admired were made of wood. But these didn't look like painted wood but hard, unforgiving material, like the hardest of lab-created plastic. As I was considering the parlour's material properties, a point of black appeared in the middle of the white wall of infinity. It grew and stretched backwards like a vortex into blackness. "No!" I wailed. I didn't want to return to Dark.

Suddenly, it was like I could feel those creatures bumping my ankles and biting me. I jerked my legs up. The sight of my legs horrified me. *Not my legs! Not my legs! They're a hallucination. A drug-fuelled hallucination!*

A gelatinous arm slithered around my chest, pulling me into itself. Coolness enveloped my torso as my legs rose under the vortex's power and extended feet first towards the enlarging vortex. Way in the vortex's distant core, red appeared. Red like red dust swirling and whirling. Round and round, faster and faster. My head vibrated. I wanted to lose consciousness. The desire gripped me; not since I was a child had I yearned so much for sweet oblivion. The vortex won. With a sucking sound, it pulled my legs into it first, then my head, arms, and chest out of Desire's grasp. I gave myself up to its force.

Chapter Four

IGNORANCE

I landed face up. A reddish sky stretched over me and into the limitless distance. *Mars?* I shook my head at my foolishness. *Of course not Mars. I'm on Earth. Hallucinating. In oxygen deprivation.* I turned my head and saw I lay on a vast plain that seemed reddish black. My face touched the plain, and it felt like beach sand caught between skin and bathing suit. I sat up to see it better, rubbed my face, almost fell backwards, and braced myself on my palms behind me with my fingers bent. Charcoal lines of black delineated the plain into squares turned sideways. In each huge tile, reddish charcoal coloured the surface. I stretched out my fingers until they too lay flat on the plain's foreign hardness. It had felt like sand glued to my face, yet my hands sensed an unknown quality. The plain didn't feel cold and thin like metal. It wasn't slightly smooth, slightly rough like concrete. It wasn't warm like plastic or vinyl. Yet somehow I knew humans had created this hard, unyielding surface, even though the charcoal lines made it appear as if drawn by an unknown artist, not real.

I thought, *I'd like to stand*, and I was standing.

The landscape's unfamiliarity beguiled me into noticing it, and I surveyed it, ignoring how my thought had lead to an instant change in my position. The sky curved like an enormous piece of red fabric stretched and tightly stapled to the plain, yet I couldn't see where nails or staples or thread secured it to the plain I stood upon. *Thread?* I queried myself. Since I was alone, so completely alone, no sound, no smell, no visible creature or human, I allowed myself to snort derisively at the idea that thread could hold a landscape together. *Proof right there that I'm still alive and in some sort of delusion. Existence doesn't continue beyond death*, I assured myself. Dr. V had nodded when I'd said those words after our conversation about near-death experiences. "It's all explainable," he'd said as he'd patted my hand lying there on my lap.

I'm alone: completely, utterly alone. The thought fell into my consciousness. No orbs dancing and coruscating blue lines and pink or yellow or silver highlights. No booming voices or wiggly blobs. No person or baffling entity demanding I think, say, or do what they wanted.

Relief curved my lips, or so I imagined they did like when I shut my bedroom door noiselessly against my family's pronouncements when Mom would dismiss me.

Darkness didn't obscure my vision, and I could see where I was. I scanned my body with my mind. No pain. Actually, I felt nothing. I flung my arms out high and wide and bent backwards as I closed my eyes in happy relief. Dr. V had promised me the end of pain, and he'd delivered, even if I still seemed to be conscious and therefore existing. Bringing my arms down and straightening up, I sighed and opened my eyes. I gazed at this limitless reddish landscape. *Where was I? No, it didn't pay to think.* I'd wanted so much for my unpredictable life to end, had disliked how my heart disease had ruined my routine. The uncertainty of when my heart disease would end my existence, imagining my heart forcing me to return to my family, having to depend on them while leaving the safety of the home I'd built for myself during the one time I'd managed to buck their desires for me. I'd saved up money in secret until I'd accumulated enough for a down payment on a small property in Old Toronto, enough to tear down the leaning house with its crumbling foundation and build a new one. My home. Memory of it salted my eyes. I missed my home, my safe place: the one thing I missed. The magnetism of my skin dropped, and my being began to bleed out into the space between sky and plain. If I had to hallucinate, better to be alone and safe.

Thump.

Thump. Thump. Thump.

Thud.

Thud. Thud. Thud.

Bang.

Bang. Bang. Bang.

If I could catch my breath, I would've. My skin regained its magnetic strength—or maybe atoms fused again? My atoms reconstituted back into the inside of the magnetic force holding my skin together. I refused to contemplate these bewildering sensations. I shifted my mind away from them; instead, I strained to determine the sounds' direction. I needed to focus on the menace aiming at my back. The threatening thunder of angular wheels thumping, thudding, banging towards me, closer and closer, raced prickles up my back. I feared to look behind me. I tried to scan as far left as I could, then as far right, but the menacing wheels remained hidden from my sight. Not seeing is less dangerous than seeing, I reassured myself. I yearned to hide. I had nowhere to hide. Against my neck's resistant stiffness, I gradually turned my head to the left. Nothing.

A movement on the far left horizon blurred the charcoal black lines. I stared at that spot, scrambling for ideas on how to flee and where to run. I couldn't flee inside myself because I was inside myself, and my inside self was creating this terrifying landscape where things came at me. *Would these thumps and thuds and bangs ask me questions, too?* I trembled, and little sparks of magnetic energy hopped across me, one way, then the other.

I swallowed, and nothing went down. Only my magnetic skin moved; it constricted what I knew as my neck.

The moving blur sharpened into three unknowable things.

The three things rolled towards me awkwardly. Each roll forward looked like a stall followed by a sharp fall followed by another stall as the thumping, thudding, banging things became recognizable to me. Hexagonal wheels. Three of them. Each a different size. With charcoal lines sketching out eyes, eyebrows, and mouths. Charcoal lines also delineated their shapes.

My feet merged into the landscape, calling my attention. I couldn't move. I dared not, but I wanted to bolt. If I couldn't retreat into myself, maybe I could run back to that ice cream parlour. Green blobby Desire was safer than here. And the parlour offered ice cream with my favourite candies. I could get lost in those candies and frozen cream. Maybe Desire had frozen custard, too. I recalled the rich frozen custard I'd had down at Union Station during their summer plaza of foods from all over. Go in and gorge. Forget the world.

Laughter erupted above my head and assaulted my face like wicked cackles in a horror movie in an IMAX theatre.

I raised my eyes from my feet and craned my head. The three wheels had stopped in front of me. Giant hexagons, rising higher and higher above me, with pencil-drawn eyes grinning at me, pencilled-in eyebrows angling downwards towards each other, and pencil-sketched mouths lengthening into curves that conveyed intense humour at my distress. Conflicting smells wafted towards me out of them. Unwashed jeans. Expensive cologne. A medical clinic's antiseptic air. They stopped laughing.

"Where are you going?" asked the thumping one, the one closest to me, dousing me in the acrid smell of unwashed jeans.

Words refused to come out of my mouth. I wanted to not breathe anything in. Thoughts left me.

The second one sniggered, blowing cologne around like a hot hair dryer, in contrast to its thudding awkward rolls. "She thinks she's dead, doesn't she?" Laughter thudded my head like pattering bombs. "Dead. She doesn't like that word."

The third one said in even tones, its antiseptic scent dousing the unwashed jeans and cologne, "She's confused. We must be kind to the confused. They've been mislead by the news." It banged forwards.

The first thumping one said harshly, "Answer me! Where are you going?"

"I...I...," I stuttered, unable to utter any other word. I thought, *Existence ends. But I still exist. I'm hallucinating. And I get to be covered in the stench of unwashed jeans, too.*

"Yes, you do," said the second thudding one. "Existence is a joke."

"What?" I blurted out, trying not to take in the powdery perfume of its cologne.

"It's a joke!"

The first one laughed, its laughter like thumps of packed-dirt-balls machine-gunning compliant wood. It mocked me. "She thought it was real."

"Life is real," I inadvertently retorted, desiring to get away from its smell. I shut my mouth in horror. I thought, *I mustn't say that out loud.*

"It's okay," said the third hexagonal wheel, its clean-air smell calming my overwrought senses. "We can hear your thoughts. That's how we all communicate here in Ignorance. I'm Ignorance." It pointed to itself and the other two wheels.

I furrowed my brow or thought I did. My confusion magnetized the space between my eyebrows, making it feel like pulling two opposite magnets coming together with effort. I ignored that sensation, let go, and said, "You are all Ignorance? Isn't it 'we'?" I couldn't believe I'd queried it. I crunched into myself, waiting for the blow.

"I are not we. The three of I are Ignorance," explained the third wheel.

"I," said the first wheel, "are asking you, 'Where are you going?'"

"Answer me," demanded the second as the third one soothed a beat behind it, "Answer, please."

The battling smells diminished. *I must be habituating, at least enough to ignore them, like I'd learned to ignore the smells on the TTC back when I had no choice but to use Toronto's public transit system.* I shuddered at the memory.

"Speak up!" demanded the first.

I spoke. "I...I...don't know. I was in the hospital room. In reality."

"Reality? Reality is a joke! There is no material life." It guffawed so hard, it rocked itself back and forth. Thump. Thump. Thump. Thump. Thump. Thump.

The shock of its statement overcame my need to give them what they wanted. I said, "But we only exist in material form. Dr. V said when the physical body dies, there's no more brain activity to produce consciousness. We, pain, and suffering, don't exist anymore. We get to rest forever."

The third one leaned down towards me, the inside edges of its eyebrows angled up, creating an open-drawbridge effect. "It's okay."

A gentle force patted my hand reassuringly. It calmed me, and I wanted to cry. I'd mastered swallowing tears decades ago, and I did it without thinking now as I straightened up. "I still exist, don't I? You are my hallucination? My brain cells are starving for oxygen, and they're creating this world in an attempt to restore order, aren't they?"

The first one roared, "She thinks her material existence is real, and her Doc-tor Ver-i-tas was real. No, you simpleton, it was all a joke. A figment of the universe, created just for you. All a lie."

My mouth fell open. A faint light appeared high above them and to the right. I gawked. The luminescent light hurt my eyes. Unlike any light I'd seen before, its purest white somehow pushed the reddish fabric of the sky away and punctured rays through the upper edges of the giant wheels towering above me. I had no other sense of it but sight.

"Don't look at that!" the second commanded as it thudded once, twice nearer to me.

"It's okay," soothed the third one. "Rest is good. Rest in us." And out from itself, an arm appeared, extending a forming hand, from which fingers appeared, dangling a pair of glasses. The glasses looked real.

Physical.

Black plastic frames.

Thin lenses that reflected the reddish light.

The hand holding them, though, was like a crude pencil drawing.

How did it hold the glasses? No, I wouldn't think about that. Questions lead to unpleasant consequences. Consequences always make living harder. Dr. V had promised me rest without pain. I will believe he kept his promise, I vowed. The antiseptic air floated down towards me, reminding me of my visits with Dr. V in his minimalistic office. Those visits highlighted my last days, and I'd looked forward to them. Swimming in that pleasant memory the antiseptic smell conjured, of how I'd felt heard and seen for the first time, I gazed up at Ignorance with a new perspective.

"These will help you erase the rest of the pain," said the third wheel, extending its stick arm, elongating its stick-drawn hand and fingers until the dangling glasses swayed above my head. I reached up to grasp the glasses, and the light seemed to shine sadness upon me. I paused. *Was I wrong to trust it?*

I dropped my arm.

Thud. "Don't listen to it!" commanded the second wheel as it moved closer, its musky cologne wafting into my face.

"The glasses will help you, like Dr. V helped you. They'll shield you from the lying light," stroked the third wheel.

"I are Ignorance, and we know where you came from. You came from nothing, a joke, a figment created by a jokester. Do what I tell you, like you obeyed Dr. V. Believe I, Ignorance, like you believed him." The three wheels spoke in unison as the third wheel's fingers stretched their black-pencil lines until the glasses touched the back of my hand. It rippled.

I resolutely shifted my eyes to block the light out of my sight. I complied with the three wheels.

"Call I Ignorance," the three said in unison.

"Ignorance," I repeated as I sought their eyes and ignored the light shining through their edges. *No, I hadn't been mistaken about Dr. V, so I'm right about Ignorance, no matter what it called itself. This was my hallucination, and I could trust myself. I could trust the science that explained the odd things a dying brain does to a person.*

Their eyebrows angled down, their charcoal-etched eyes narrowed, their drawn-in mouths curved upwards. They held my gaze, and I flipped my hand to grasp the glasses.

Chapter Five

WRATH

$\int$ulphur irritated my senses. Growling crawled towards me, staying my hand from covering my face. A belching "tcha" then nothing as thunderous clouds enveloped me. Black light fractured my senses. A void of light, sound, and smell. Nothing touched me. *Am I in that dark tunnel that vacuumed me from the Dying with Dignity Suite? No! I can't face those creatures!* Time had no meaning as I waited. But I remained in a nothingness. No water swirled at my feet; no heat abraded my skin. Neither warmth nor cold surrounded me. *Maybe this is the perfect room temperature, where warmth is not too warm, and cool not too cool, and so you feel nothing?*

I waited for a voice to ask me a question.

Nothing.

After time shifted into eternity, I shifted my right foot forwards a centimetre. Nothing happened. No crackling energy or magnetic pull. It was like I was in mid-air yet not floating. My senses began to bleed out from me, and my edges blurred. I swallowed hard, except, again, I didn't swallow, only my magnetic skin tightened, a kind of constriction where my throat should be. *Is!* I reprimanded myself. I eased my arms up and straightened them outwards. I touched nothing. I spread out and stretched my fingers, and no sensation told me where I was. I wiggled my fingers and felt no resistance, neither gravity's pull nor underwater pressure. If I could feel my heart, it would pound, depriving me of breath. I didn't know whether to be glad or sad I felt neither.

No heart beating.

No lungs breathing.

No ears registering sound.

No senses.

"Where are you coming from human-killer? And where are you going destroyer of realms?"

I jumped.

My skin's magnetic field loosened, and I almost blew apart before the field remagnetized and gathered my atoms back into myself. Atoms and magnetic fields—how else can I comprehend these sensations? *I don't want to!* Instead, I searched for the voice above me, below me, to one side, the other side, my mind whirling and nothing to anchor my vision on. *This is not happening!*

"It is happening human-killer. Answer my question. Where are you coming from? Human-killer."

I'm not a human killer! I'm a human saver. I saved myself from endless, undignified pain!

"Pain," the voice from out of this nowhere place rattling my being, spat, "is not undignified. Pain just is. Darkness just is. You are a human-killer."

"I'm not!" I gasped at my insolence. Again, I'd spoken back. *This never ends well. I have to keep my thoughts to myself.*

"Your thoughts destroy. You are a destroyer of realms."

I heaved. *How can it read my mind? How can any of these...these...things read my mind?* My mind is my safe place. No one can grab my thoughts, shake them in front of my eyes like a raggedy doll, tell me they're bad, tell me I shouldn't speak such things, I shouldn't speak back, shouldn't speak at all. Now these things, these places are reading my thoughts, knowing everything I think. My skin's magnetic field rippled; my lips that weren't lips trembled.

A voice shushed out of the darkness; an apparition with a faint blue line circling it appeared in front of me. It reminded me of the fairy tales I'd lose myself in as a child. Tinkerbell. I'd loved Tinkerbell when I was three years old. So sassy and bright. How I'd wanted to be that brave. Sally and Sincerity had asked to see the Disney movie when I was five. So Mom took us all to the movie theatre up at Eglinton and Bayview. She hustled us by the popcorn and candy, my head twisting around as she pulled on my arm. "Popcorn!" I'd demanded. Then I spotted chocolate-covered peanuts, shiny and yummy. I'd blurted, "Please could I have some of the chocolate peanuts?"

Mom had snorted. "You're chunky enough as it is." She'd yanked on my hand and hustled me forward as my older half-sisters Sally and Sincerity hurried behind her. They didn't say a word. All three, my sisters and Mom, were so slim. "You take after your father," Mom had hissed as we walked down the darkened red-lit side aisle to a seat midway between the screen and the exit. I knew taking after my father was the greatest sin. She'd flung my hand out of hers and grabbed Sally to push her first into the seats. "Make sure she doesn't try to sneak out to cadge some candy." Sally had nodded and slipped into the fourth seat from the aisle. Mom shoved me forward. I toddled in the space between the rows and sat next to Sally. Mom next to me. And Sincerity on the aisle. She usually needed the bathroom halfway through and none of us wanted to be disturbed. Tinkerbell soon had me enthralled, distracting me from my growling stomach.

The ghostly blue twinkled, catching my attention. I'd forgotten for a blissful moment where my oxygen-deprived brain had taken me. Even that memory was blissful compared to this void with its apparitions. Pink spoke into my thoughts, "You're okay, you're not alone."

No, I thought sourly. *I'm not alone. Darkness surrounds me; I'm existing in a void so intense, I see and feel nothing. Threatening, lying voices are invading my mind's safe place. I don't know where I am, and Dr. V had assured me I'd be ended. No more pain of existence. He'd promised me! Why had he lied?* I hushed myself. Dr. V had not lied. I mustn't countenance such treasonous thoughts of the only doctor who'd been kind to me, who'd listened and heard me.

"Human killer," boomed the darkness, like I existed inside a massive drum. "I am Wrath. I am the fourth power you must go through. I take seven forms. And you will answer me. In one form or another, I will wrench the answer out of you."

Dr. V is not a human killer, I thought. *I will not allow myself to think that!* I struggled to thrust the thought into the locked box where I kept my dangerous emotions and thoughts and to drive the voice out of my mind.

Pink's blue light twinkled again. I turned away from it. The voice bellowed. "You will answer me!" Lightning red glared into my vision, leaving streaks that grooved down far-away walls. *Walls! There are walls here!* The grooves glowed like coals, angry and streaking pain. *Huh? How did that light emit pain?*

"You will call out my name and answer me!" The red grooves faded, and the walls vanished. The voice regained its nothingness.

Once again, I found myself lost for words. I couldn't speak. I wanted to faint, but I'd learned fainting couldn't happen here—just like my existence's end hadn't happened. No, no, I slapped that thought away from me.

Pink's voice lulled me, saying, "It's okay. Existence doesn't end."

"It does! Dr. V promised me, and it's true. He wouldn't lie to me. Other doctors didn't listen. But he did. He knew. He understood." Fluttering my lips, a sob erupted, a sob of gulping heaves without tears, without wetness flooding my cheeks like when I was alone in my bedroom. This was in my mind.

"I am not your mind," the voice grated as red flushed my sight and red lines seared shrieking scars down the far black walls. *Like nails dragging through skin*, I thought. The lines faded. *Why would it harm itself?* I gulped and whispered, "You're not my mind."

"Say my name human-killer!"

"Darkness."

"I am not darkness. I am the fourth power, Wrath. Dark is my first form. Would you like to see my second? Or my third? Or fourth? If you will not answer me?"

I shook my head. No, this was bad enough. Worse I didn't want to face.

Pink coruscated sound towards me. "You don't have to face anything alone here. We're glad to be accompanying you. It gives us joy to be by your side."

Joy? I thought. No one feels joy travelling with another through their disease and pain. Except Dr. V. He did. He welcomed my calls, reminded me I could email him anytime. No other doctor I saw, from my GP to my latest cardiologist, cared enough for me to call. Their emails returned an autoreply with instructions to not send confidential information and to please call the office to make an appointment. Mom and Sally had told me to buck up and get on with things when I'd shared my heart disease diagnosis. Sincerity had set up weekly dates at the ice cream parlour. I softened. The outlines of my being loosened like threads unweaving themselves.

"Destroyer of realms, use my real name!" Sparks of blood red flew towards me. I ducked and twisted. I felt heat rat-a-tat my back, like molten glass. Crimson drops zipped past me, and they boomeranged back towards where they'd appeared from and scatter-shot holes in the wall far ahead of me. *How can I see what's so far away so clearly? No*, I shook my head. *Asking questions leads to trouble.* Darkness re-descended, and the void sucked all sensation out of me.

"My name!"

"Wrath," I replied obediently.

"Good. Now answer me, 'where are you coming from human-killer and where are you going destroyer of realms?'" The questions burrowed themselves like worms into my thoughts, distorting my sense of self to believe they were mine.

But they are mine, I thought.

Pink said, "No they're not."

Pink's words also found their way into my thoughts.

"This is how we communicate after death."

"Don't say that!" I yelled. "Death is the end of existence! I still exist! I'm having thoughts because I still exist! This is not resting!"

My anger, ignited so unexpectedly, vanished as suddenly. *Thoughts? Is this the problem I must solve?* I pondered that idea.

The air shimmered around me. The void dissolved like a film effect into blown-up dots resembling a newspaper photograph. Black dots against white dots. They overwhelmed me, and I longed for consciousness to end.

Pink twinkled against one of the black dots, casting pretty blue highlights on its surface. "You're not alone. You don't have to be overwhelmed."

I'm always overwhelmed, I replied to myself.

"Maybe you were. But you don't have to be anymore because we're your soul family. We knew you before you met Dr. V. We waited for you, anticipation increasing our joy when we met you."

I couldn't imagine anyone being joyful at the thought of meeting me, never mind when they met me. My clients liked me. They were loyal to me. Some even expressed sorrow when I told them about today's Dying with Dignity session. But joy? Oh, please.

"Yes, joy—"

"Enough! She has not answered my question. She's in my power, now. And I demand an answer from this human-killer!"

The dots mushroomed like miniature nuclear bombs, changing my dying brain's hallucination from a void to...

I raised my head up and up. I stood at the bottom of a hill covered in fluorescent green. Baby blue sky surrounded it. I looked down at my feet. Rust red covered the floor. But not rust, more like the reddish charcoal plain of Ignorance. *Where has my mind taken me now?*

Weariness dragged at me.

"Destroyer of realms, now you will answer me. You are in the Foolish Wisdom of the Flesh. That is you."

Confusion leadened my arms and legs. I sank down onto the hard artificial surface and contemplated the garish hill in front of me.

Chapter Six

WISDOM OF THE FLESH

"Here we are," Silver carolled cheerfully.

I groaned, drew my knees up, clasped them tightly to myself, and dropped my head on my knees within my enclosing arms.

"Hey, you should be thankful we're here. This hill deceives."

I unburied my head enough to peep over my arms at the hill. Except for its garish colour, it was just a hill. *How can a hill deceive?*

"You'd be surprised." Silver tinkled laughter.

"Hush," said Pink. Pink's tones washed over me, soothing me like my pink noise machine. I didn't want to be soothed. I wanted an end.

"It's okay," said Pink. "You can call us whatever you want. We're your soul family, here to accompany you on your journey on this soul track."

Soul track? What's that? What's a soul? I buried my head again and attempted to retreat beyond hearing.

"It's difficult, we know. We've heard of raucous journeys where the soul resists all the way. And others find their families have paralyzed souls and struggle to get them unstuck. Don't get stuck here."

Stuck? Who's stuck?

"You're in danger of being stuck. God doesn't want you to be stuck."

God? I'd vaguely heard that word on a drive home when Mom had barked at me, "There's no such thing as God. Nonsense people make up." After that nothing until I was settling my legal affairs with my lawyer. He'd asked me as we went over my will what my plans were, and I'd uncharacteristically shared I had a date with welcome rest in two days' time. He'd asked me where I was going to rest. I told him the Dying with Dignity Suite. He'd paused, seemed speechless for a moment, then mentioned near-death experiences. "Some of my clients have told me they call them death experiences because they were what death actually was."

I'd nodded and grabbed the brown envelope containing the legal documents. I'd stood up, pushed my chair back into its place, and hurried out the door before he saw me out. Turns out I was so eager, I'd mixed the dates up, and my rest date was a week later than I'd thought. I'd fretted over the delay and heard my lawyer's words nagging me whenever I'd find myself not busy. His words became so incessant, I'd googled "near-death experiences." The stories I read had horrified me. A few mentioned God and Jesus. *Who was Jesus?* My fingers had touched the keyboard when Mom's words smacked my memory. I'd dug my fingers into my palms. *No, Charlotte Elisabeth. Does it matter who they are?* I drove my head between my knees as I remembered that day.

"Of course they matter, silly," Silver interrupted me.

Were they listening? My head shot up. The three blue-streaked orbs were facing me, oscillating up and down in an unseen, unfelt wind, between me and the hill. *Where did they come from?*

"We're with you whether or not you can see us. We were concerned that you'd get up and climb-descend that deceiving hill."

I leaned forward to see the fluorescent green hill better. The ground I sat on impelled pain into my being. I vaulted up and jogged on the spot, trying to pound the pain out, to busy my body and mind against the lawyer's disturbing words that seemed to have continued into this bizarre existence. After uncurling my fingers, I'd called Dr. V's office. He'd been happy to squeeze me in that afternoon once he'd heard my reason.

"I bet," Silver said.

"Hush," Pink said.

My thoughts banged and crashed and zipped away from my attempts to corral them as I began to realize, not just on an intellectual level of " that's odd" but really realized that this existence, these orbs, were actually happening, that places and beings were conversing with my thoughts. *I can't allow that.* I attempted to shut down my memory, yet the emergency appointment scene with Dr. V. churned on. He'd eased me into the chair in front of his desk, pulled his own chair from behind his desk, and sat on it, his knees close to mine as he leaned towards me and asked me to tell him in my own words what was upsetting me. I'd described the experiences I'd read about, and when I'd mentioned God, he'd guffawed. He'd leaned back, clasped his hands in his lap, and smiled. "God!" he'd exclaimed. "There is no God." He'd waved his hand as he draped his right leg over his left. "God is a fantasy people afraid of no longer existing made up. They comfort themselves with the idea of immortality. You and I, though, Charlotte Elisabeth, aren't afraid to face reality. We see our consciousness as the evidence shows us. Evidence-based God doesn't exist. We know the signs when we cease to exist. Our hearts stop; our brains no longer produce brainwaves. Even the ancients understood it to a certain extent in their limited capacity to understand things. Science has taught us so much. Science created electrodes and diagnostic machines to show us what the brain is doing. No brain activity, no pain, no existence. It's as simple as that. I assure you, Charlotte Elisabeth, science is certain. Science reveals reality. That's your evidence."

I'd been afraid he'd want me to know more about God. I'd blurted out my fear.

He'd laughed and told me not to worry, patting my hands again. "God isn't worth learning about. You're lucky, you know, you haven't been burdened by God and hearing about Jesus in all of your sixty-one years." He'd smiled, leaned forward again, and patted my clenched hands until they relaxed.

The remembered relief poured through me. I'd smiled back, sinking into rare praise that I'd done something right, even though I knew deep in my heart, it was because of Mom. She'd kept knowledge of these things out of my head. And I was glad for it.

"You shouldn't have been," chimed Silver, interrupting my memory, wiping the memory-resonating smile out of me.

"Hush," Pink said louder. "She's not ready."

"She should know the truth."

"In due time, when she's ready. We can't be like that other family who in their mad rush to show off their knowledge and truth halted their new soul member's journey in Wrath. We can't have her stuck here!"

Why not?

"Why not?" The question deafened me. I thought Wrath had remained behind in the void, that it was that void. *Where did the voice come from?*

"I'm the hill you see before you, Wisdom of the Flesh. Some call me Foolish Wisdom of the Flesh. But do I look foolish? No!" the voice bellowed. "I'm a hill, one of the forms of Wrath I told you about, the fourth power. Don't you listen, human killer? Come. See. You'll learn the light always lies. There is no God. The light lies. Always. Climb me, so you can answer the questions. Where are you coming from? Where are you going?"

Two questions. I didn't want to answer even one question.

"You must human-killer!"

Oh gosh, it can read my mind, too. Yes, Charlotte Elisabeth, they can all read your mind. You know what to do! Drain your thoughts away.

"No!" Pink's voice forced me to hear the words, "Stay with us!"

"I don't want to," I spoke out loud. Then I dived into myself. I excavated a cavern in my mind. I imagined an open drain hole at its top and drained my thoughts through that hole into the cavern. I visualized a lockable lid, slammed it shut, and turned a lock on it.

"Is she thinking?" the silver orb asked as it hovered towards me.

"No," said the yellow-highlighted one. "I sense no thoughts from her."

I heard their words inside my mind. I couldn't stop that from happening. I wondered if I should or could build a wall against hearing their thoughts. *Oh no, I realized, thoughts have slipped up out of their locked cavern into my consciousness. This is going to be hard.* I reminded myself how many years it had taken to build mental walls to protect myself from Mom and Sally, from so many others who'd sought to hurt me, belittle me, tell me what to do when and how. *This'll take time*, I reassured myself.

"Time!" bellowed the hill. "You think time exists here!" Laughter rang out from the hill. Yet the hill didn't move. I scrutinized it, sending my gaze up and up, and noticed a faint light behind it. It hurt my vision. I lifted a hand to block it out, but the light shone through my transparent hand. I shuddered. Fear vaulted into me.

"Don't be afraid," the pink voice said, sliding towards me mid-air.

I need to brick up my emotions, too.

The orbs' highlighted colours shifted from harmonious coruscating to sharp wiggles. *It's not possible for energy and floating objects to look worried*, I told myself. *You're hallucinating, remember?* I sought again to drain my thoughts out.

The hill said, "My name is Wisdom of the Flesh. Climb me, and I'll tell you the truth. Fear not, the light will fade as you climb."

I stepped forward. The orbs vibrated and moved towards each other to create a barrier line between me and it. I swung my left leg forward. They vibrated harder. I slid my right leg forward and almost bumped into them. They hovered backwards. "Don't listen to Wrath's Foolish Wisdom of the Flesh form," the pink orb pleaded. "Only God's wisdom gives integrity. This kind of wisdom lies."

I pushed forward.

"I thought you said in due time to tell her the truth," har-rumphed the silver orb.

"I'm desperate," the pink orb retorted.

I stepped onto the hill.

"That's it. Climb me. Ignore them. They lie," encouraged Wisdom of the Flesh. "Learn that God is not real. That spiritual is not reality. We are all material. You are a human-killer, a destroyer of realms. I allow you to climb."

I took another step forward and through the orbs, sending them spinning away from me. The fluorescent green depressed underneath my foot. I slid my left foot over this green. Artificial fur burred the sides of my ankles. It felt pleasant. Safe. Familiar, like the rug in my bedroom. I imagined a brick rising against these errant memories, and I moved my right foot forward. The orbs bubbled worry as I left them behind me.

The hill purred, "That's it human-killer, look up. You'll see that lying light is fading."

I looked up. The light dimmed. It still hurt my vision, though. *But if I keep going, it'll disappear, and I'll be in less pain, like Wisdom of the Flesh promises. Anything to be in less pain.* I walked as I drained those brief thoughts back into the cavern where they belonged, locked away, unable to be read. As I walked up the hill, the light dimmed more and more. I neared the crest.

"Come back," the pink orb called out from below me. "You don't know where you're going!"

"You know where you're going human-killer."

Yes! The thought leapt out of its locked cavern: *I am a human killer. I signed the papers to kill myself, and I'm proud of it.* I threw my shoulders back, lengthened my neck, and sharpened my vision to greet the crest, my climb's victory.

"So you should be proud," Wisdom of the Flesh said. "Ah, you say my name. That's good. Now come to my apex. Come to where you belong. Come and be proud."

"No! Stop!" the three orbs shouted together. Their voices reverberated in my mind, scattering my few thoughts, halting my feet. "Look around you. Really look!" they commanded.

I obeyed instinctively.

Suddenly I saw I was not on a hill but in a pit. Horror engulfed me. I scrambled up, but my feet slipped on the slick artificial fur, now somehow matted down and wet. I fell, face angling upward, arms and hands reaching to where the orbs hovered, bouncing and jerking sideways, unable to reach me or help me. I clenched my transparent fingers around a tuft of the slippery fur while averting my gaze from my hands. *They're not transparent*, I decided. *They look that way because my dying brain cells are making them look like that. I am material. I still exist. And Dr. V has to finish the job.*

"Your Dr. V was right," Wisdom of the Flesh vibrated my magnetic skin until my insides' atoms and molecules rumbled. "There is no reality but evidence-based materialism. You think you know me? You think you know them? Do you want their help? Help from your imagination that's created all this for you?"

"Yes, of course you do," the silver orb chimed. "Because we're real, not your imagination. Why do they always think we're figments of their dying oxygen-starved brains?"

I dropped my head, and my feet slid backwards to the bottom of the pit. My arms and hands strained to keep me in place.

"Come," said Wisdom of the Flesh. "Not much farther now to the end."

The end? That was what I'd wanted, why I'd lain down in that bed and had watched Dr. V push those plungers.

I let go of the artificial fur. I slid faster and faster towards the bottom. My atoms suddenly let go of each other. They merged with the floor of Wisdom of the Flesh. They slid between its molecules. They reconstituted themselves together as I fell through particulate-laden air. I fell and fell and fell.

Into garbage.

"Oomph."

Plastic shreds and styrofoam peanuts flung themselves up around me. Caustic air invaded me. I coughed and coughed and coughed, but plastic- and diesel-laden air didn't cease ravaging my being. I opened my eyes to see a cracked monitor staring back at me. It said, "Welcome to Hell Track."

Chapter Seven

HELL

The monitor grinned at me, the crack across its glass widening. I screamed and screamed, hearing my screams' harmonies echoing into me. I stopped screaming and panted at the monitor. Screams flew like fiends in whirlwinds all around me. Not mine. Others were screaming and shrieking and keening.

"Welcome to Hell Track," the monitor cheered.

I scrabbled back. Thick plastic bags slid out from under me, jerking me down, and I clutched them to halt my slide. Thin, crinkly bioplastic bags scrunched under the force of my fingers. My bottom sank down; I folded in on myself. Reaching up, I grasped unfamiliar textures, but I didn't care. I heaved myself up by my arms; leaned my weight on my hands, relieved they held me; and lifted my bottom up, which rotated my shoulders and left my hands behind me. In bridge pose, I scrambled backwards away from the grinning monitor with its bulging back and beige frame. It leered the 1980s, a time of bling and nightclubbing, a time I hadn't belonged in, like all the other decades, but worse, for I'd been in my twenties.

I walked myself backwards, my hands finding purchase on paper bags held up by unknown solid things and my feet following in their wake. I quickened my pace as I gained rhythm. My leading hand landed on a mango peel. The squishy interior splurged up between my fingers like a mushed larvae, and I screamed.

My bridge pose collapsed. I lay flat on my back. Things crawled underneath me, and I flung myself sideways. A glass eye looked up at me. And winked. I vaulted up, and the monitor said, "Welcome to Hell Track."

A plume of smoke erupted between me and it, obscuring its cracking visage. Through the plume appeared a face with two depthless wells staring at me. The face said, "Have you seen my father?"

What? Heat radiated into my bottom. My lower atoms were vibrating faster than my head's atoms.

"Have you seen my father?"

All I've seen is a monitor, and this dump I'm in is heating me like a frog in a pot. Why do I care about your father?

The smoke dissipated, revealing the monitor and a male form attached to the face. The eyes captivated mine. I about-faced from the monitor and apparition and stepped onto a slab of meat. Its softness gave way, flinging me backwards onto it, wrapping its edges around my bottom.

A sob hiccupped out of me. I slumped in the meat. My hands fell from my lap and lay palms up on either side of me as I wept waterless tears. Atoms flowed down my face. I didn't know how I knew they were atoms. The atoms melted the edges of my chin and transformed into waves that drummed on my palms like fingers hitting piano keys. My hands rested on blood-soaked, torn paper, and the waves spread further afield, tearing apart the already-present rips. I stilled myself. I bricked up the sobs, and the atom flow and waves stopped. The tears in the paper remained under my hands. I carefully lifted my right hand, then the left. I scanned the dump for a safe place to crawl onto; I needed to escape the meat.

"Welcome to Hell Track," repeated the monitor in its computer-generated voice.

Frustration rose in me like bile. *Hell! What is that?* The word "Hades" nudged my memory and something about a River Styx and a ferryman. I grabbed at the memory and shoved it down the drain hole into the cavern. I viciously locked the hole closed.

My eyes darted here and there over my immediate surroundings. I spotted a flat cardboard box. I stretched myself towards it and cautiously placed my left hand on it. It creased underneath my palm, the crease stretching outwards. But the cardboard kept its flatness. I lifted my bottom end out of the gross meat; must and mould tickled my nose. I sneezed, and my outstretched hand jerked, bending the cardboard down, upending me and landing me on my side. *Will I never get out of this wretched dump?*

"Welcome to Hell Track."

I yelled, "Shut up!" and clamped my right hand over my mouth, tasting plastic and stale moisturizer. My hand dropped. I lunged towards the flat yet bent cardboard, scrambled onto it, and searched ahead for an exit. I found the edge of the dump. I scrabbled over rotting fruit and meat, intact plastic bags, crinkled up plastic bundles, popped bubble wrap, hard plastic pill bottles, poly mailers with their tops open, plastic bowls partly inside ripped cardboard packaging, and coffee cups torn and strewn among all the other detritus. I scrambled through drifting, spouting smoke, my hands feeling singed as my hands and knees and feet contacted whatever was on top of the burning.

The screams wailed on.

The closer I ran like a bug to the edge of the garbage dump, the louder they became. I didn't stop; I sped up until I reached the edge and somersaulted off it. Whomp. I landed on cobblestones. I gasped, let my mind catch up, then lifted my head to sweep my surroundings. I couldn't hear the monitor anymore. Vast blueness opened above me for as far as I could see. I twisted around, searching for the monitor. The garbage dump rose high above me. I neither saw nor heard the monitor. I relaxed onto the cobblestones and lay there soaking in the blueness. Someone ran by, disturbing my magnetic field. I shuddered, sat up, and stood.

Ahead of me, people filled the space. Some were grabbing things off the dump. One woman shoved her arms into the dump at my head height; deeper and deeper she drove her arms up to her elbows, her shoulders chugging with the effort. She halted, and with a triumphant cry, hauled out her quarry.

A blue purse.

Wide at the bottom, clasped together at the top with a single silver clasp, and a thin, short strap ran from one corner to the other corner. A couple of white stitches which sewed the strap to the corners dangled loose. She slid the strap over her arm to her elbow. With a smile, she hugged the purse towards herself, swivelled around, and forced her legs away from the dump. The purse began to turn into little squares; the little squares began to space out; the little squares streamed back towards the dump. The purse disappeared from her arm and reconstituted itself on the dump's vertical side. Then, with a slurping sound, the dump sucked it into itself. The woman patted her midriff, glanced down at her arm, cried out, and ran back to the dump, where she began grabbing and pulling things out in her frenzied effort to reclaim her purse.

I turned my head to look ahead of me.

Fear marking their faces, people were running parallel to me towards a freakish mist way to my left, away from gates way to my right. I sensed the word, "Gates," as if they were sentient and named.

I squinted at the Gates. The most enormous gates—the only Gates—I'd ever seen. They rose higher than the dump. Thick cast-iron poles held the gates up on either side. Horizontal iron bars, blackened to light-sucking black, immobilized similar vertical bars, which were evenly spaced across them. The top horizontal bars curved towards each other, ending in finials like towering black-metal versions of wooden ones found at every hardware store. The bottom horizontal bar lay flat against the ground. People bent themselves away from the Gates' pull. "Help me! Help me!"

I turned away from the sight. I covered my ears, but the voices penetrated my mind.

A woman, her blonde hair in waves, with green pools for eyes, leaped off the dump, and molecules shivered around her. Their shivering grew into shaking back and forth until a green Jeep Cherokee Sport erupting from the dump caught her sideways, tumbling her neatly into the driver's seat. Its heavy steel door slammed shut, and the molecules whipped themselves into a vortex, lifting the Jeep higher and higher. Oblivious, she cranked her window down and yelled out of it. My mouth fell open as I bent backwards more and more, watching her go round and round, and round and round the vortex, she appearing and disappearing.

Who is she yelling at?

An ephemeral object appeared outside her driver-side window, the target of her blue-letter words. The object took human form. A small woman standing on a slab of asphalt with her arms hanging by her sides.

"I'm dealing with something!" the blonde bellowed at the small woman. Just before the Jeep and the small woman whipped out of sight, I noticed its passenger-side wheels were up on a concrete sidewalk, leaving a narrow path between it and a slatted wood fence.

I stood stunned.

The Jeep, with the woman still at the wheel, still glaring out her window, reappeared, and the vortex slowed like a film projector running at half speed.

"...there's room for you, you bitch!" the green-eyed blonde yelled at a slender man who was clutching the harness of a guide dog. He'd replaced the small woman in this whizzing scene.

He snapped, "Not for me. You heard about accessibility, right?"

The blonde thrust a blue-and-white disabled permit out the window. "Don't talk to me, you fucking..." her voice faded as she and her Jeep spun out of sight.

I stayed put to hear the rest.

The vortex shuddered as it zig-zagged towards the Gates. I followed it with my eyes. The blonde in her Jeep spun back round to the front of the vortex, her face level with the edge of her lowered window. "Get out of my business, bitch," she spat at a stocky woman leaning heavily on a cane and panting.

Why did the ephemeral person keep changing? Why did the scene outside the blonde's window change with each spin round the vortex while she didn't.

The woman retorted, "You're in my business."

What was this business? I took in the road under the stocky woman's feet; the sidewalk under the Jeep's wheels. My mind cleared: the ephemeral people's business was the sidewalk. The blonde's business was whatever she wanted to do.

"Stop talking to me, you c—"

The blue sky siphoned the vortex with its tableau, cutting her off. *Where has she gone? Was she real?* I shuddered and severed myself from these involuntary questions.

Red robes off to my left caught my attention. A trio garbed in red robes stood together, demarcating an inward-facing circle, their backs to the cacophony of screaming people running towards the mist, up ramps, along the cobblestones in any direction they could. Yet the Red Robes stood still, chattering and laughing to each other. I couldn't hear them, only see the outlines of mouths moving in their featureless faces.

Suddenly the circle opened up a gap in the direction of the mist. They raised their heads, calling out to a figure emerging from the mist. Another Red Robe. It was walking confusedly. Then it spotted the trio of Red Robes, and it smiled. It sped up into a determined, certain walk. The trio raised their arms, and the one out of the mist raised its arm in greeting. The new one tried to hug the others, but they stepped back hurriedly, shook their heads while smiling, and mimed bowing. The new one bowed back, and the four re-created the circle.

Thick books emerged out of their robes. They bent their heads over the books as, one by one, they opened them up. They conferred with the books. They nodded at each other. The molecules between them began to circle. Round and round. Faster and faster. A man with thick, wavy black hair appeared on the side opposite me. Another with a paunch and greying short, back, and sides joined him. Another with a brush cut. Another with the strangest, thinnest hair, fluffing up and settling down over speckled baldness. More men arrived, stocky, fat, thin, handsomely slim. Skin shades from waxy white to pink-white to florid to grey-stubbled brown. Women with metallic blonde hair or long brown hair supported them, holding the men up so that they appeared strong and surefooted. The men halted near the Red Robes, and the foursome opened their circle to listen while the women stood behind, heads lowered, hands holding the mens' backs. The Red Robes nodded to the men's moving mouths and recreated their circle. The men walked away from the circle and each other. The women, retaining their supportive hands on their mens' back, slid their feet forwards as they increased speed to catch up and walk side by side, sliding their hands across their mens' backs to clutch their hands or arms. Only the man with the fluffy hair covering his speckled, bald dome walked alone. A dark mist waved in and out of his skin, sending heavy musk into the air. All the men ignored people running towards them, crying for help, except for the one with the dark mist. He waved to the people running on the upward track. People nearby tried to grasp onto him, pleading for his help. His mist twisted around their arms, pulled them in, merged them into his speckled skin, and the man and mist grew. A few veered from him to grab onto the other men and women, for these men and women planted their feet with confidence and stable solidity, whereas no one else did in Hell Track. But their hands pinwheeled through nothing, and they stumbled.

"Ah-ha!" a cry shot up from the Red Robes foursome.

A large rectangle of parchment paper emerged in the space between two of the Red Robes. Black ink calligraphic letters decorated it. The foursome grabbed it, and began to scratch out some of the lettering. The molecules between them began to circle, then spin in their midst yet didn't touch them. The spinning quickened and fattened. The four Red Robes, oblivious to the spinning molecules, kept referring to their tomes and wrote letters over the scratched-out ones. The molecules became a vortex. The vortex rose and became a tornado that lifted up the skirts of their robes, billowing them outwards. Yet still they chattered and laughed over their texts and didn't pause in their rewriting of the parchment. People nearby who'd been running towards them for help spun on their heels to get away from the tornado. The tornado rose to the blue sky and spun clouds of pain into its blueness. The pain clouds crashed into each other; heat poured down like an expanding explosion. Thunder followed and flattened people. Rain burst out of the clouds and pelted my face, drove into my head, threw up the stink of stagnant mud puddles from ravines in the Spring. The cobblestones turned to mud, and the ground underneath me became a sliding, mucky river rushing towards the Gates, its stink rising like a chemical vapour cloud. The mud flung itself over people as they slid and slipped in their attempts to run away from the Gates. Some fell into the river, which churned into rapids near the Gates.

My eyes widened at the sight near the Gates. The violent mud river suddenly became cobblestones again, with a thin slide of liquified clay over them. The tornado blew the air from near the Gates towards me. The freshness of a pottery wheel hit me. Then the ravine-mud-pool stink returned as the tornado veered its edges away from me and towards the Red Robes. I kept watching the action near the Gates. People scrambled on to their feet again and away from the Gates, except the ones who'd given up and were repeating, "I'm sorry. I'm so sorry." Their apologies crashed into each other like opposing waves as they each spoke what they were sorry for. They fell and became part of the mud slip. They slipped under the bottom horizontal bar. Some who had found their footing after the churning river had spat them out onto the slick cobblestones, but who hadn't stopped saying sorry, entered the red spaces between the bars.

And vanished.

I gulped.

I turned my head away and saw rain lashing near the Red Robes. They alone stood dry and stable, untouched by spinning molecules, tornadoes, rain, or mud. I looked around for the men who'd approached them as I slowly, slowly slid to my right like a car hydroplaning on a slick road. I spotted them, each far apart from the other, each also solid in their footing, none screaming or crying or apologizing. The one with dark mist stood apart, watching the Red Robes, his mist snatching errant people as they slid by too closely, fattening him each time the mist merged them into his speckled bald dome. In this maelstrom, he and the men seemed as comfortable as the Red Robes. Neither the hot wind blasting nor the teeming chilly rain affected their footing as they walked towards wherever they were walking towards.

I slanted myself against the sliding mud and tried to step towards the ramp that angled up to the mist to my left. Only on the ramp could people move away from the Gates. They clutched their stomachs with one arm against the bone-chilling wet as they extended the other forwards, their legs straining against the heated circling winds and the Gates' magnetic pull.

"Help me!" a hand clutched at my arm as a person slid past me. I shook my arm free.

Lashings of rain blinded me. I shivered. Smoke belched from the dump behind me, suffocating me with the chemical smell of a cheap department store perfume. I lost any sense of direction, and the scenes faded as if filmed over by slicked-on mineral oil. *Which way is the ramp?* A glimmer of blue appeared before me. I followed it as another and a third joined it.

The soul family.

"How do I get out of this hallucination?" I yelled above the screams, and the driving rain, and the clashing apologies, and nuclear thunder. I resisted the force of the tornado trying to spin me towards the Gates. I thought heaviness into my feet so I could keep my footing as mud slid underneath them from the left and tried to drag me sideways towards the Gates.

"You're not in an hallucination," Pink shouted. "This is Hell Track. We can't tell you why you're in Hell Track. You have to figure that out for yourself."

"What's the point of asking for help if you don't get it," I muttered to myself. "Why are you here?"

"We're your soul family."

"There's no such thing."

"Yes there is," Silver shot back. "We exist because we're here."

"No!" I screeched. "No!"

Chapter Eight

HELL CONTINUED

"It's okay," Pink consoled.

"Stop saying it's okay and get me back to Dr. V so he can end me properly."

"God, you're so obsessed with that man!" the silver orb snorted.

"Hush," Pink replied. "We are here to guide Charlotte Elisabeth, not tell her what to think."

"Then guide me back! This is not real. It's my oxygen-deprived brain hallucinating. I wanted an end, not exist here!" I flapped my right hand at the cacophony. The tornado wound down into the ground. The clouds flopped onto the upper ramp, engulfing the people struggling towards the mist. Choking and coughing, they emerged up the ramp, still struggling upward towards the mist way to my left, still crying out, "Help me!" I heard another word embedded in their pleas, but I was in no mood to listen. I wanted out.

61

"There is no out—"

"Yes, there is. There's always a way out," the yellow orb spoke up. "First, believe you are where you are."

"I. Am. In. My. Brain. That's. Created. This. Hallucination," I ground out.

"No. You're. Not!" echoed silver orb. "You know you can call us by our names. It won't kill you." The orb jiggled like silvery bells giggling.

Pink said, "I think it's time we need to tell you one thing. This place is Hell Track and isn't you hallucinating. It's not oxygen deprivation. Oxygen deprivation results in loss of focus. Have you lost focus? Have you found yourself not paying attention at all to what's going on around you?"

"No," I replied sullenly. Then I thought of the memories those strange places elicited. "Well, actually," I said, regaining my certainty, "My mind did wander off into memory."

"Oxygen deprivation leads to memory loss. How could you remember if your lack of oxygen was eating away at your memory?"

I stared at the pink orb. I disliked its sudden bluntness. Its blue energy bands undulating on its perimeter, the orb continued, "Have you had trouble moving your limbs?"

"No," I reluctantly agreed.

"Loss of motor co-ordination is another sign of oxygen deprivation."

How can I have motor coordination when I'm not a physical body? I fixated on the horizon, cudgelling my mind for answers.

"So are seizures!" I retorted, remembering Dr. V had quoted a famous author. I repeated his words. "Dostoyevsky experienced seizures, he has a type of seizure named after him. He described these seizures in his novel *The Idiot*. I quote, 'he had always experienced a moment or two when his whole heart, and mind, and body seemed to wake up to vigour and light; when he became filled with joy and hope, and all his anxieties seemed to be swept away forever. When I recall and analyze the moment, it seems to have been one of harmony and beauty in the highest degree—an instant of deepest sensation, overflowing with unbounded joy and rapture, ecstatic devotion, and completest life? I would give my whole life for this one instant.'"

The head orb remarked, "You have a wonderful memory to recall verbatim what Dr. V quoted at you."

I opened my mouth and shut it again.

"Have you experienced any of those things yet?"

Doubts about Dr. V slipped out of the locked cavern and sliced pain through me at the idea he'd lied. I whacked the doubts back in. "Deepest sensations," I volleyed back at Pink. "I've had those. Each sound. Even the horrible stench around me here is deeper than I recall. Ravines didn't stink as much as this mud."

"What mud?"

I pointed downward and followed my finger's direction. "Uh..." I frowned at the cobblestones in deepest purples, maroon reds, and greyest greys, dry as the desert sand. I raised my head. The bluest of sky blue arced overhead, over the racket of screams and sobs, the jarring smells of musks and lavender and vile mud, the scratchy fumes of rotting vegetables and mouldy fruit. Movement caught my eye to the right and behind me. I twisted around to see the woman haul the blue purse out and, with a satisfied huff, slide its strap over her arm, whereupon the purse disintegrated and streamed back towards the dump as she crossed the cobblestones to the ramp. When she squeezed her arm against her torso and glanced down, she howled in frustration and stomped back to the dump. I shut my vision against this sight and concentrated on bricking up despair and its parasitic emotion of futility.

"No seizure, no oxygen deprivation, is causing this reality. You continue to exist because you do exist."

I rubbed my forehead, feeling a slight magnetic push against my fingers. I intoned Dr. V's last explanations for near-death experiences. "Highly-trained professionals, NASA astronauts and USA test pilots, the toughest of the tough, the smartest of men with agile minds and resilient bodies were put into centrifuges during the Cold War to dissect what happens during loss of consciousness and its subsequent recovery. They measured the cardiovascular system stopping blood flow to the brain," I paused. I sank into myself. I straightened up and said, "That's what happened to me. That's what was supposed to happen to me. No more oxygen. No more blood flow." I resumed my recitation. "The pilot faints. When consciousness returns, they are briefly confused and disorientated, like I was when I was seeing the Dying with Dignity Suite from the ceiling. These men recount tunnel vision and bright lights, a feeling of awakening from sleep. I'd like to note here that I was asleep then I was not, as if something awakened me and planted me on the ceiling looking down at myself and Dr. V. Looking down upon oneself is part of near-death experiences." I glared at the three orbs.

They bobbed in front of me like rhythmic balls in calm water.

"Well?" I queried. Silence was their reply, as if they were listening. I kept going. "They had a sense of peaceful floating, of out-of-body experiences—like me on the ceiling—pleasurable and euphoric sensations; short but intense dreams; conversations with family." I paused and gathered myself. "You call yourselves my soul family. It's the same thing, isn't it?"

"Where is the euphoria?" Pink asked.

"There can be negative euphoria. Euphoria means a state of intense excitement. I allow that it usually means pleasurable excitement. But this," I waved my hand at this unmelodiousness place, "is excitement. They're all screaming except...," I frowned as I turned my head towards the Red Robes, "...them."

"Do you know who they are?"

I shook my head. "I'm not interested. The only thing that interests me is to get back to where Dr. V is and tell him to finish the job. I always provided my clients with complete jobs."

Some familiar sound beeped behind me. I turned around and craned my neck. Just above my head sat my favourite computer display. "Oh!" I exclaimed. I reached up to grab it and noticed the new tax code sitting beside it, the one that had arrived the day before my euthanasia date. I'd unpacked it, using my exacto knife to slice the tape holding the box together, pulling the two half lids apart, sticking my arms into the box, and hauling the brand-new tax code into my arms. I'd carried it reverently to my desk and stroked it. I usually laid it at the top left corner of my long desk, a familiar presence connecting me to my first accounting days, but this being my last time, I'd wanted to savour it. I stroked the code's cover and smoothed my hand over the top of my computer display, the wide, curved screen reflecting the bookcase behind my desk. I liked the feel, the heftiness of the code in physical form, but I used the CPA's basic online tax code package. Computer searches, I had to admit, were more efficient, and I respected every dollar my clients spent on my services to not waste them.

As I stared up at the display and tax code on the dump's edge, I thought, *Never again will I work on someone's complicated taxes*. Regret twinged my heart, but I knew I'd made the right decision.

Shaking myself free of the memory, I extended my transparent, magnetically-held together arms towards the display.

"You know what will happen," said Silver.

I ignored them. I grabbed the display with one hand and the tax code with the other. Surprised I could hold each with one hand, I brought them down and hugged them. I turned to face the three orbs, "I'm returning to the hospital's Dying with Dignity Suite one way or another."

Pink bobbed higher than the other two.

I set off for the ramp, and cracks running in grid patterns scratched my hands. I looked down. The display and the tax code tome had transformed into small squares; the squares began to flow back towards the dump behind me. "Argh!" I raged. I stomped my feet as I hadn't since I was a small child. "I want what I was promised!"

A person passing by, sliding down the dry cobblestones towards the Gates, screaming "Help me God!" stopped screaming and contemplated me as their body careened towards the Gates. Before they left hearing range, they yelled, "Ask God for help!" Then they screamed over and over, "Help me God! Help me God!"

Chuckling nearby swivelled my gaze towards it. The fluffy-haired man, his dark mist swirling and bending and reaching, was observing me. I ignored him.

"God is a figment of cowardly people too afraid of the end to face the inevitable. We all move on to rest," I hissed the familiar words, drilled into me over my six decades. Cauldrons of sparking thoughts simmered revenge against these three orbs torturing me. A vacuum brushed and sucked at my skin. As I turned to find out what was happening, I saw simultaneously dark mist dragging at my skin and the yellow orb zip between me and it.

"Don't let Hell Track's staff get close," the yellow orb warned. "Else you won't exist any more. Second death is no joke."

I didn't know what second death was, but the non-existing part appealed. I contemplated the retreating dark mist.

A sigh floated towards me from the silver orb, distracting my attention from the fluffy-haired man vanishing towards the ramp. "First oxygen deprivation, then seizures, then loss of blood flow. Now no such thing as God."

"What will be your next defence against the reality so obvious around you?" the yellow orb asked.

I stared at the yellow one, forgetting all I'd just seen. I fantasized taking its roundness in my two hands and crushing it, grabbing the pink one and twisting each pole until it tore apart, and slamming the silver one onto the cobblestones. They seemed unperturbed by my imaginings. I knew they heard my thoughts. They'd said often enough that thoughts were communication means here. I intensified my stare. I added blood and gore spouting from their insides, screams curdling passersby' blood.

"It's okay," said Pink. "Your rage is natural. We know what you've been through. We understand."

"Argh! You don't understand!"

"We've seen you your whole life. God gave us to you."

"What is God? No! Don't answer that. I don't want to know. I'm not a coward. I simply wanted my pain to end, my existence to end. I wanted peace at last. Why is that so wrong?"

"It's not wrong," Pink replied. "It's not wrong at all. Just like your rage is not wrong, wanting peace is not wrong. You're only going about it the wrong way."

I tunnelled my vision to the pink highlights. They shot into high-definition focus. I thirsted to laser cut the pink out of the blue orb. Pink bobbed as if nodding. I suddenly realized I'd let them in.

I covered my vision with my transparent hands and narrowed my focus to my emotions. One by one, I bricked them up. Replacing my rage with calm; replacing despair and futility with a sense of nothing; expelling my shame over copying the woman with the purse when I'd known better, a habit Mom had called out many times. I aimed my thoughts, one by one, down towards the drain hole into the cavern. I inserted the circular lock, twisted it shut, and locked it.

"Do you feel better?"

The orbs danced like floating fairies.

The silver-highlighted one rotated and spoke to the pink and yellow orbs, "I think she feels better."

The yellow one replied, "She feels nothing at all. That's not better. It's easier."

"It'll work for now," the pink one commented.

Chapter Nine

AND HELL KEEPS ON

"Maybe we should tell her about God?"

The Red Robes nodded at each other, and they opened their circle.

"She doesn't seem to know anything."

The Red Robes walked towards me, heads angled towards each other, carrying their tomes, the parchment nowhere to be seen.

"Is it our job to tell her?"

The Red Robes discussed this question as they stepped closer.

"Of course it is! Since her parents and schooling taught her nothing about religion, not even its legal history—"

The Red Robes tacked direction to my left.

"I wonder how she understood English literature?"

They stopped short of the dump as their conversation livened.

Pink asked, "Does it matter now? She has all of eternity to read those works with a full background of knowledge. Right now, we must consider if we tell her about God?"

One of the Red Robes raised their heads. "God? Of course, we will tell her." The other Red Robes paused in their debate and looked at the three orbs.

Pink orb rotated languidly. "Charlotte Elisabeth has not heard of God's role in our existence."

"That is of no occasion," said Red Robe Two, standing next to the first one.

"Of course it is," Pink replied. "God is everything."

"No, God is the domain of religion. Religion had its place in its time. But we are the law, and the law is the foundation of a modern, progressive society," Red Robe Three answered.

"Why do you say that?"

"It has always been that way," remonstrated Red Robe Four.

"No, remember it has been that way since the Enlightenment," Red Robe One corrected.

"Ah yes," replied Red Robe Four. "That is when humans became understanding of humanity."

The other three Red Robes nodded sagely.

"Really?" replied the silver orb sarcastically as it floated up to hover beside Pink. Yellow followed suit, and they fluttered in front of the Red Robes out of their usual order of pink, yellow, and silver.

"Yes, really," Red Robe Two said aloofly. "The Enlightenment is when men put their reason to the test and found that reason created a higher order of thinking about the things that matter. Law, ethics, and behaviours that run life."

"How so?" Silver asked.

Red Robe One raised their eyebrows as if the answer was obvious.

"Take her, for example," Silver said, pointing to me.

"No, we will not use her for fodder for debate!" Pink interrupted.

"Why not?" Silver pushed back. "She's here now before her time because of them."

I goggled. *Say what now?* Alarm clanged in my head; I didn't want to be used as fodder, and Silver's...no, I wouldn't repeat her words.

"In what way are we to do with her?" asked Red Robe Two, bowing superciliously towards Pink.

"You're here, comfortable," Yellow responded. "You claim reason is your metier and allows for higher-order thinking that God disallows. You've watched people coming and going in Hell Track, yet you don't know why she's here? Use your reason."

"You are not a lawyer, are you?"

"I am Blair. That's who I am. Career choices, labels, no longer matter in this stage of life."

"Life is governed by a set of laws. We," Red Robe Three pointed to the other three, "reached the highest echelons of understanding and interpreting the highest laws of the land. We attended short courses on physics and medicine in order to execute our judgements. We listened to select experts. We often find the public doesn't understand the law sufficiently to understand our rulings. You cannot understand if you are not a lawyer that reason requires facts. Take this fact we were just discussing. The fact of life. It's a fact that death as we traditionally experience it is inhumane. We have given physicians permission to provide health care to ease the suffering of those who wish to end the cruelty of life in a dignified and non-dangerous way."

"Why do you suggest life is cruel and death inhumane?"

Red Robe One reared back. "Why everyone knows that. Cancer, heart disease, depression. These things are terminal. They bring on pain and suffering that medical professionals agree is intractable."

"The Supreme Court didn't agree in 1993."

"The Supreme Court didn't have the Constitution and laws in front of them we do now. As Heraclitus said, 'The only constant is change.' That includes our Charter of Rights and Freedoms."

"Heraclitus said, 'potamoisi toisin autoisin embainousin hetera kai hetera hudata epirrei,' that is, 'On those stepping into rivers staying the same other and other waters flow.' When we know the originators' words, we can see their meaning better. The river is, by its nature, flowing water; flowing water changes. But the people who step into the flowing water remain the same. You may change the course of the law, but you can't change human beings who step into the law. Their nature will distort the law's intended course."

"We cannot say the 1993 Supreme Court erred in their judgement," Red Robe Four nodded, and the other three nodded in unified agreement. "Judges can rule only with the facts presented to them and the laws as they have been interpreted. But we looked through the Charter carefully. We determined that the original judgement was not about being against suicide in any and every circumstance but to protect vulnerable persons from being induced to commit suicide in a moment of weakness."

Blue fire spat and sparked from all three orbs. Yellow glowed blue fire into green. "A moment of weakness? Isn't suffering a moment of weakness? Isn't that when a person needs humans around them the most to support their life energy?"

"People with terminal illnesses understand they are about to die. It is not a moment of weakness to want suicide."

"What?!" Blair hollered. "Most dying people don't want to suicide."

"We've seen the tens of thousands who've hailed our judgement and asked their physicians for the health care they truly need. We have done an ethical service to them. It is unethical to make people wait for curative health care. Dying with dignity is the ultimate humane cure."

The three orbs quaked. "How? In that case, is it unethical to make a fetus wait to be born? Is it unethical to make one of a couple wait to be married? Is it unethical to require children to wait to graduate?"

"What?"

"Those are specious reasons," waved Red Robe Four. "We are, of course, against suicide. And we understand waiting is part of life. But dying is the end. A person who requests medical assistance in dying knows what they want."

"Do victims of domestic violence know what they want?"

Red Robe Four smirked. "Of course not. That is why we progressed the law to protect them from their own errors in thinking."

"How is it that in their suffering they don't know their mind, but the ones who seek a doctor to kill them do?"

"They are entirely different situations," Red Robe One condescended. "The woman must be protected from being abused. Too many women die at the hands of their spouses."

"Why are their deaths not okay? After all, they are in severe and intolerable suffering, so severe that they remain with the abuser because they see no way out."

"They do not wish to die," Red Robe Three snorted.

"Are you sure of that? Some suicide because killing their spouse is the only other option they can see. Will you consider it good and ethical for them to seek medical help to die?"

"They are not terminally ill. They are not suffering from pain. And obviously, they don't want to die."

"You don't read case law."

"How dare you!" fumed Red Robe One. "We are judges. We are familiar with the laws. We have clerks and staff to help us with our research. We attained our standings through diligence and ethical applications of the law. We will not be lectured to by a nobody who doesn't understand."

Silver meandered closer and hooted, "You have no choice because in this stage of life, you can't escape us if we choose not to leave you."

Red Robe One reddened with indignation.

"Answer me this," Yellow barked. "In the case of the neurosurgeon and the family physician. She wanted divorce, yet she stayed living with him. The family physician agreed to the neurosurgeon's pleas to better himself and hold off on divorce. Did she need to be protected from herself? Why did she remain with him after years of physical assaults when she knew that staying with him risked her life? Her acquiescence to stay, was that not a request to risk death? Perhaps even to die? Or had she fooled herself into thinking it love because however men treat women, it reflects love?"

"How dare you suggest such a thing," raged Red Robe One.

"If the law believes that a suffering person who through her actions states she's willing to die for a chance at repaired love, needs protection because the suffering makes her vulnerable in her weakness, then why not the same for the suffering ill and disabled?"

"When one has tired of life, and pain is all there is—"

"Is pain all there is when people are seeking a physician to kill them? Is it not more that the human beings around them are not providing pain relief, that trauma has perverted human social structure to such an extent they've created a language of pain rather than a language of health, life, and vitality? Jesus said you can't serve two masters. Caesar and God. In your parlance, you cannot serve death and life. Death is the end stage of life on Earth, but a physician's purpose is to heal, help, and support life on Earth, not end it prematurely," Yellow huffed.

"How do you know it's premature?" Red Robe One demanded, leaning in to Pink and away from Yellow's cold blue fire.

Yellow floated closer to Red Robe One who stepped back. Yellow gestured to me. "Here is one example in front of you. She hadn't yet reached the necessary time and space to repair her relationships and to finish her Soul Track, mature in her material form."

"We gave her the freedom to make her own autonomous choice. Her life did not end prematurely. It ended on her time."

"She can't know her future. The present is not the future. Change is inevitable. Her suffering blinded her to that knowledge."

"Your God gave her free will."

"God also gave us each other to sustain us during our weaknesses, not to create laws to accelerate death prematurely."

"You cannot prove medical assistance in dying leads to premature death."

"Would you say capital punishment ends life prematurely?"

"Of course. Capital punishment is barbaric. That's biblical. And as we said, the Enlightenment separated church and state. We have come to understand that God does not judge like man does. Man's judgement is reasoned and humane. Capital punishment often catches the innocent in its grasp. We have come to understand that we cannot allow that. Capital punishment allows for no other option, no other finding of fact, once it's executed. In order to protect even the one innocent, the law cannot allow capital punishment."

"Then why is the same protection not afforded to those with suicidal ideation? Is the one vulnerable person not deserving of protection?"

"The terminally ill are dying. Suicide is a natural response to a life condemned to severe and intolerable suffering."

"Who condemns the sufferer to intolerable and severe suffering?"

The Red Robes stared. Red Robe One said sarcastically, "Perhaps it's your God."

"God created a good universe, a beautiful Earth, creatures to inhabit it, and humans to tend and nurture it. Humans chose to decay and abuse it. You're right God doesn't judge like humans do. God wants to save it all."

"God has nothing to do with Earth, the universe, laws, and the ethical and constitutional judgements. Man uses his reason to improve it. Every generation progresses it."

"Yes," Pink agreed. "In the nineteenth century, physicians and the law locked up the insane and the suicidal. Ashamed families barricaded their ill indoors where no one could see them. Thus they couldn't cast their families out of society. Now you simply kill them. Cheaper to kill. There's no cost to housing them, to protecting them, to creating chemical addictions, to offering health care for decades in order to sustain their lives and allow them to fulfill their purposes that God created them for."

Red Robes chortled and chuckled, laughed and roared, and choked.

"God created every human being," Pink continued over their coughing. "God thought carefully about what each created being was to be like. Like a potter considers their creation, so God considered every human being before bringing them to life. God gave them talents, the potential for skills. God placed them in a place and time for those talents and skills to be used best. God infused each person with purpose. We're all God's children—even you."

Red Robe One gasped with one last cough and, pausing, smirked at Pink. "I beg your pardon but I have long since grown up."

"Grown up and listened to your own rationalizations. What have you wrought? You've allowed governments to cut health care funds and services for the chronically ill. You've given doctors permission to no longer seek cures or accompany their patients in the long decades of chronic illness. You've given governments an out for providing income support to the vulnerable. Instead, the vulnerable exist in intolerable poverty and mismanaged illnesses, lonely in societies that shun them because of their very health status, not listened to nor cared for by their physicians until that moment they express a desire to end it. Then suddenly the wheels of health care turn. Physicians snap to attention. They rapidly provide access to death. To receive care, the vulnerable must express a wish to die. Isn't that the core of suffering? And once expressed, the options are to change their mind and return to the loneliness of being ignored, impoverished, shunned, and mismanaged—or to end it. Which would you pick?"

Red Robe One sniffed.

Red Robe Two said, "It is not in our purview to decide how our judgements will be executed."

"The wise consider the consequences of their thoughts, words, actions, and judgements," Pink noted.

"That is up to the Legislative arm of governments. We merely interpret the Charter of Rights and Freedoms."

"Merely?" Yellow-tinged blue sparks shot towards Red Robe Two. "You claim you must be wise in all areas in order to execute the law. How then are you so unwise to not see how human behaviour on Earth works? The foolish wisdom of the flesh contradicts itself. You said capital punishment captures the innocent, and therefore can't be allowed. Yet you see no problem with euthanasia capturing the vulnerable?" Yellow snapped.

"Medical assistance in dying. Please use the appropriate term."

"Very well. Doctors killing their patients capture the vulnerable as capital punishment captures the innocent." Rage suffused the faces of the Red Robes. Red Robe One tried to interrupt, but Yellow was blazing yellow streaks in its blue fire, its voice a flame thrower's roar. "You said capital punishment allows for no other option, no other finding of fact, and thus cannot be allowed. You said to save one innocent life, capital punishment must be banned. Yet you blind yourself to how doctors can call a person terminal yet be wrong. Do you believe that doctors and surgeons are better able to understand the past and predict the future, to discern who's vulnerable and who's not, than lawyers and judges?"

Red Robes glared at yellow orb.

"You don't see that when pain becomes intractable, it isn't because pain is unable to be alleviated, it's because physicians, lazy and egotistical, deafen themselves to their patients and refuse exercising their brain cells to help their patients live and die with the true dignity of surrounding love. Love carries the suffering but demands compassion and vulnerability from the person who loves the needy. That's hard! It's easier to kill than heal. In your august judgement, you ignored your governments underfunding of palliative care. You accelerated death above all findings of fact for those who society used to barricade behind locked doors."

"And where is your God in all this? If God created human beings, why has he not alleviated their suffering?" Red Robe Three scoffed.

Pink said, "God sent us each other to alleviate each other's sufferings."

"Then why didn't that happen?" I blurted out as thought became speech before I could stop it.

"That's a long story. It's why we're here for you. And they are why you're here now instead of where you were meant to be."

Red Robes flounced away as the orbs floated closer towards me. Yellow orb's glow returned to its normal pleasant blueness with yellow highlights.

"I don't understand. How are judges the reason I'm here?"

"They gave Dr. V permission to kill you. They didn't order government to fund the health care you needed. But they're only arbiters of the law and tunnel their vision to rationalizing arguments. They're not arbiters of humanity."

I shook my head. Red Robe One approached the dump and reached up. Red Robe Two reached up as well, and together they pulled out three tomes with worn leather covers. I anticipated what was about to happen. Red Robe Three slid the tome they were carrying into the slot from where the first two had taken out the heavy text. The dump accepted it, and shifted the returned tome down into a stable upright position. Red Robe Three took one of the hefty leather-bound texts from the first two. And Red Robe Four received the third. They strolled back to their circle area. The tomes didn't disintegrate. My mouth fell open.

"They belong here. The dump knows it's own," Silver said sardonically.

I switched my gaze to Silver. "Why are you here?"

"We're your soul family," Pink replied. "We're here for you, with you. We won't abandon you."

"Why not?"

"Because we love you!"

"Love always abandons. It's cruel and looks for ways to get at you."

"That's wrath. Not love," replied Pink.

I shook my head. But curiosity sidled up into my mind. "Who are you?"

Pink replied, "We're triplets. I'm Bailey. They're Blair and Blake. We're your soul family."

I allowed curiosity to remain in me. "Bailey," I said as I glanced at Pink. "Blair," I said as I shifted my gaze to Yellow. I eyed Silver. "Blake. You're here for me? You want to know me?"

"Yes. We do know you. That's why we came to you. It's why we're here," Pink-Bailey replied.

I reeled back. *They knew me yet they still came?* I focused my vision on them. I took them in. "Am I existing? Where are you going?"

"Yes, you exist. We go where you go," replied Bailey.

Oh, my mouth shaped the word without sound. "All of you? Blair and Blake, too?"

"Yes," the three said in unison.

Lightning flashed to our right, between us and the Gates. I gasped, and I swear the orbs smiled, relief suffusing their highlights with stainless colours of pink, yellow, and silver. Lightning flashed pure white. Hell Track vanished from my sight.

Chapter Ten

FLOWER POWER

Flowers danced into infinity on my right. Red-striped pink tulips, their pinkness so glorious they hummed. Bluebells upon bluebells like miniature blue lights glowing out their heads. Yellow asters and golden daisies, with their coal-black eyes shining like black pearls under an arching sky of such intense blue, it drew my gaze. Grass greener than any I'd seen, blushing blue stripes along their edges, lay under my feet and accompanied the flowers into the disappearing distance.

"Welcome to what I like to call the Flower Power Track," a Golden Lab said to me as it walked up and sat at my feet. Brown eyes blinked up at me.

I jumped backwards.

The Golden Lab's puffed-up inner eyebrows gathered together. Fluffing out his lips, he cocked his head and looked towards the soul family swaying on my left side. I twisted my head to follow its action.

Beyond the three, a booklet of giant postcards waited as if for someone to unfold them. I stepped to my left. Fresh grass scents powered up into my nose, and I suppressed a sneeze. But my nose hadn't twitched, and neither of my nostrils experienced irritating tickles; I'd only felt a sneeze coming on because grass and flower pollen always made me sneeze.

A breeze caressed my cheeks and wagged tulips and asters and daisies' heads. They sang to the breeze, the bluebells harmonizing underneath their melody.

I needed to bolt. So many allergens in such vibrant colours and singing! *What kind of madhouse is this?*

The front postcard unfolded and slid towards me as if on silent rails. I stepped back. The second postcard unfolded itself and followed the first.

"Don't be afraid," Pink-Bailey said.

"I'm not afraid!" I countered. "I don't want them near me."

The front quickened towards me, training the others behind. The picture on its face sharpened: walls of a nursery. Creamy white, and—

I averted my gaze. I scouted behind me for a safe exit. The same mist that bookended Hell Track bookended this one. I faced the three soul family and focused my vision on the postcards beyond them, but a glare far, far in the distance distracted me. Its rays shone out in sharp lines in all directions, waiting to impale an errant body walking or flying past.

I re-fixed my gaze on the postcards that were now a metre behind the soul family. I stepped backwards and twisted my head to check behind me then back to check the postcards' position. Several had unfolded themselves and streamed back towards the glare in a giant, colourful zig-zag.

"Don't be afraid," Pink-Bailey repeated. "They're your life review."

I shouted, "Get me out of here!"

"This is a good thing, and you're not alone."

The front postcard shot past the soul family, its wake swirling the orbs towards the flowers that bowed in greeting. I leaped to the side and away. The postcard changed trajectory to meet me face on. *No!* my mind yelled. *I want no part of reliving my life.* Once had been enough. I crouched. It zipped up to me. I leapt and grabbed its edge. I swung my legs up and towards the flowers and landed on my feet, the green grass cushioning my landing. Fresh mown scent sighed upwards. I ran deep into the flowers, repeating to myself that their pollen can't harm me. I checked behind me. The zig-zagging unfolding postcards curled themselves like a scorpion's tail. A rushing wind arose and flattened the tulips and daisies and bluebells in a path towards me. The soul family zipped upwards over the bent flowers out of the wind's way.

"It's okay," Pink shouted over the gale.

"It's not okay," I gritted out. *I. Do. Not. Want. To. Relive. My. Life. Ever.*

The fourth postcard's edge rippled my skin. I grabbed it to prevent it from dragging me into its picture of the old blue car with me in the front seat. Never did I want to relive this memory. The postcard twined its other side towards me and hauled me into the pictured memory.

"HOW COULD YOU embarrass me like that?" Mom yelled. "It's only the dentist. You have strong, white teeth like a Trent does. We don't feel pain."

Pressed against the blue car's ceiling in a futile effort not to witness, the memory played.

MY SMALL SELF sat silently on the car's rough fabric front bench seat, a rare honour Mom had bestowed because it was only me and her. Shame suffused me and my small self as I relived the high whine of the dentist's drill in the next room penetrating my skull. My whole self had vibrated in tune with that whine. It made me want to run.

Mom kept yelling. "You only had to sit still for twenty minutes! Twenty! That's all, and your cleaning would be over. But no, you had to run out screaming! What did the other mothers think? They thought I can't handle my child. A six-year-old! What mother can't handle a six-year-old? Only an incompetent one! I'm not incompetent," she screamed at the windshield, her knuckles white, her chest contacting the steering wheel, her stiletto-shod foot smashing the accelerator. That's how Mom drove: accelerating, daring the other cars to get out of her way, until a red light forced her to brake, rocking the car on its front wheels.

Shame flooded me from my small self and from Mom. And rage. *Why rage?* I wondered and received an immediate answer. I hadn't screamed. Shame-birthed rage spewed out of her, drowning my small self's shame as she shifted centimetre by centimetre to the passenger door and crushed herself against it. *I know Mom's rage, but what is this shame-rage? And why do I have to feel it?* I repeatedly hit my transparent head with my transparent hands to force their emotions out of me.

Neither spoke as the engine roared, and the car tore down the middle lane of the three-lane road.

My small self slid forward on the seat and stood up to look over the dashboard.

Mom gritted her teeth. "Get back on your seat. How many times have I told you."

My small self sat back down and scooted backwards. I somehow felt the fabric scratching the backs of my legs. My child self wore a short skirt that ended above her knees.

Mom braked hard, vicious satisfaction flying out of her and smacking me as my child self flew off the seat and catapulted into the space underneath the dashboard. I'd learned soon after that day how to curl my body so that I landed safely in that space. I unwound and, one hand at a time, crawled back onto my seat stealthily. No emotions came out of my six-year-old self as I concentrated on not letting Mom hear me, as she remained fixated on the red light. Yet my current existing self picked up that Mom knew what I was doing. *She did?* Like in this memory, her eyes always remained on the lights or the car ahead, her body canted forward, hands squeezing the steering wheel, her foot hovering over the accelerator, ready to slam the car into speed the moment the light turned green or the car ahead rolled forward.

My small self squished herself up to the door and lay my arms across the open window, hands folded over each other. I watched her gaze out the window. I cringed as I remembered what came next.

"Mom what's that building?"

"What building?"

"That building over there," one arm unbent to point towards the church kitty corner to where we waited for the light. "That pretty one with the two rods on it. The rods crossing each other."

"That's not a pretty building, Charlotte Elisabeth."

"It is. It's got a pointed top like a fairy tale."

"They teach dark fairy tales in there. They have talking snakes in there." She leaned towards me and commanded me with the force of her eyes to look at her. She kept her hands on the steering wheel as she pushed her face into mine. "Would you like a talking snake?"

My six-year-old self's eyes widened and my mouth fell open at such a thing. But I absorbed not just her words but pain, fear, shame. *Mom was afraid?* Yet my curiosity, which still burned bright back then, compelled me to ask, "What's a talking snake?"

"It's a snake that talks."

"Why do they have one?"

"They make up tales to scare little girls and boys."

My small self pondered that idea. It sounded like Mom. "Maybe we could go together to that pretty place, Mom?"

"How dare you! I do not ascribe to people who talk about God and Jesus."

"What's God?"

"None of your business. Why's this light taking so long?"

My small self stretched my neck up to see over the dashboard. To my left, black horses with feathers on their heads pulled an elegant, black rectangular carriage with tall windows. A long box lay in it. "What's that?" I asked and pointed to it.

"Just what we need. A funeral."

Black limousines glided behind the horses and carriage, crossing our lane.

"What's a funeral?"

"It's for dead people."

"Oh. What's a dead—?"

"Enough!" Fear radiated out of Mom. Grief engulfed her and broke through me. Rage followed it and suffocated the grief. *Oh no,* I thought. *This is why—*

My small self asked, "Are they going to that pretty building?"

"Do you want to go into that pretty building?" Outwardly, Mom smiled, lips closed, eyes sparkling. But I knew and, in this moment, lived her baiting a trap, desiring me to enter her hell.

My small self nodded, eager to see inside that pretty building. I'd seen it a few times and hadn't had the courage to voice my curiosity because Sally usually rode with us. This rare drive alone with Mom had been my chance.

"I could go see the horses, too?" I yearned to pat their fuzzy noses.

"Maybe we could do that, too. Would you like to?"

My head nodded like a bobblehead.

"Okay then. I'll send you in. They only like little girls and boys. Adults like me know better to stay outside, but you need to learn what's in there. Witches."

My mouth fell open. Horror and fascination mingled as I asked, "Like a fairy tale?"

"Yes, exactly like a fairy tale. God is the witch's boss. He told that witch who imprisoned Hansel and Gretel how to do it. Entice them in with candy."

My small self searched the building's walls for gumdrops and candy canes and peppermints. "I don't see any candy."

"Of course not. You're too far away. They offer a different kind of candy in a special glass of silver and gold and is deep red. They break off pieces of sweet bread for you to eat. But what you don't know is it's a person you're eating. They get you to eat a person before you know it. Then they brainwash you to like eating a person. That person could be your father."

I gasped. I still remembered my father at that age. "No!"

"Yes." Her smile widened as she savoured my horrified expression. The black limousines crossed in front of us, one by one. "They give you books to read and demand you read them whether you can or not. You have to tell each other stories and act them out. If you don't do a good job, God will turn red with anger, and he'll send you into a furnace that'll burn you forever and ever." Terror fogged out of her into my witnessing self. I leaned towards her, trying to understand her emotions. I'd only remembered my growing wariness.

"They eat Father," I squeaked. "Would they make me eat Father?"

The last limousine cleared the intersection, and Mom sat up and set her eyes on the traffic lights, waiting for the red to flash back to green. "Yes," she replied curtly to the windshield. "They'll start by telling you you're eating Jesus."

"What's Jesus?"

"Don't ever say that name or God again," she suddenly shouted as she mashed the accelerator. Terror, horror, unescapable claustrophobia leapt out of her at the same time. The sudden acceleration flattened my small self against the back of the bench seat. "Say it!" she twisted her head around as the car barrelled down the asphalted road. My small self thought, *She told me not to say the names. What do I do?*

"Say you won't speak those names again. You won't think about them. You won't look at those buildings with their crosses of tortured death on them. Say it!"

"I...I..."

"Clap your hands over your ears if you ever hear those words again. Say it!"

"I...I'll...I'll clap my hands over my ears, Mom."

"Promise!"

"I promise." Fear and dread emanated from my small self into my existing self. I gulped with her. Mom demanded so many promises, it was hard to remember and keep them all.

"If. You. Break. Your. Promise," she spat out like a slowed-down machine gun. "I will give you punishment number three. Do you want that?"

My small self shook my head hard as fear blossomed in me and determination to ensure complete compliance bloomed in Mom.

"You understand?" she demanded as the car careened down the blessedly empty road. But I knew there was a light coming up. There always was.

My small self said in a small voice, "I understand." My small self slid off the seat like a slithering seal and tucked into the space underneath the dashboard.

"Good," Mom said, satisfaction drowning out the receding terror. She slammed her foot onto the brake pedal, but neither my small self nor my reliving self got hurt.

I LANDED ON the grass beside the postcards standing in their zig-zag formation. The three orbs floated beside their enormity. The Golden Lab padded over to me and sat.

"We're so honoured to witness your first scene in your life review," Pink said.

"I don't know who you are or what you want, but I'm supposed to be at rest. At rest means the end of existence. It means never reliving the last sixty years. It means an end to the pain. Take me back to Dr. V."

"But your life review isn't over yet."

"This is not real. You're not real. You're my brain sending up desperate signals, trying to make sense of things. Wake me up so I can tell Dr. V to finish the job."

"You're so obsessed with that nincompoop," Silver huffed.

I bricked up fear, bricked over shame, encased grief and pain. I drained away the lingering stench of that memory into the cavern with its twisting lock.

"You are not real. This place is not real." A breeze wafted intense scents of rose and lavender over me. "Those are not real. I know they're not because I'm not sneezing. That dog is not real. These things are my brain making up something so I'll stay. I'm not staying. I'm going back to Dr. V. I'll wake myself up to tell him to finish the job." I dropped my forehead into my hands, closing off my vision from the ghastly artificial sight, the lying orbs, old desires and early terrors waking up. *I am in the Dying with Dignity Suite, and I'll wake up*, I told myself. A vacuum glommed onto me.

I drew my hands down and opened my eyes.

Where am I? University? This makes no sense. Oh, another postcard sucked me in.

MY UNIVERSITY-AGE self stood in line at Sidney Smith's coffee shop at the University of Toronto. Frosh Week had ended. Classes had begun. I'd noticed my classmates buying a cup of coffee and muffin every lunch hour at this cafe and had followed them. Autumn sun lit up the echoing space between the glass entrance doors at each end but not deep into the space's centre where the cafe stood. Sounds played in the background: clomping footsteps, the rhythmic squeak of the doors opening and closing, the hiss of the coffee machine, voices bouncing off the terrazzo floor and painted concrete walls. My 18-year-old self tuned out the noise as she hoisted her knapsack up. Heavy textbooks pulled it off my shoulders.

"Here," a baritone voice said behind my university self.

My university self turned to look. I met brown-black eyes. Before I drowned in them, I averted my own.

He grasped my shoulders and turned me to face the cafe.

Who is he? Why am I reliving this scene I don't even remember?

From out of him and into my witnessing self came a sense of wanting to ease my physical burden, to take the books' weight off my shoulders.

Huh? Why would he care? I wondered.

He adjusted the straps up. Then stepped around to my front and buckled my knapsack's chest strap. Instantly, my 18-year-old self felt the weight lighten.

"Better?" he smiled.

I nodded.

He checked his watch. "Ah, crap! I'm late again!!" He sprinted towards the back exit doors. With no curiosity, I smoothed the straps as I waited for the line to move. I hadn't remembered him, though I'd taken care to buckle the chest strap since that day. I'd forgotten he'd been the one to show me. *Is this important?*

No! It isn't!

I shut my eyes and repeated silently, *Wake up, wake up, wake up.* Nothing changed. *Wake up!* I scanned myself. No change. I spoke out loud, yet my voice sounded the same as when I'd thought the words. "Wake up, wake up, wake up. Wake up. Wake up! Wake up!!"

Chapter Eleven

BACK TO WRATH

"Where are you coming from human-killer" The wrathful voice echoed like slapshots above me, below me, beside me. I sensed artificial ice reflecting artificial lights, fans shouting in the stands, yet I couldn't see or hear anything in the all-encompassing black. I didn't answer the familiar voice.

Despair flooded me. I hadn't woken up and returned to the Dying with Dignity Suite.

"Where are you going destroyer of realms?" The voice slapshotted my hearing, reverberating my mind. Sickly sweet refrigerant smells assailed me. Darkness enclosed my vision. Again. I struggled to wake up, to refute what my mind was hallucinating. I only had to apply my willpower to waking up, the same force against my fear the day I'd walked out of Mom's house and into my own.

"Wake up! Wake up! Wake—"

The darkness snuffed out my words mid-flight. It vied with the sense of being in a bright place, filled with fans' shouts, cheering on the opposing players. The voice cut through me like a blade slicing through ice. "Where are you coming from human-killer?"

"They called it Flower Power Track."

"Answer me truthfully!" The words hit me with all the force of a puck smacked hard.

"I am. And I'm going back to Dr. V. I'm going to wake up and tell him he didn't finish the job."

"You think you know everything, human-killer?"

"I know I'm not at rest."

"How do you know that destroyer of realms?"

"Because you called me a human killer."

Light buzzed garish green, slashing illuminated streaks on the far-off walls where the grooves bled red. Then I was in absolute darkness again. The voice roared, "Do not mock me human killer."

"I'm not."

Light spots peppered my vision. I scratched at my face as I screamed, "I don't lie. This is all a lie. I'm not dead." I squeezed my eyes as shut tight as I could, forcing my eyelids' magnetic fields against their repulsion towards magnetic closing. I disappeared into my mind's safe recesses as I'd taught myself decades ago, until the buzzing of the light and the roaring of the voice echoing, echoing, echoing, diminished into background brown noise.

Unpleasant, but no longer distracting. I focused inwards as if meditating, but instead of focusing on a mantra or a calming scent or a pleasant vision, I focused on one thought: *Wake. Up.*

I envisioned the hospital, the Dying with Dignity Suite. The sweet goodbye suite as the nurse had dubbed it. I heard a giggle escape me and ring around as if hitting one arena board after another in a concrete box. I refocused on the thought, softer this time: *wake up.* I removed the urgency from my thinking. *Wake up.* I envisioned the room as I'd entered it, seeing the soft lamplight, seeing the bed made up with the sheet and blanket folded back. I brought back to mind how their softness invited me to lie down under the warm incandescent light. The nurse had remarked, "We have a cache of banned incandescent bulbs. They give the right amount of warmth for our patients. We don't want you going out under a glare or cold blue light." I'd nodded in agreement. Warm incandescent light pleased the eye.

I focused on the silkiness of the Egyptian cotton sheet, sliding underneath them with their tightly woven threads, and the warm weight of the blanket as the nurse pulled it up to my shoulders in a vaguely familiar way. My brain plays tricks to think the nurse's actions felt familiar. Mom had never tucked me into bed at night.

Wake up.

Feel the sheet over your body. Feel the weight of the blanket comforting your body.

Wake up. Wake up. Wake up.

I remained in this icy chemical-smelling place. My feet slid as if on ice. I sent heaviness down to my feet, and they stopped. The brown noise intensified. I refocused and resisted it. I must wake up and tell Dr. V I remain existent and am hallucinating. If I'm seeing things, I must exist. I spoke out loud, to hear the vibrations of my voice above the brown noise. To hear and sense my desires both.

The environment shifted around me. Light tried to penetrate my vision. Coins clinked as someone drew their hands through a pile of them. They snatched up a handful and let them fall one by one. I heard each coin landing on a chinking pile. Ignoring my will, my attention wandered towards it. Desire tore at my eyelids to part them. I drew in the scents of this place, as if trying to find which direction to look in first. The smell of fresh leather, the distinctive artificial perfume smell of new clothes, the clean, metallic scent of gold, a scent I'd never noticed before, so strong, so compelling to me. Desire heaved at my eyes to open.

I shook my head hard. *No, no, no,* I thought to myself. I strived to regain my thoughts. *Where am I in them? What am I thinking?* The coins clanged and jangled nearer, calling me to count them. I swallowed against their pull.

What do I want?

I want death!

I spoke out loud. "I want my pain to end."

My voice strengthened me to return to my mind's recesses, to push aside the sounds and smells and the bright light, to sink into my thoughts, my truthful desire. I repeated, "I want to rest. I want to see Dr. V. I want to tell him to wake me up." The new environment receded into yellow noise. And I bellowed to drive the external further away from my consciousness. "I need to speak to Dr. V. I need to tell him I'm not dead yet. I need to be awake to speak to him. I need to wake up to speak to him. I need to tell him I'm not at rest yet. I haven't stopped existing. I need to speak to him to finish his job. I need to wake up to speak to him. Wake up! Wake up! Wake up!"

Nothing.

"Wake up. Wake up. Wake up."

Nothing.

"Please let me feel the silky softness of the Egyptian cotton sheet. Feel the comforting weight of the blanket on top of me. Wake up. Wake up. Wake up." I descended into a drone. "Wake up. Wake up. Wake up. Smell the lilacs and the freshness of the room. Wake up. Wake up. Wake up. Hear the murmuring voices bringing an end to my pain. Wake up. Wake up. Wake up."

"What are you doing to her!" Mom's voice screeched into my ears as my eyes shot open.

Chapter Twelve

AWAKE

"She's dead, Nurse. I gave her the dignity other doctors didn't have the courage to give her."

I opened my eyes.

The Dying with Dignity Suite's ceiling greeted me. I sighed with relief and happiness. Reality, sweet reality. I stretched my ears out. I couldn't hear Mom. Had I imagined her? A hand grasped my arm and pushed it back underneath the sheet as the nurse said, "Some dignity." The door flung open, and I sent my eyes in that direction. I couldn't move, yet somehow my eyes still worked. I refused to consider why, only deliberated on how to do the necessary task of telling Dr. V he hadn't finished his job.

"Her Mom is yelling at us to stop," a security guard said. His white shirt that had looked crisp white when I'd passed him this morning in the waiting room seemed kind of dingy. Must be the lamplight washing out his shirt's white and the room's colours.

Dr. V was speaking. "I'll come out to speak to her in a few minutes. She can't do anything now. It's over. Charlotte Elisabeth is where she desired to be."

The security guard nodded. "I'll tell her." He swivelled on his heel and paused. He pushed the door open wide. A cart appeared. The guard held the door open long enough for someone to push the cart further past the door's edge. He left, and the cart kept the door open. Dr. V and the nurse had fallen silent.

Now was the time to speak.

I tried.

I willed my mouth to open.

Nothing happened.

My flabby body lay inert underneath the sheets. When once the sheets' silkiness caressed my skin, now they scratched it. I sent my eyes down to the bottom of their sockets. Maybe staring at the top of the blanket and sheet would direct my muscles to move.

I swivelled my eyes to the far right, straining to creep out Dr. V's back to get his attention.

He said to the cart person invisible on the other side of the doorway, "We're wrapping up here. You can leave the cart over there and come back when we're done."

I regarded the cart. Tall, pink candles sat on top, the pink looked kind of drab. A crystal-mimicking vase held fresh pink roses next to them. A silver-ish bowl heaped with shreds of bark and dried rose petals took centre stage. The fragrance of pot-pourri drifted to my nose, a pale imitation of the pot-pourri sold by my local home decoration store sold. *Cheap*, I thought. I wanted to sneeze but couldn't.

The next client can't spring for decent pot-pourri for their last hour on Earth and only muddy-looking pink roses and washed-out candles? I stopped my thoughts for a moment. They didn't seem like me.

I dropped my gaze to the cart's second shelf. A quilt lay folded there on top of white Egyptian-cotton sheets, the same kind lay in between. The quilt's colours were grey in the dim light from the lamp and underneath the blue-ish glow of the LCD display. The cart moved into the room, and a young woman appeared, wearing a greyish blue smock over her simple short-sleeved white cotton-polyester shirt and pants. *How can grey cast its dull tones in the whites, the pinks, the roses and pot-pourri, the blues, and even the LCD display? Had everything been this grey when I'd first entered the Dying with Dignity Suite?*

The cart person's long, straw-blonde hair hung down her back in a thin curtain. She let go of the cart's handle and lifted her head to nod at Dr. V, and mid-nod she spotted me staring at her.

She dragged air deep into her lungs, expanding her chest as her mouth dropped open. Her eyes turned to round pit-holes of blue. Slowly, her right arm lifted with her hand extended and her forefinger pointing towards me.

The nurse whipped her head around as Dr. V admonished, "Get a hold of yourself. You see dead bodies several times a day."

"She's not dead, Dr. V," the nurse stated baldly, staring down into my eyes staring mutely up at her. I put all my begging for Dr. V to try again into my expression. The nurse looked away and at Dr. V, and he aimed his scowl at the nurse.

"I have never not once in the hundreds of patients I've administered dying with dignity to have failed. I've made them all well at last."

"You mean dead," the nurse intoned.

"They received what they most desired."

"Well, she hasn't," the nurse said, jerking her head towards me.

Dr. V switched his angry gaze on me. My heart skipped a beat at seeing his anger flaring into my eyes. In an instant, his eyes softened, his mouth turned up at the corners, his shoulders dropped, and his face relaxed. He bent towards me. "Oh dear, Charlotte Elisabeth. You seem to still be alive."

I tried to speak.

"It's the drugs we gave you. We'll have to reverse the muscle paralyzer so that we know your wishes."

He swiftly turned to the medication cart with its drugs and plungers. He and the nurse, their backs to me, spoke in hushed tones. The young woman had fled, leaving her cart and the door open.

They hadn't taken my IV out yet. The nurse handed him a syringe, and he inserted it into the tubing. My muscles came alive, and I worked my jaw to speak. Garbage nonsense issued from my mouth.

Dr. V patted my shoulder. "Wait a moment. I know this is not what you wanted. I'd measured the doses out so carefully to ensure the most dignified health care I could provide you in your final moments."

"You screwed up," the nurse said.

Dr. V ignored her.

"I'm sorry," the nurse sighed. She approached the bed, stood beside him, and laid a hand on my arm underneath the blanket. "It's okay honey."

"It's...not...," I breathed in.

The nurse mused in sotto voce, "It's funny she could still breathe on her own."

I dragged air deep into my lungs, feeling the oxygen expanding my chest, spreading through my lungs. The life the air brought felt good. I forced that thought away. "Dr. V...I...had...a...terrible...experience." I breathed out the rest of the air and drew breath in again. "I...knew...I...," I exhaled, "was dreaming." I rested for a moment while my breathing relaxed into automaticity. "It was like those near-death experiences, but I remembered what you'd told me about oxygen deprivation. But they said—"

"Don't worry about that now," he purred, laying his hand on my right shoulder. "You're here with me, and I'm going to listen, and you're going to tell me what you want. Do you want me to finish the job?"

I nodded.

He waited.

"Yes," I said. "Oh yes. And this time, please complete it quickly. I don't want to hallucinate those places again or that soul family that deceived me into thinking existence continues on. I held on to what you told me, Dr. V, I held on and used science to push back the lies they told me, and I willed myself to wake up out of that nightmare.

And here I am. But I don't want to see Mom again. She's so selfish. She only thinks about herself, about telling me what to do. But she can't tell me here." I gasped at a sudden thought. "Is she here?" I remembered her voice had been so close to my ear.

"No." Dr. V patted my shoulder while the gentle pressure of the nurse's hand sent steady waves into me. "No, she can't get to you here. We're keeping you safe. I'll prepare the dosages again. And we'll do it right this time, I promise."

I nodded, sagging into the bed. He turned his back to me as he began working on the dosages.

"It's a good thing we hadn't taken out her IV yet," the nurse remarked as she smiled down at me, her hand still on my arm. I'd paid no attention to her before, yet now, wondering what her name was, I searched for her nametag on her yellow cardigan. Funny, earlier the cardigan's yellow shone like buttercups, but now it seemed dull, and the fresh scents that had greeted me when I'd first walked in had dissipated. Even their voices, the shush of the cart on the carpet, the subtle rattle of instruments on the medication cart seemed muffled or dampened.

I shook off these thoughts. *It's the drugs*, I decided.

"Here we go," Dr. V said, turning round to face me. "I've double checked all the measurements. I have your whole file here. It's one of our safety protocols so we can track your measurements over time, the medications you've been on. I see no change in your weight or height, and you didn't look significantly bigger or smaller since I last saw you."

"My weight doesn't change, Dr. V. It's been the same for the last many decades. Fifty-six kilograms."

"You're lucky," the nurse said. "Most people's weight goes up and down."

"I'm glad you confirmed the measurements my staff took. I've reviewed my calculations," Dr. V continued, eyeing the iPad in his hand. "And I see no errors in them at all. It is rather strange that you had no pulse when I checked yet now you do. I listened to your heart stop, too." His brow wrinkled, and confusion darkened his eyes.

The nurse said, "I knew something was wrong. I had an intuition."

Dr. V smoothed his expression into inscrutability. "Yes, well, enough of that." He stepped closer to me and bent his head to penetrate my eyes. "You want to be at rest, Charlotte Elisabeth? You want a dignified end to your pain now, here, with us?"

"Yes," I breathed out.

"Good. Let's get to it."

I closed my eyes; my cheeks fell slack; my arms and legs sank into the bed. Finally, an end to the mind pain that wracked me every day, except when I'd been near him. An end to having to listen to Mom. An end to the worries my heart sent up to my mind. An end to my nightmare.

"Sweet dreams," the nurse said gently as she patted, then let go of my arm.

Reality faded like black mists receding. Bliss, then—

Chapter Thirteen

DARK REALITY

My atoms—because what else could they be?—streamed under the mighty force of a dark will, the spaces in between each quantum inflating. I splashed reconstituted into cold, swirling water. Heat blasted my skin. Teeth, two tiny teeth, sank into my left heel.

"Nooooo!" The absolute darkness absorbed my scream.

"Why are you here?" the familiar voice boomed.

Exquisite awareness left no hiding spaces.

The cold water iced my feet; heat papered my skin like the coarsest sander roughing wood; unseen creatures stirred up the waters to fight the swirls, churning them counter-clockwise, then clockwise, then in a paisley pattern. I smelled flesh rotting, eggs turning green. Walls pressured my body with their presence close at hand.

A second set of tiny teeth sank into my right heel. I jumped forward and landed on both feet. Freezing waves like upside down icy rain pockmarked my calves.

"I. Am. Not. Here!" I thought the words as I screamed them, my voice silenced by the deadening atmosphere.

"But you are here," exploded the darkness. "Why?"

"I don't know why!" I yelled as loudly as I could, straining my vocal chords, wanting to hear my voice, not understanding why no sound came out of my mouth.

"I can hear you. And I need an answer."

"Why are you hoovering up my voice?" I slashed my right hand diagonally. "No! Don't answer. I don't want to know. All I want to know is why am I still conscious. You. Do. Not. Exist."

"I exist. Dark has always existed. You created me, and you have existed since before time. Why are you here in me now?"

I shook my head hard, wanting to feel my hair slap my face, begging an unknown to let me feel the sting of my hair ends, and, at last accepting I felt nothing, I sloshed forward. "Where are you? I demand you show yourself."

"But I have. You can see me. Why don't you know? Is that because you refuse to tell me why you're here," the voice sneered.

I growled; my vocal chords vibrating my neck, Dark swallowing up the sound waves.

"Good. You know my name. Now tell me why are you here?"

"I don't know! I won't tell you what I don't know. You. Tell. Me. Why. I'm. Here," I gritted out.

Dark roared, sloshing wet, cold burns on my heat-abraded skin. The walls moved in as I bulldozed through the icy waves. *I'm supposed to be at rest. Dr. V rechecked his dosages. The nurse assuaged my fears that I wouldn't remain existing. They're scientists who know what they're doing. They cannot be mistaken.*

"Yet you are here," Dark blasted. Heat shock-waved into me. My skin flamed, and my feet anchored themselves as fat snouts thumped into my arches and slithery bodies twined themselves between my toes. I fought the urge to hurl. *I must move away from these sliding bodies. I must. I must.* My feet remained paralyzed.

"Answer me. Why are you here?"

I croaked, but the creatures, the absorbing darkness, the closing-in walls snatched sound and breath out of me.

Blue sparked up ahead. I narrowed my vision. A second spark. *Them!* Fury breathed motion into my feet; I strode away from the snouts, and the slithering things slid out from between my toes. I stomped down hard. Something squished under my feet.

Satisfaction galvanized me.

Dark roared. Ice water swirled and spun around my ankles, rising into a waterspout. The waterspout followed me as I sloshed faster towards the now three sparks of blue. They'd answer me. They'd tell me the truth. Hot granules cannonaded my face, my chest, my stomach, my thighs, sizzling the waterspout's edge. Heat and cold confronted each other, capturing my knees and bending them to their will. I shoved through the pain towards the spark. Pressure on my right and my left. Massive forces pushed in on both sides as I kept going. *I will have my answer.*

Dark laughed. "You are so futile. You think you can conquer me? You don't answer my question yet think you can defy me?" Dark's laughter stopped. Silence. Absolute silence sucked all senses out of my ears. Into it dropped menace: "You can't."

The massive forces felled me. A wall behind me joined the two beside me. They funnelled me like a cow into an invisible small box whose sides, floor, and ceiling repulsed me like we were opposing magnets. A box that felt like many boxes, each box containing me and parts of me. My atoms strained to stay together. Tears erupted, yet I couldn't feel wetness on my cheeks or lashes, only a stream of atoms. "I should not exist," I whimpered.

"Yet you do," Dark gloated. "I have you. You are mine. And here you will remain, under my will, until you answer, Why are you here?"

I collapsed into myself. My atoms seeped away from me, each into their parts.

"Stand up!" Pink commanded.

I ignored the command.

"Stand up," chorused the three. "You exist!"

"Death is final," I sighed. "The end is known. We see the body end. We see the cells die. We see the maggots move in and eat the flesh. We see organs liquify. We see we need special embalming spices and fluids to keep the body together. Without them, the body rots away until only the skeleton remains. The skeleton falls apart into each separate section. We know this. Generations have witnessed this certainty. Scientists have documented it. They can't all be wrong. There is nothing else."

"Yet here you are," Silver drawled.

I can't explain this, I realized. I'd seen Dr. V recheck and the nurse look over his calculations. I'd seen her nod at me he had it right. I'd seen what I didn't want to, that the calculations were correct the first time. *How did I wake up?* The question clanged alarms of *no, no, no*. I covered my ears from the thoughts and imagined squishing my doubts and questions into the cavern. But they refused to drain out of my consciousness.

"You have to face them," Pink said.

Why? I whimpered. *I'd only wanted an end to my endless pain. Was that so wrong?*

Dark chuckled. "It's why you're here. And you remain here."

"There were other ways," Silver chimed.

I tucked my head into my stomach as far as it would go. With shock, I realized I could contort into a C. My being had acquired feats of flexibility I hadn't had since I was a baby. Even then, I'd sometimes wondered if I'd been born the most inflexible baby ever. Mom used to...memory didn't need to be pushed away, it simply faded into blank mind.

"Get up," Yellow demanded. "You can't stay here."

"Yes, this is where she belongs," Dark retorted. "I have her, and she can't elude me."

"We will help her," Pink replied.

"How? You think you can defy me?" Dark snickered.

"We can," Pink said. "Time doesn't matter here, as you know. We know what you are and who you are."

"But she doesn't. And it's her who has to answer me. Not you. I have her where I want her. She will be the first that'll never leave."

Silver's laughter rang out like bells shining in the sunlight. "You've said that before. I've heard tales of you boasting that no one can escape you. Yet here you are, alone."

"Look at her. Curled up. A quitter. Defeated. She won't defy me. She cannot answer me. To answer me is to doubt. She can't doubt. Science has her in its snare of certainty," Dark spat, and the walls spewed spittle on my head, my exposed arms wrapped around my knees, the water that lay over my feet. The spit hissed as it hit the water's iciness.

The grossness of being spat upon lit resentment in me. I curled in tighter. The resentment transformed into rage.

"Your arrogance has defeated you," Pink stated.

I clenched my abdomen and used its potential power to thrust my being upwards, slamming into the ceiling, my rage power-drilling holes, caving in the ceiling. I stood up.

"Who are you?" I demanded in thought and voice. Dark snatched my voice before it could leave my vocal chords. I ignored that strangeness. *I will speak and think at the same time.* "Why am I here?" I demanded. "I should be dead."

"You are dead," Pink replied. Pink's voice somehow overcame Dark's arrogant reply. I couldn't hear Dark, only Pink. "You're dead, Charlotte Elisabeth. You've begun life in your next state."

"There is no next state."

"Yet here you are. Why are you in Dark? Do you know?"

"What is Dark? What is this being, this space that's haunting me, anyway?"

"Look around you. What do you see?"

"Nothing! I see nothing!"

"What do you feel?"

"What do you mean, what do I feel? I'm outraged that I'm still not dead!"

"We'll leave that for the moment. Right now, focus on what you feel. Do you feel hot or cold?"

"I feel both!" Anger expelled my outrage at the obvious answer to the simplistic question.

"We must begin with basics. Ground ourselves in what our senses are telling us so we can then begin our journey out. What else do you feel?"

"I'm being bitten by snakes. Why are there snakes?" I screeched, my screech not being allowed to express its sound. Frustration clenched my hands into fists.

"Good. Good. Anger is good. Anger gets you to think. You must think Charlotte Elisabeth. You must think and feel. What else do you feel?"

"I'm trapped," I huffed.

"Yes. Yes, Dark has you trapped, but Dark can't keep you trapped."

Dark's voice underlay Pink's, yet Dark's words remained soundless. I wondered at this phenomenon that Pink's words over-powered his words.

"Good, good. You're getting it Charlotte Elisabeth. Thoughts and emotions that question will overpower Dark. You need the bravery to doubt. Can you doubt?"

"I doubt Mom. She never listens. She does what she wants me to do—"

"Don't let your focus waver. We're here, in this moment. Focus on that. Why are you here?"

"I sought rest," I replied.

"Rest? Wasn't it death?"

I shook my head. "Yes."

"You were lied to about death, weren't you? Admit it!"

"I'm still conscious."

"What does that tell you?"

"I'm not dead. Dr. V failed again." Sobs heaved my insides. The words "you're dead" echoed in my head. My legs weakened; my knees buckled. Dark blasted me with his satisfied roar, which smacked me sideways. The ceiling exerted its force against the top of my head. "Dr. V failed me." My hands covered my eyes as I bent my head, and my body sank.

"Yes he did!" stated Pink baldly. "But he knows only what he's told himself. Are you going to mimic him?"

I cried into my protective palms as my body froze in bent-knees, bent-at-the-waist position. Dark roared underneath Pink's voice, enraged at its futility of trying to punch through Pink's dominance.

My hands fell away from my eyes. I straightened my knees. "Why am I here?" I whispered to the light-absorbing water. My whisper escaped my mouth and stroked my cheek on its way out into Dark.

"That's it," Pink replied. "That's the question you'll answer as you journey through the Distortans because now you can face it."

"What's the answer?"

"The answer will come. But you won't find it here. For now, the first part of the answer is in your thoughts."

I contemplated the drain hole into the cavern I'd created. *Which thought's the answer? Which thought could I face? The only thought is the immediate one. I'm here because I sought—*

I turned aside from that word. "Think it!"—the words barrelled into my thoughts at the same time as that word "death." Dr. V had promised it to me. *But he doesn't know death, I realized, so how can he promise peace and no more existence with certainty?*

A happy clap sang through the air. "Dark can't keep her now!"

A familiar gel stroked my cheek from behind me, wrapped its arm around my right shoulder, down across my chest, and clasped my left side. I folded into its tug and merged with the wall behind me as Dark's teeth sank into nothingness, its cold water no longer icing my feet, its heat abrasion softening into fine sandpaper warmth.

Dark was no more.

Chapter Fourteen

DESIRE AGAIN

Desire's familiar green wobbliness greeted me. The mirror behind the ice cream parlour's counter reflected their back. "I didn't see you go to Earth; now I see you return."

I glanced around the space. Walls glaring white purity. White marble floor with an artificial sheen. The plate-glass windows separating me from the people passing by at a clip. And the soul family hovering on the other side of the chrome-handled glass door. *It's as if I'd never left.*

I wiggled my bottom on the chrome stool and checked out the candy jars. *If I must exist, then ice cream can keep me company.*

I raised my hand and scrutinized it. My hand, yet not my hand. Transparent yet outlined. I squinted at its edges. *Can I see magnetism?* I raised my left hand to face my right and extended my left forefinger towards my right palm. *Did the lines on my hand still exist?* I searched my palm, then millimetre by millimetre I edged my forefinger closer to my palm. As I poised my left forefinger a millimetre from touching my palm, I pondered, *What do I feel?*

"I didn't see you go to Earth," Desire flubbered in my face, startling me backwards as I dropped my hands. "Uh...," my voice bounced off the chrome-banded white counter and disappeared into Desire's jelly mass with a small burp. "Now I see you return," Desire continued.

"Yes," I reacted.

I flopped around in my mind. *What am I supposed to say?* I cudgelled my mind. *Ice cream!*

"May I have a bowl of ice cream?"

Desire frowned.

"I desire ice cream."

Desire's wiggly eyebrows lifted, and a groove appeared below its green bulging eyes. The groove stretched and curved upwards on either side. "You desire ice cream."

"Yes."

Suddenly, Desire straightened its mass, a blob emerged from its left side and elongated to a pointing hand. "Feast your eyes. I provide you with desires from Earth. This is your desire. Remembering it will return you."

I shook my head. This place satisfied me. Earth did not.

I followed its gesture, and somehow a chiller had appeared filled with tubs of ice cream. The labels were as clear to me as if I was standing right in front of them. Macadamia nut. My favourite nut. Salted caramel chocolate. The only chocolate ice cream I'd slurped up. Fresh strawberries churned into whipped cream, a melange of early summer and tongue-coating fat, creating contentment and safety. Roasted banana caramel ice cream. I'd had that once with marshmallow. My mouth dropped open, for right beside it was burnt marshmallow ice cream. *Where to start?*

Movement in the corner of my vision caught my attention. Soul family remained on the other side of the door, vigorously jumping on legs that had emerged from beneath their orb shapes. Arms emerged from their upper perimeter, waving to catch my attention, to tell me to let them in.

The ice cream triumphed.

"All there is, is earthly desire," Desire said.

"I'll have a scoop of salted caramel chocolate and a scoop of burnt marshmallow and in between the creamy strawberry."

"You feed your true self. Your material self."

"Is there any other kind?" I asked rhetorically, my eyes glued to the ice cream, anticipating sweet chill and their luscious deliciousness

"Why stay here, when you can return to Earth and have your satisfaction in your own ice cream parlour?"

I shook my head. People stayed securely outside here. They didn't jostle me as they single-mindedly headed to their tables or endanger my clothes with their sticky fingers.

Desire dropped its gesturing arm and squared itself in front of me. I frowned into its glistening green face. *Where's the ice cream?*

Desire said, "The ice cream is your want. But it exists on Earth in material form. You need to be material to eat it."

I pointed at it. "It's here."

"The real thing is down there, on Earth."

"Earth is down?"

"Earth is material. It exists where you exist."

"If I must exist, I prefer to exist here." I sat up straighter. I set my eyes on it.

"You can exist only in material form. You're not material, therefore you don't exist."

"I am existing because I can see you!"

"If you're talking to me but you're not on Earth, you cannot exist. There is only material."

I huffed. Desire's senseless babbling annoyed me. I twisted my head to contemplate the chrome-handled glass door and the three bobbing orbs. They said they were my soul family. They said they were here to support me. Maybe they could get me the ice cream.

I slipped off my bar stool, walked to the plate-glass door, reached out to turn the knob, and found no knob. I searched fruitlessly. *Maybe I should push?* I flattened my palm on the diagonal chrome handle and leaned into it until the door popped open outwards with a sucking sound. The people hurrying behind the soul family stopped and swivelled their heads to stare at me. *Oh-oh*, I thought. The three orbs floated through the gap as I stood stock-still guarding against alerting the people to my presence.

Pink said, "They won't come in."

I remained rooted.

"It's okay, you can let go of the door."

I still couldn't move.

"Drop your hand," Pink commanded.

I dropped my hand, and the door hissed shut.

I eyed the people through the door. *Who are these people? And where are they going?* They turned their heads to their previous direction and resumed walking, as if on a mission.

I slumped and turned to face Desire and the soul family.

Desire planted its jelly arms on the counter. "You are material. You cannot exist in any other form but corporeal."

I shook my head free of Desire's words. I would not contemplate them and began to address the blue orb with the pink highlights.

"My name is Bailey," Pink said gently.

"I'd like some ice cream but Desire won't give it to me. Desire showed me my favourite kinds, yet won't scoop any out. How do I get a bowl of ice cream? All I want is a sundae."

The three orbs levitated at my eye level, and a gentle hum emanated from them until it resonated with some unknown knowledge deep inside me. I squared my shoulders. If I had to stay in this alien consciousness and ice cream was here for the taking, then I was taking ice cream. I pushed myself between the pink and yellow orbs, planted my bottom on my stool, leaned towards Desire, and said, "I'd like my sundae, please."

Silvery laughter erupted behind me. *Hush*, came the responding thought.

I heard that! No, I'm not contemplating thought communication, either. All that matters is ice cream. Ice cream made me feel good, feel loved. I smacked my head to free it of such thoughts. *Stop thinking. Stop feeling.*

Desire loomed towards me, its green jelly exterior filling my vision, its refrigerant chill tickling my skin's magnetic field, its presence dominating my attention. "Matter is material, and matter exists. You are not matter, therefore you do not exist."

I opened my mouth, but no sound came out. Pink drew abreast of me over the bar stool on my left. I turned to watch. Pink said, "Charlotte Elisabeth exists. You can see her here, in front of you. She no longer exists on material Earth, but she's still here, Still alive. Still thinking and feeling."

My chest rebelled. Burning spread and pushed outward.

Pink shifted as if pointing towards me. "This is her true self. Or part of her true self. For now, all she needs to know, is that she still exists. And this place is not for her to rest in."

Desire wobbled into place in front of Pink. "Her true self is the body on Earth. The material, the matter, what she can touch and see with her eyeballs."

"No, that's only one aspect of herself."

"Stop!" I cried out. "I give in! I won't get ice cream here. And I don't want to return to the parlour on Earth. I died. I tell you, I died! Dr. V said so. His nurse confirmed the numbers were right. I am dead!"

Pink jounced. "Yes, the material form of you is dead, but you are not."

"I don't care! If I have to exist and live in some sort of permanent dream state, then I want to do it eating ice cream by myself, my favourite flavours by myself with no one to bother me and touch me with their gross sticky hands. Why is that so wrong?!"

"It isn't," Pink said. "It isn't wrong. But it won't get you to where you want to go."

"I really wanted to end!" I yelled, my voice ricocheting off the artificial walls and floor, the glass that wasn't glass, but a transparent human-created material. I didn't care how I suddenly knew that the people passing by had created the environment and that I'd created the glass out of my subconscious, my buried thoughts and emotions. I yelled to drown out that revelation and stop contemplation in its tracks. "I wanted to stop thinking! I wanted to stop feeling! I wanted no more pain! Is that so wrong?!" My words slammed onto and bounced off of surface after surface before smacking Desire, who absorbed them, their exterior dimpling with each word before reforming itself over them, as if they were food.

Pink spoke over Desire's reply. Like with Dark, Pink had the power to diminish Desire's words into background noise. Pink soothed, "No, it's not wrong, your wants are not wrong. But your grasp of reality isn't complete. We're here to help you understand reality. This is only one stop on your journey of discovery. This usually happens on Earth, but you weren't given that chance. We're here to—"

I jerked up my right arm. I bent my right elbow. I chopped my hand across and down. Tension, the tension of held breath, of waiting, filled the room. "I don't wish to discover anything," I shouted-thought. "Discovery brings unwanted knowledge. Unwanted knowledge brings pain and betrayal. Unwanted knowledge throws people you know into hideous light that reveals too much. I don't want to know anything. I only want to sit here and feel ice cream in my mouth and enjoy my favourite flavours. Over and over and over and over and over again. But since none of you will let me, what do I do now?"

"It's your decision what to say to Desire."

I glared at Pink.

Bailey. The name resounded in my mind, as clearly as if Silver had said it.

"Bailey," I stated, and Desire drank in the name, like all my words had been moments after I'd heard them leave my mouth.

None of these bizarre beings spoke. Silence expanded and stuffed the room with waiting. The tension drew my eyes towards

Desire, whose green jelly form reclined on the counter between me and...Bailey, and snapped my fear.

"I don't know what you're talking about," I said. "But you don't know, either. So I won't listen to you anymore." I thought for a moment. "No, I wasn't listening to you. I won't talk to you anymore. You take in my words and exit gibberish. My words are feeding you. I won't feed you anymore." I crossed my arms. I swivelled my stool around, my back to Desire, my face to the white wall. A vortex opened up. *Oh no!*

Chapter Fifteen

IGNORANCE STRENGTHENS

The vortex swelled, whirling into a wind tunnel that extended into infinity and reddened farther and farther into its core. Silver jumped in. Yellow and Pink leapt in after. I clung to the counter behind me. I thought heaviness into my bottom, but the vortex's power swooped into the parlour, glommed onto my chest, and its inflexible vacuum inhaled me. I shot through its core, smashing onto the reddish plain with its charcoal lines, and somersaulted towards the soul family awaiting me. From behind them and in a distant corner of the reddish sky, a pure-white light flared rays into my pounding mind. I raised my hand to try to shield my vision. Futile. The rays blasted through my transparent hands.

Silver rotated, lilting a high-pitched tune. "It's a nice light, isn't it?"

I turned my mouth down. I twisted my torso, but the plain held my feet in place.

"It's okay," Pink said. "You'll get used to it. God's breath is as far away as possible."

Breath? I thought. I rolled my eyes. *Breath is air, not light.*

"God's breath is light that—," Silver began.

Pink interrupted, "No, she's not ready. She needs to journey through the Soul Track first."

Silver blew out her lips, as if she had lips. The burring sound was the same.

Thump. Thump. Thump.

Thud. Thud. Thud.

Bang. Bang. Bang.

Fear vaulted from its domain and gripped me. I dared not untwist my torso or move my head.

It was them.

The three, taller than me.

Far, far taller.

Ignorance.

"Don't be afraid," Pink soothed. "We're here. You're not alone."

God glaring or Ignorance-in-three thudding or three orbs pretending I wasn't alone: I didn't know which was worse.

Ignorance's three wheels appeared on the horizon, their eyebrows, eyes, and mouths drawn in as if by a hand wielding charcoal. They accelerated, thumping and thudding and banging towards us. I untwisted myself and scrabbled on the plain, seeking an exit back to the ice cream parlour. *Why had I agreed with the soul family? I always make the worst moves.* As Mom had remonstrated over and over, my decisions about people land me in a pickle, and I force her to rescue me.

The image of my house dangled in my head. Yearning squeezed me into myself for the home I'd chosen and decorated alone. No one else had helped me. I'd not needed anyone. In my space, I was safe.

Maybe I should've stayed there, not sought out Dr. V. No, he found me. But I allowed him to talk to me. If only I hadn't needed to be heard. If only—

"You're back!" The three wheels were towering over me. *How'd they suddenly appear like that?*

A stick arm with a stick hand stretched out from one of them.

"Don't look!" Pink barked.

The far left one, Thump, interrogated, "Where are you going? There's only material, and you're in a joke."

"You're not in a joke, Charlotte Elisabeth. You're on a journey. Journeys are serious, but they're also fun. They're not jokes."

"Take the glasses, shield your eyes from the glare that we all hate." The third one, Bang, with the lengthening stick arm said. I began to obey.

"No, don't listen to them. The glasses will not help you. They'll make it worse for you."

"How can sunglasses make things worse," the middle wheel, Thud, scoffed. "Sunglasses protect your eyes." Its mouth's line waved, like a shaky hand had drawn it—like Charlie Brown's grimace-smile in the Peanuts Halloween special.

Thump shattered my thoughts. "Your eyes are in no danger. It's your vision that is."

I shifted my vision to the soul family, appearing small and crushable next to the ginormous wheels. I returned my gaze to the glasses dangling in my eyesight. I gasped. *My reading glasses! The ones I use outdoors.* My optometrist had manufactured polarized reading glasses so that I could read outside without harming my eyes from the sun's glare.

Pink shouted, "Ignorance turns lies into truth and truth into lies."

What does that mean?

"Those glasses work opposite to your reading glasses! They're—"

I stoppered my hearing and craned my head, bending my neck back, back, back to see up, up, up. Ignorance blocked most of that pure white light, but the painful rays blazed above and through their transparent edges and, like pressure cups, pressed and squeezed and opened my eyes. I wanted to squint yet couldn't. I grabbed the glasses and slapped them on. The last thing I heard was Pink yelling, "No!"

The glare vanished.

The pain left.

The soul family disappeared from my senses.

"Better?" laughed the one who'd given me the glasses. My glasses.

"Yes," I replied. I sighed, satisfied at having an object I'd chosen, one I'd directed an optometrist to make for me with no one else telling me what to do, on my face.

"Of course you feel better," said Thump. "There's only material, and you have the material back."

I nodded happily. All the fear, all the pain gone. Ignorance's three wheels no longer intimidated me. I had become part of them, and they me. I'd joined them.

The three jostled each other. Thud bent to peer into me, not towering over me as much anymore. "It's all a joke, you know. Reality is."

I gazed between Thud and Thump and realized I was growing to Ignorance's height. They weren't shrinking. I was becoming like them. *Is this how it ends? I grow until what?*

"This is all there is!" Thump said, its sides expanding out until its left side hit Thud, its right side obscuring my vision of the plain on that side.

"Hey! Watch it!"

Thump retorted, "I'm in charge."

Bang said, "I have the glasses. I'm the one who gets them to see the truth."

"So what?" replied Thud.

Ignorance's three wheels spun towards each other, their eyebrows drawing down, their crooked mouths flattening. Thumps, thuds, bangs racketed and crashed, slamming my atoms into each other as my feet merged with the plain. *How do I get out of here?*

"Time to choose again."

"We already chose. I'm in charge."

"We've changed our mind. I should be because."

"I have the glasses. I'm the one who changes their vision. I should be."

"Enough! We agreed. And I was first."

"Who cares? You think you're so good because you were first? Well, you're not. You're just like us."

"Yeah, you've gotten too big for your angles. You think your angles are sharper than ours. Mine bang. That makes mine harder and louder and better than yours."

"Thuds shake the ground. People listen to shaking ground. They freeze. The stupid tricksters and the gullible, all freeze when the ground shakes."

"They don't just freeze. I know them better than you, that's why I'm first. I'm in charge. They run, too. They flee because they know they exist in a joke. The joke's that death takes them in the end."

It hasn't taken me, I thought. I brooded on that thought.

The cacophony stilled.

Three sets of eyes, with angled eyebrows, stared into my face. *How do awkward angled wheels bend and contort like that?* If I could have felt my heart, it would've been hammering. Instead, my skin felt like an electrical current shocking chaotic waves into its magnetic field.

"Yes, you should fear us. But we'll be nice to you when you believe us."

Believe? I thought they'd said I should fear the light.

"The light is deadlier. The light lies. Lies are bad for you. How can you know you're in a joke when the light is burning out your sockets?" The three spoke in unison, the power of single-minded Ignorance reverberating through me, exacting acquiescence.

I nodded.

Charcoal-drawn eyes intensified.

I spoke in a strangled whisper. "The light hurt my eyes. I'm glad you gave me the glasses."

Their mouths' flat lines curved until they resembled smiles. They unbent themselves, raising their top angles until their broad middles, angles, and sides touched each other and dominated my vision. I felt cocooned. I raised my right hand unthinkingly and touched the hinge of the glasses.

"Don't touch those!" commanded Thump. "The light will hit you hard if you move them even a bit. You want to be hurt?"

"We are on your side," Thud reminded me. "Reality is not what you thought. You thought it was there for you, certain, knowable. But it wasn't. It's a joke. It's a cosmic joke. Death doesn't exist. We're the truth."

I stared way up at the three faces grinning down at me. My right hand fell and hung by my side. Their eyebrows' inner ends lifted as their eyes grew large, their lines softening. Their inflexible smiles didn't change.

Chapter Sixteen

IGNORANCE RESISTED

Reality is what we make it. The cliché flashed in my mind and pummelled me. I didn't know who'd thought it or why they made me hear it, but I didn't care. I stopped resisting merging with the plain and sank deeper.

Thump clanged, "That's the truth, right there. The evidence is before you. Reality is what humans make it. We exist because of you humans. Look around you, Charlotte Elisabeth. We're it. The rest of it, is all a joke."

I dropped my vision to their broad middles.

"Evidence!" scoffed Bang. "We're into the scientific method now. That's what humans call evidence. Not of the eyes but of the science."

"And what is science?" condescended Thump. "We see. We know. What else can we desire?"

"There's more to reality than what we know."

"Evidence is all around us. Are you challenging me?"

"You don't know what you're talking about. You won't admit the truth."

"The truth? Whose truth? We all know reality is a joke."

Thud cracked up. "The humans. They think they know everything. They're certain their material world is more than material."

"Not all humans," sniffed Thump. "The ones who understand evidence know that what their eyes see is evidence. What we tell them is reality."

"It's materially a joke," Thud flung back.

"You're stuck in the past," growled Bang. "You're always certain. You think you know everything."

"The humans made us. They know everything," Thud replied.

"I'm talking to First. I don't care what you think."

First? I wondered. *I'd named them from their sounds, but they have real names?*

"And I don't care what you think!" Thud retorted.

"Come, come, we're Ignorance. We think as one."

"Yes, the scientific method shows us the truth today."

"It's the evidence-based truth that matters. She knows nothing. She thinks what she sees and feels is the truth. But here she is with us in reality, the reality she created."

I started. "What?"

Thump sneered down at me. "You didn't know? You think you know death? But you didn't know this is of your making? You don't even know my name!"

"I didn't make this," I stuttered, shocked. "I didn't imagine this up. I'm supposed to be dead! How can I know your name? You're not being fair!"

"Fairness is for sissies. There's no such thing as death," First sneered.

"Because there's no such thing as reality as you know it," Ignorance three chorused.

"The world is real," I replied. "It is! I existed. I did!"

"Of course you think that. You think you exist now. But do you?"

"What?" My mind spun.

"Reality is what you make it. Isn't that what you believe? And you made us. You made this plain, you made us three Ignorance. You even made up that light that devils us throughout existence."

What light? I concentrated on pulling memories out, but they stuck fast, giving up faint traces of my vision hurting but not showing me a devil light or annoying light. I raised my right hand towards my right temple, a memory of Bang giving me my polarized reading glasses to wear, but I couldn't recall why Ignorance had retrieved them for me.

"Stop!" commanded Thump.

My hand froze in mid-air, my right arm bent at ninety degrees. After eternity, my arm flopped down.

"I didn't create you," I said sullenly. Tears trickled out of my mind's cavern, winding their way through my heart and lapping against the walls imprisoning my unwanted emotions, eroding my protection. I swallowed and imagined mortaring bricks against the tears. But they slid through like Teflon floss through teeth. Yet I didn't feel like Teflon. Confusion spiralled me. Ignorance made no sense.

"We are sense," Bang replied haughtily. "We exist because of you. Billions of you traipse through the Earth-Heaven Interdimensional Expanse with your chaotic thoughts, your wants, your demands, creating us as one after another of you built up thoughts and your emotions empowered your thoughts to create us. You are just another human building on to what came before. You are us. And we are you. You belong to us. This is reality. Material is all that exists, and you don't exist because you're a joke. Your life was a joke. You think you're dead. But you're not. You're imagining us."

I gaped up at Bang.

"I am Third!"

What the actual fuck? The words thudded into my mind, my memory vomiting them from my meetings with young clients seeing their prepared income tax returns for the first time, and they, as they say, 'No like.' "You make no sense!"

"She's right," First declared to Third. "You make no sense. This scientific method of yours is too new. We know what's true from the evidence that we've declared is true from time immemorial."

Third wheeled ninety degrees to face First, its side banging into me. I canted to my left side like a flailing doll, my feet stuck in the plain, until at the zenith of my left movement, I whipped back towards Third, unable to stop myself. I screamed and raised my arms as I slammed into Third. My entire being vibrated like a tuning fork. I rebounded left as First pivoted and squared off to Third, and I smacked First's front, shock reverberating my mind. "Reality is what you make it," repeated in my mind like a spinning wheel squealing against a doorstop. *What is reality?* I raised my arms higher to cover my head as I careened back to Third but failed to brace myself in time, and its rigid front connected with my right arm and shoulder and my protected head. I gave in to being a ping-pong ball between the two as they clamoured and caterwauled way above my oscillating being.

My bounces between the two slowed, and I was glad that the law of physics held true here.

First fell quiet.

It looked down at me.

Third followed suit.

First said, "Reality is material. Physics is something experts made up. It's why they called it theoretical. It's an inside joke you all believed." First chuckled. "You are dead because you don't exist. We have the evidence that you've created us, and you live on in us, and we in you. We are the real truth. The only thing that matters is what we can observe."

" We don't make up information through any means," added Third.

"True," conceded First. "We add to our evidence using the scientific instruments you gave us. We know what we see down to quantum level. Nothing that isn't material exists. You're not material. You're a joke that no longer exists, and you're us. Just a different form."

A screech materialized deep inside me; from behind the bricks and inside the cavern, frustration and outrage birthed. I heard a scream from far away. The scream became a bellow. "I exist!" My hands flew up of their own volition. They clutched my hair. The spaces between my squeezing fingers buzzed like bumblebees fighting. I yanked my angry hair forward and accidentally grazed the arms of the glasses. They rocketed off.

"How dare you!" Ignorance exclaimed in unison.

A powerful light winked on high above them. I ducked my head to my left side as I raised my right hand to shade my vision as I attempted to observe this light. Three transparent orbs with jet streams of blue energy appeared between me and the light. The far left orb had pink highlights, the middle yellow, and the third silver. The silver one exclaimed, "She sees us!"

Bailey. Blair. Blake. *How do I know their names?* I lowered my hand, for it wasn't shielding me from the glare, anyway. I tried to squeeze my eyelids together to block out the light while I contemplated how I knew these orbs and their names.

"Stop looking—," First began.

"You remember us," interrupted the pink orb. *Bailey*, I thought. *Its name is Bailey.*

"Yes, you're right. We're your soul family. We're here for you."

Anger flowered in me. "If you're here for me, where were you when Ignorance was ping-ponging me?"

"That's a good question," replied Bailey. "God is forcing you out of your comfortable, familiar thoughts. Ignorance feels comfortable until it blindsides you."

"Yeah," Blake interrupted. "That hurt is sooo familiar. Who wants to leave it?"

Bailey's coruscating blue light seemed to frown. "As I was saying. God, that light that's watching over you up there, wants you to confront and question your beliefs."

Blair replied, "We've learned to trust God when they forced us, too, out of our comfort zone."

"We'll tell you more about that later," Bailey said. "But for now, remember this struggle is for you to learn and grow on your Soul Track."

I growled in frustration. *Why didn't she answer my question?! Who is this God? That overbearing light glaring judgement at me? I already know what I need to know. I don't want to know anything else. I don't need to know anything else. Why should I be forced into learning something new when death was supposed to have ended all the questions, all confusion, all pain, all my suffering?! Why does everyone say existence is good and learning is fun like exploring?! Here I am being mocked, talked down to as if I was a high school student needing to be taught a lesson and Mom humouring me as she set me up like smart people like to do. My life was real! I existed! I'm not a joke! I didn't create these...these...things! I don't know what this place is! And I don't want to be here! I don't need change. I hate change! Change only brings bad things! I liked my routine! There's no point to suffering. Every rational being knows that!!* I huffed and glared at the orbs.

They floated placidly.

I stormed, "Just leave me alone! I'm ready to end my existence!" I moved to stomp away from Ignorance three and the three orbs, away from the glaring pure white light. But I'd forgotten one thing: my feet were one with the plain. "Aaarrrghhh!"

Tears sprung, and I collapsed onto the unyielding plain and wept into my see-through hands.

Chapter Seventeen

IGNORANCE PERSEVERES

The plain lay silent around me. My sobs rent the silence like glass shattering. I couldn't stop. And none tried to help me stop. Ignorance towered unmoving behind me as I collapsed further and further into myself.

An impatient sigh blew down on my bent back. Thump. I felt the molecules around me being pushed into me.

"How do—," First began.

"It's okay to cry," Pink-Bailey said, interrupting First. Like with Dark, Ignorance could not be heard once Pink-Bailey spoke and I listened. This peculiar ability hiccupped my sob mid-eruption.

Grief volcanoed out from the depths, exploding all my carefully bricked up walls, flinging emotion shards hither and yon, leaving trembling fear behind, exposed and puncturing my heart. I scrunched into myself, tensing against their strike, against remembered attacks using words revealing my inferiority, words so silky and nice on the outside, hiding venomous tones on the inside.

"You don't need to fear us," Pink-Bailey said. "It's okay to cry. Your heart has been fed so many lies and mis-truths, like too many humans before you, it's normal that you don't know what's happening. Crying is normal. We've been here before you."

Yellow-Blair agreed, "Yes. It's normal. Crying, weeping, sobbing, we've all done it. Even me."

Silver-Blake jingled, "Crying is nice. It's like your emotions saying to the world, back off, I can't take anymore. Leave me alone; surround me with a blanket of love."

Her words startled my sob. I spread my fingers apart, glancing up through the spaces between my fingers, even though I could see through my hands. I just didn't want to acknowledge their transparency. *Is Silver-Blake being nice?*

"Yes, I can be nice," she retorted.

I expired and stayed in place. My feet couldn't move off the plain, anyway. *What now?*

"That's right, that's the question you should be asking." Silver-Blake was back in form.

"Hush, Blake. Give her time. We were all given time."

"Some of us need less time."

"And some more," Pink-Bailey pointed out. "Time is immaterial here, Charlotte Elisabeth. Don't worry about time because it no longer matters here. Time flows, and we flow with it so that we become one with time, and we can be how we are at any point and not lose time."

An ache began in my temples. I uncovered my eyes to rub tiny circles into my pulsing temples. *Why does pain never end?*

"It will end," Pink-Bailey said. "We're here to help you through that journey to the end of your pain."

Pausing in my futile motion, I angled my head up. "Why?"

"Because we love you."

I snorted. "Love! How can you love me? You don't know me." I dropped my voice and muttered, forgetting they hear every word, "If they knew me, they wouldn't love me. My father left me, and Mom told me Father left because of me and my boisterous, interrogating ways. Sally concurred. If Sally hadn't concurred, I might have doubted. Sincerity and I both heard the same story, and Sincerity said it must be true because they didn't lie to her or lead her on like they did me. Love is being fed when convenient for them, not when you're hungry or need to eat before an exam. Love is buying the clothes they like, not what you like. Love is conditional on good behaviour. No, scratch that, conditional on behaviour they approve. Love is following Mom in all things and ways. Love is Mom's words and actions and Father's absence. Love slanders and shouts. Love is—"

Thump. I felt First's flat front against my left hip.

"You have it wrong," Pink-Bailey interrupted my rant. I stared up at the orbs, horrified they'd heard me.

Thud thudded towards me.

Bang. Bang. Third clunked up alongside.

"Ignorance cannot hurt you. Love is not any of those things. Paul wrote a famous list of what love is."

Who's Paul? I wondered.

Yellow-Blair said, "Paul called himself the twelfth apostle of Jesus, God's messiah."

Apostle. Jesus. God. Foreign, meaningless words.

My family's familiar words birthed the love I know.

Thump. First pushed me onto my right side, and I lay there, gazing up at it glaring down at me. Its charcoal-drawn mouth squiggled. I giggled. Thud thudded until my vision beheld only an endless wall soaring over me.

"Ignore them," Yellow-Blair said.

Pink-Bailey said, "It doesn't matter who they are. What matters is that we're here because we love you. We saw you when you were birthed, and we've wanted to be your family ever since. You were so cute as a baby."

"I wanted to throw you up in the air and watch you giggle. I envied your father being able to do that," Silver-Blake said.

I failed at imagining Father wanting to play with me, like I saw other fathers do in the park while I swung on the swing set, sometimes with Sincerity, but usually by myself.

"He did," Pink-Bailey said. "But his story comes later. Right now, all you need to know is that we love you."

I raised myself up on my right hand and twisted my head forward to stare at the three orbs wafting towards me. "I don't believe you. How can you love someone you've never met?"

"But we did meet you," Silver-Blake said. "Don't you get it?"

Third banged and clunked to get between me and them. But somehow, it couldn't insert itself. I frowned.

"Ignorance has no power over us," Pink-Bailey said. "When we wish to speak and you listen, it cannot speak. When we want to relate to you and you us, it cannot get in between us. We grow stronger the more you accept we exist. We are real not apparitions. Not hallucinations. We didn't spring out of your imagination. Even though you may invite Ignorance three and are merged with its plain, it has no power over us. You've removed the glasses it deceived you into believing were yours. But this is not the material world." Pink-Bailey paused.

First cackled, its laughter rat-a-tatting into the back of my head. "It's the Earth-Heaven Interdimensional Expanse, and humans created it."

I didn't look behind me. It's easier not to fear what you can't see. That name, "Expanse," again, a name I'd never heard. Maybe I didn't contrive this place.

Pink-Bailey huffed, "We didn't want to get into the name of this expanse yet. It's difficult enough for you to understand that we love you, that we want to be with you, that we came because of you, not because you did something bad, or made us angry, but because of you, your being, your existence!"

"How can I exist? And what is this earth-something-expanse? Nothing exists outside of the cosmos. Everyone knows the universe is stars and galaxies and nothing in between."

"You know part of the universe."

"Yes," I conceded. "Theoretical physicists and cosmologists are still exploring. But we know enough to know that there's no expanse, or whatever you call it." I heaved and let my anger drive me up onto my knees, flailing against my planted feet pulling my back against First's rigid flat front. Thump. It tried to push me back down, but I rocked into balance, locking my thighs straight, and staying up on my knees. I shouted, "And there's nothing after death!"

"How can you know what's beyond death?"

"We know death is final," I shouted at the three orbs floating in front of me. "There's nothing! No expanse! No life! No existence! And no love!!"

"That's scientific dogma. Not the truth. Dogma states that existence ends on death so dogma prevents exploring what happens after the material body's cell death. You can't state for certainty, Charlotte Elisabeth, what exists after what you call 'death' when you've not explored it. Scientific dogma stops curiosity in its tracks. It prevents exploration for fear of being mocked. No one enjoys being mocked, and human biology drives us not to be cast out from the social hive. Only the brave and nine-lives-cat-curious can brave such social opprobrium. It's not safe to ask what's beyond death in case you're cast out. Only the stupid and religious think anything lies beyond death, right? Isn't that what you're taught? But right now, none of that matters. What matters is that we love you. We're here for you because we love you. We want to accompany you."

Soul Track. The words flew into my mind.

"We should tell her," Silver-Blake said.

Pink-Bailey sighed. "Yes, Ignorance can't be allowed to speak these terms and make them sound bad. You're right, we should explain."

"Simple will do," Yellow-Blair said.

"I wish she'd stop calling us colours," Silver-Blake said.

"At least she's using our names," Yellow-Blair pointed out.

Pink-Bailey breezed nearer. I tottered up onto my feet, and Pink-Bailey rose to my standing eye level. "You're in the space that exists between Earth and what most call Heaven. It's a space that material beings cannot enter. There's more to being human than material existence. We're a multi-factorial species, as are all the creatures on Earth. But I'm getting ahead of myself. All you need to understand now is that Earth exists in one dimension; Heaven in another; and the space that allows one to transit between the two dimensions is called the Earth-Heaven Interdimensional Expanse.

"It comprises three tracks, one of which humans created when they brought all their thoughts and words into the Expanse with them. The Creator, what we called God, created the other two tracks. You're in the Soul Track of this expanse. Many humans don't enter this track because they've journeyed on Soul Track while in their material selves. But unfortunately, you didn't. You'll have to go through this expanse as part of your Soul Track before you can reach the barrier that protects Heaven from Earth as it exists currently in this slice of time.

"The Earth-Heaven Interdimensional Expanse boasts two other tracks. Hell Track and Flower Power Track. You've seen those other two. Your journey will shift you from track to track as you mature and become ready to exit the expanse through the Barrier. It's a tricky, arduous process. We've all travelled through the expanse. Some never see the Soul and Hell Tracks in the expanse, while some remain in Hell Track willingly or unwillingly. With increased medical power over bringing people back from the dead, more and more enter one of these tracks only to be sent back to Earth, for their work is not yet done. Sometimes, as with you, they can't be sent back. Not yet, anyway. Maybe every now and then, scientists and the public at large can chalk up waking up from death as a miracle, but if in the numbers currently being killed by doctors, executioners, soldiers, and torturers, chaos would encase Earth as people wrestled with the to-them incomprehensible. Evil must play itself out to its fullness."

"Huh?"

"I think you went too far with that last sentence," Yellow-Blair declared.

Pink-Bailey nodded.

"Forget the last part about evil. Did you understand the rest?"

I dropped my head and clasped my cheeks. I rubbed my temples. The ache advanced down my face and into my skin, soaking my being. A golden energy suffused with peace seemed to blanket it, and arriving with peace: *it's okay.* My shoulders dropped; my arms relaxed; my hands fell to my side.

Thump. Thump. First's angles hitting the hard surface of the plain menaced. First pushed me from behind. Thud. Thud. Thud added its heft to First. Their hard fronts crowded me from behind and to my left. Bailey, Blair, and Blake hovered, keeping me in their line of sight, or rather them in mine. Bang. Bang. Bang. Bang. Third rolled around. It towered behind the three orbs and blocked the high-up light, which I suddenly realized no longer burnt the retinas of my eyes, or whatever existed in my face. I raised my head and squinted into the reddish sky or whatever that arc was. Rays prickled above Third. Third's charcoal eyebrows slanted downward towards each other. Its drawn eyes narrowed. Its mouth drew down at the corners. Its colour deepened to black-red. Bailey, Blair, and Blake resembled marshmallows against its implacable front. It heaved and juddered, attempting to smoosh them, but they remained unperturbed.

Love, I thought, and tilted my head to the left as I contemplated their courage in staying with me. *This is love?*

I didn't understand it or this place or why Ignorance assaulted them.

"Where are you going?" First shouted from behind me.

I jumped, and the plain released my feet before my startle separated my ankles from my feet. I gawked at them as I landed back down on the plain's reddish surface. Gingerly, I lifted my right foot. It came up. I lifted my left foot. It also obeyed my command.

I twisted my head to look up and up and up until I met First's intimidating eyes. "I don't understand, but I'm staying with Bailey, Blair, and Blake. I don't belong to you, and I don't believe you anymore. You lie."

Chapter Eighteen

FLOWER POWER GREETS

The heady scent of roses flooded my senses. Ignorance's angry towers and reddish plain faded from my awareness as the roses lead me into the Flower Power Track. That's what Bailey had called this place with grass greener than the greenest lawn and diverse flowers nodding their beautiful heads in the gentlest breezes. My memory of Flower Power Track metamorphosed into reality. I stepped forward and released fragrance like springtime's fresh-mown grass. Ahead of me the postcards waited, semi-folded up, standing on their long edges zig-zagging into the distant horizon of soundless white. The melding scents distracted me from the postcards. I closed my eyes and drew the scents down into my deepest depths and savoured their pleasurable effects. Opening them, I discovered the postcards had slid towards me.

A MAN STOOD between an open door and a white-painted crib, his arms holding a baby underneath the armpits, powering the baby high in the air, his eyes gazing into the baby's and the baby's into his. I was in the postcard, I surmised.

Laughter burst forth. I knew who the baby was.

Me?!

The man threw the baby up again. And I, baby and me observing both, shrieked. Baby-me shrieked with laughter. I shrieked with horror. *Would I fall? No.* The man caught the baby easily. His grin widened, dimpling his cheeks.

"Who is this man?" I asked.

Bailey thought into my mind from somewhere, "Your father."

My father? The thought confused me.

His emotions revealed themselves to me. Happiness. *No, joy. And something else?* I contemplated his laughter-creased eyes, his laughing mouth, his dimpled cheeks as I attempted to identify his complex mix of emotions. I'd bricked my emotions up for so long, I couldn't identify nuanced emotions anymore, only strong ones like anger and joy. *When had I lost my knowledge of emotions?*

I shook that thought away as I watched, shocked, my father gleefully throwing me up into the air and catching me, over and over, as baby-me giggled and shrieked in a well-known-to-baby-and-Dad game. *Dad?* I wondered.

Yes, somehow I knew that's what the baby called the man. *Dad.* I tasted the word on my tongue. I tested it out by saying it. It felt foreign. A burning started within me as I watched baby and man play.

"You and your father," Bailey said. "A delightful scene."

Delight! That was the emotion I couldn't identify. And pride. Not boastful pride, but pride in another. *Pride in me?*

These revelations reeled me backwards. *My father was proud of me?* My eyes prickled, and my vision blurred, and confusion spun my head. *How can I feel tears when I'm no longer material?*

"Everything's possible in this next form of yours," Bailey responded. "This is a beautiful scene. I'm thankful we three get to share it with you."

I averted my gaze. I didn't want to watch anymore. But I couldn't block out their shared laughter.

"Wheeee," trilled the man.

"Dad," whispered Blake from behind me.

"Nooo," I moaned. I had no father, no Dad. He left me because Mom and Sally had said I'd driven him away. Yet baby-me's laughter rang and his expression echoed baby-me's love.

"Who's the good baby?" The man cooed.

"Your father," said Blair. "He's your father."

"Hush you two. Don't rush her. She'll get there in her own time."

I brushed my face roughly with the side of my right hand and turned to face the three orbs, avoiding the man and baby. "Get where?" I asked Bailey.

"Flower Power Track wanted you to see this memory in your life review. It's the first scene."

"But I don't remember it."

"I know. We rarely remember our baby years, or infant years. Some even have their life review start in the womb. But these memories fed who you became. They're the start of you. Look," Bailey said, moving in a gesture towards the man and baby.

My eyes obediently followed Bailey's gesture before I could stop them.

The man caught the baby under the armpits. I noticed his brown eyes were both joyous and watchful. I shifted my gaze towards baby-me. The baby looked like she was tiring. The man...Father?...lowered the baby...me?...down towards his chest and snuggled her close. Dad and child. My breath caught. My heart stopped from surprise and not wanting to disturb this moment—or what felt like my heart stopped. I gawked and absorbed and processed the emotions emanating from baby-me.

Safety.

Sleepiness.

Contentment.

Closeness.

From...Dad? *Dad.* I tried to speak the alien word out loud, but my throat and lips snapped shut like powerful magnets closing. I let myself feel his emotions, though.

Pride in another.

A sense of temporariness.

Trying to keep the moment going.

Fear. *Fear?*

Not wanting to let go.

Wishing for the moment to last.

Wishing to be alone with me. *Why alone?*

"Why indeed?" Bailey echoed.

I scanned the small room with its bare, white-painted walls. The crib held only a thin mattress and a duck-decorated soft blanket over a similarly patterned sheet, and a small teddy bear lay haphazardly in the middle as if abandoned. Thin curtains hung over the small window behind the head of the crib on the wall perpendicular to the wall the open door was in. As I looked at the all white room, tremors started in my lips and spread outward. I trembled. I didn't understand why because, as I lowered my gaze to baby-me and Dad...Dad...

Thoughts fled. Observations halted. Grief heaved me up against the ceiling. Baby-me slept in Dad's arms against his chest in a cocoon of safety. I once was loved just as I was and I once was safe.

"Take me away," I sobbed, pushing my back into the ceiling. "Please. Take me away."

I covered my vision with my transparent hands and cried. I curled myself into a comma, my face tucked into my abdomen. I stretched my senses out to will the flowers to return. But I felt nothing move around me.

"It's okay," Bailey soothed.

"What are you doing?" Mom's harsh voice shattered the cocoon atmosphere of my first bedroom.

"She's sleeping in my arms," Dad whispered.

"She should be sleeping in the crib. That's what it's there for. Put her down. I don't want her waking up Sincerity."

"She won't. Her half-sister is a deep sleeper."

"No thanks to you. She's my daughter."

"I see Sincerity like my own."

"She isn't. Put Charlotte Elisabeth down."

"Charlotte Elisabeth is safe."

"You'll drop her. You're so clumsy."

"I won't." My father's voice sounded strangled and defensive.

"Here. Give her to me."

I didn't want to peek. But without thinking, I untucked my head and dropped my hands. Mom was grabbing baby-me out of Dad's arms, and baby-me shrieked, my shriek pitching into a heart-shattering wail.

"Look what you've done," Mom scolded.

"I...," Dad's hands flopped by his side as Mom plopped me down in the crib, arranged the teddy bear in a corner away from my face, and pulled the blanket up over me. "I don't want her catching cold. You need to keep her warm, Greg." Guilt emanated from Dad. Envy from Mom. *Envy? Why envy?* And also concern. *Concern for me? Since when had Mom been concerned about my welfare?* I puckered my brow and failed to recall such a time.

Baby-me wailed sirens of fear and confusion, of wanting comforting warmth back, of not knowing where Dad had gone to, of not wanting to be alone. Mom pushed Dad out of the room and slammed the door shut. Their last thoughts disappeared as they disappeared: Mom yearned for what Dad had with me and if she couldn't have it, then neither could he; Dad feared confronting Mom yet yearned to hold me again.

Fear won out.

He left me.

Love had left instead of brazening it out for my sake.

I returned my focus to baby-me, who saw white everywhere. No other human. White blared aloneness. Fear became terror. The wailing vortexed into a hurricane of need. I cringed. I tried to not feel, see, and hear. I didn't know whether to cover my eyes or my ears. Suddenly, the wailing stopped. The silence deafened me. I cautiously looked baby-me's way. Baby-me's eyes, wide open, were watching the door. The door remained shut. Baby-me watched and watched and watched as the minutes and hours ticked by. After a time, watching transformed to confusion to helplessness, and helplessness buried need. I felt her disappearing into herself. And then her emotions were gone.

MY FEET SCRUNCHED Flower Power Track's sweet green grass. Springtime scents assuaged my soul. "What happened?" I asked.

"That was the start of who you became. You weren't meant to be buried. You were meant to flourish and live a long life on Earth before you arrived here."

"But now you're here, so we gotta start again," Blake interrupted.

"We?"

"Yeah, we're with you, you know," Blake reminded me. "You don't have to start again alone."

I dismissed that thought—I'd always been alone. I wasn't comfortable with the idea of not being alone. Inevitably, relying on others for friendship lead to being violently abandoned against my will, like baby-me had been. So many times people had taught me I was not lovable. *No, it's better for everyone for me to be alone.*

"No!" I stated. "I'm alone. It's better this way. I know how to take care of myself. I took care of myself when I asked Dr. V to end my existence because ending sixty-one painful years is the best way to deal with...with...with...whatever that scene was. You and those alien postcard life forms can't deceive me into thinking someone wants to be with me. Everybody leaves. Death is a welcome rest from the hell of life. Whoever invented life should be punished! So what if I, and not some random event, choose when to end my life? That's my right, my prerogative to do that! It's my life to do as I please with," I stated firmly. "I wanted a dignified end to a life...a life...that...," I gestured feebly to the postcard standing by. "...It was right for me to ask for death on my own terms. To have a dignified, peaceful death. Why can't I have it?"

"Death, no matter the circumstances, is always peaceful," Bailey said. "It's that science hasn't investigated death to know that no matter how awful, how painful and rude it looks on the outside, death is always peaceful."

I swivelled on my heel. "You're mistaken," I shot over my shoulder. "Death is uncontrollable unless we control it through choice. My body, my choice."

"Where is your body now?"

"Dr. V understood my body, my choice. He understood being in control is the ultimate dignity. I wanted death. I want it now. The end of existence. Why can't I have it?" I stomped my foot. I didn't care that I looked like a frustrated toddler having a tantrum. I craved death; my craving seared this energy carcass version of me that my brain had created in its dying-but-not-yet-dead state.

Bailey sighed into a darkness that swirled me into its cape-like self. *Finally*, I thought, *blessed death.*

Chapter Nineteen

WRATH'S ZEAL FOR DEATH

The ground reversed beneath my feet, and I slid, tottering, backwards. I stepped forward with my right foot to rebalance myself, then my left foot swung forward. I was walking, but I wasn't in Flower Power Track anymore. Black mists obscured my vision, and white noise my hearing. I locomoted forward, going nowhere, blind and deaf, touchless and smell-less, to my surroundings.

Dark! A figure emerged before me as the black mist transmogrified to gloom. Somewhat taller than me, its hood veiled its face, and a cloak draped over its shape to the ground. A scrawny hand emerged out from its centre fold, clutching a staff with a curve on top that bent back down towards the ground and a crossbeam below it. Its hand rested on the crossbeam. I kept trudging forward; yet, though it didn't move, I remained no closer to it, to my mixed relief. Its silence menaced, yet its hidden mysteries captivated me.

I began to pump my arms in rhythm with my feet. Still no closer to this hooded figure; I bent my elbows and swung my arms with my legs as I powered my feet. Yet I remained in place. I tried to run and slammed into the edge of something. I grabbed it, and my feet sailed backwards. The ground required I walk if I wanted to keep upright.

A treadmill?

I craned my neck down and was startled to see I was on a treadmill band. My swinging hands hit an invisible console, its buttons and displays darkened, and I grabbed hold of its bar by touch and discerned where the console's lights should be shining from.

My walking fell into a rhythm, as I wondered, *A treadmill? And who's the hooded figure?*

"I am Wrath. I am Zeal for Death form," announced the figure. It neither moved nor revealed anything about itself.

My thoughts drained away. My emotions fled behind my crumbled brick wall.

A light flashed on above right and behind the figure. I blinked once against it, then I stopped noticing it as I fixated on the figure in front of me. *How do I reach it?*

"Where are you coming from human-killer?"

I groaned. Not this again.

"Who are you?" I asked.

"I told you. I am zeal for death. You've been seeking me all your life. I am wrath, and I am death. Where are you going destroyer of realms?"

"I'm on a treadmill going nowhere."

The cloak and hood shook, its silent mirth sending waves through me. Laughing at me.

"Do you know what you seek?"

"I do. Death."

"I'm here."

"So why can't I reach you?"

"I'm always with you human-killer."

"How so?"

"Haven't you always courted me? You and your kind created me."

"I didn't. I was told about you."

"Yet you knew me before you remembered."

Frustration boiled up inside me like a cauldron of steam. I bent my elbows and pumped my arms and I landed on the console for all my efforts. "Oomph."

"Where are you coming from human-killer?"

I came from Earth, I thought. *Out of the Dying with Dignity Suite.*

The hood flung itself backward, and the scrawny hand clutched the staff as if holding on to keep itself upright against the laughter shaking itself to the ground.

"It's not funny," I sulked.

"You can't reach me. Why do you try?"

"Because you're the end."

"The end of what? You're still going somewhere destroyer of realms. Tell me!" The figure stamped its staff on the invisible ground, ripping open cracks in every direction, cracks that emitted a gaseous substance that stank yet called me to inhale it. I pumped my arms and set my feet forward on a determined course. Maybe if I speed-walked, I could launch off the treadmill, charge through the console, and reach the figure. In these strange places, anything was possible.

"You think so?" The figure mocked me. "You think you can do whatever you want in this place? I commanded this place. I'm Wrath. And I'm the form humans enjoy the most. Zeal for Death. You mock me, yet you've hunted for me all your life, like all of your kind. You cover your yearning with euphemisms and fairy tales, but you all want the same: the end of somebody else. The end of yourself. Suffering on another even if the suffering splatters crimson blood all over you. You revel in me, in tales of me. You worship my power and call it redemption. You raise my crossed staff higher than the light of life, calling it sacrifice and life, justifying your token of worship. You eat me. You drink me. You court me. You worship me. Without me, you'd be lost."

I stared, thinking, *I am lost. I don't worship death. I only want it.*

My feet kept in time with the treadmill's speed.

A shadow, like an elongated caricature, splayed across the console, and the shadow reminded me the light hadn't disappeared. The shadow lengthened and extended onto my chest above the console. But I was of nothing. No material body stopped the shadow, and it pierced me like a sword. I bent forward under its lancing pain and clung to the console's edge. The treadmill demanded my feet keep moving, right foot, left foot, right foot, left foot, as I fought against the thoughts and emotions the pain was slicing open. I dropped my head.

"It's okay," Bailey said somewhere near me. "Face the pain and hear what it's telling you."

I averted my head from Bailey's voice and squeezed my eyes shut against the pain.

The staff thumped the ground beneath the treadmill; the ground cracked like a giant iceberg splitting. Reverberations shook my atoms within my skin's magnetic field and empowered the lancing pain. It searched out my hidden recesses, the cavern's depths where I'd stuffed my betraying thoughts, the ones that raised questions whose answers brought out—

The scene of my father throwing me up into the air shot into my consciousness.

"Noooo!" I cried out.

"Where are you coming from human-killer? You human-killer who killed yourself! Tell me!" The figure's shout blasted me backwards. I wheeled my arms in the air as my feet fumbled to keep my footing. The treadmill drew me backwards. I was going to fall!

"Face the pain!" Bailey insisted so close to me, I jerked upright, and somehow my feet regained purchase on the endlessly moving belt. Fatigue leadened me. I stopped walking. My arms dropped to my sides. And the belt took me backwards. I slammed up against a force that wouldn't let me drop off the belt's end. The force of the belt's movement spasmed my legs. I veered my thoughts from speculating how I can spasm when I'm no longer material.

No longer material. I let the thought linger as my feet automatically began to move in time to the belt's speed and my arms followed their tempo as the knowledge I was no longer material sank in to my consciousness.

"You killed yourself!" the figure said, its accusing authority raising my head towards it to see it pointing its staff at me.

"Yes," I replied. "I did. That was my choice."

"So why do you exist?"

"What?"

"Your form is material. Only material. You killed your form. You killed yourself. Who are you human-killer? Where are you going destroyer of realms?"

"What realms?" I had no choice but to ask the question.

"The realms you destroyed on your way here."

I shot my arms downward, fisted my hands, bent back my head, and screamed and screamed and screamed, until, my voice hoarse, I shouted, "I'm not a fairy tale! I'm not a knight in shining armour. There's no such thing as a second chance at life! I'm Charlotte Elisabeth who only wanted to live!"

I clapped my hand over my mouth and gaped at the hooded figure. Suddenly, its repulsiveness revealed itself to me. Its cloak wasn't merely the colour black but comprised sweet, soft words that whispered lies tailor made for the listener. Its hood wasn't opaque but transparently hid a hideous, grinning head, its veins engorged with the blood of people worshipping its form. Its staff was misshapen—its top not bent over in a smooth switchback curve but crooked side to side and front to back. Congealed red roughened the bark on its surface while the light surged forward and swaddled it. Zeal for Death struggled to free itself from the light. This wasn't the silent white light I'd seen on the far horizon of Flower Power Track but the same one that appeared in Ignorance.

"What is—" I broke off my question. Curiosity lead to disaster.

"It's okay to ask what the light is," Bailey said.

"I don't want to know. What does it matter to me?" I asked as the words I'd spoken earlier ricocheted in my mind. *When had I wanted life?*

"You've always wanted it. But death haunts Earth. Every community, every family thinks about death. Oh, not like how after a certain age, we all know we're mortal. And how as we enter our later decades, our mortality becomes real. No, it's about the ways we see each other."

As I continued to perambulate, going nowhere, I turned my vision away from the light engulfing Zeal for Death towards Bailey's voice. The three soul family members hovered at my eye level. *How had I not seen them before?*

"You didn't want to," stated Blake.

No, I hadn't, I acknowledged to myself.

"Good of you to face up to what you really think," Blake said.

I swear I saw Bailey move as if rolling their eyes.

"How do I get out of this place?"

"You must face Wrath in all its forms."

"How do I do that?"

"That's for you to discover."

"I thought you were with me!" I spluttered.

"We are," Bailey said earnestly. "But we aren't you."

"What's Wrath?"

"Wrath is like the anger a person has who seeks revenge on another even if it means destroying themselves in the process. All that matters is the end of the one they hate."

Oh.

Wow.

Revenge had never entered my mind.

"Whether or not we have entertained vengeful thoughts, we all end up facing Wrath's question."

"Where are you coming from human-killer?" I mimicked tonelessly, almost automatically.

"Yes."

"I wanted Death. So..." I contemplated what had happened, how Zeal for Death had enticed me before it had turned hideous before my vision. *Did I really not want death anymore?*

"It's time to explore the fullness of Wrath. You're ready to stop bouncing around and journey forward," Bailey said.

"What does that mean?" I asked, allowing myself to halt, knowing I'd slam into that force but no longer wanting to walk in lockstep to Zeal for Death's command. The light fully engulfed Zeal for Death and filled the cracks, sealing in the gaseous substances, returning them to their origins.

"It means you've met Dark, the first form of Wrath. Not the Dark that you encountered right after you left Dr. V's lair, but the one that harmed itself in grooves of blood. Its next form is Desire. Again not the power Desire, which rendered itself as an ice cream parlour, to be what you most like in the world, but the other aspects of your desire, the ones built upon Wrath, the ones that act out your anger, the anger you don't acknowledge to yourself."

I slammed into the force. The treadmill stopped. I stepped off. "Okay," I said. "I'm not an angry person, but..." I reflected on those shocking words I'd uttered: "I wanted to live." *Maybe I do still exist.*

Chapter Twenty

WRATH'S KINGDOM OF FLESH

My house shimmered into existence around me. A fat being sat in the middle of my living room, a pile of jiggly rolled flesh like three fat pancakes, each smaller as they ascended, with chubby legs criss-crossed underneath the largest pancake resting on the floor. Its chubby arms jerked like robot arms; its hands, puffy and small, caressed the gold coins piled in front of it. I fluttered to attention, my gaze fixated on the gold. "Welcome to the fourth power of Wrath. My Kingdom of Flesh," the pancake-stack-being chortled. A flash captured my notice; a crown, tall and slim, slipped to the side of its head then somehow righted itself.

I shuddered. Then peeked at this...this... *What do I call it?*

"Kingdom of Flesh," it told me. "Where are you coming from human-killer…." I tuned out its voice and turned myself around and around to check I really was in my house, yet I sensed something different about it—I couldn't quite put my finger on it.

"No," it said. "Your fingers like gold. See here, this is real. It's material. This is what you killed."

I restored my gaze to the pile of gold coins. I stepped closer, and they called to me, luring me into touching them. Lifting my right arm, I stretched my forefinger towards the realistic coins. I smelled coins' acidic smell, saw the familiar wall colours I'd chosen for my home, heard the familiar faint echoes of my footsteps, and believed. I averted my gaze from that…that…whatever that was and retracted my hand as a falling coin smacked it.

"Kingdom of Flesh," it intoned in harmony with the gold coins falling from its puffy hands.

I ignored it as I drank in my comfortable home. Relief mixed with gladness sailed into me. I was in my place, the place that mattered most to me, the place my feet hurried back to whenever I had to leave it. I was home. I walked to the closest wall to touch it but hesitated. I closed my hand and let it drop. "I exist," I exhaled, smiling.

"No. You don't," it said. "You killed yourself. Your material self is gone, and that's all there is. The material world. Look here, look upon the wonders of the world."

I found myself standing in front of a painting I'd bought. The first one I had the money to afford by some obscure painter. I hadn't known the artist; I'd wandered over to his booth one year at the One of a Kind Christmas Show and Sale. He'd waxed enthusiastic about the landscape he'd painted, about his emotions as he painted, why he chose that particular landscape. I'd listened and nodded—I excelled at mimicking listening and caring about what another was saying while I observed and reflected in my own private mind. I'd discovered this survival mechanism early: listen, nod, and keep yourself guarded behind an implacable wall where none can affect you. People, I'd learned, love to hurt you then claim they didn't mean it and blamed you for feeling the wound. They only wanted to help you, they asserted, as they knifed you.

I snorted and startled myself with the sound.

Pancake-stack-being chortled and dropped a pile of coins onto the pyramidal pile sitting on the floor. Their metallic clunky clash drew my attention away from the painting. "That's right," it said. "You understand what's real. This is real." Its pudgy fingers threaded through the coins and grasped a handful. "Hear their song," it said as he dribbled them back onto the pile.

I returned my attention to the landscape painting. *Yes*, I thought, *it had been a good buy*. The colours in the landscape highlighted my wall's paint colour. Its proportions fit that wall well and its heft the frame I'd chosen for it. I'd disliked his simple wooden frame. Wretched wood. He'd said something about finding the weather-beaten wood in the vicinity and it being part of the art. I'd smiled in agreement as I'd paid and considered how to make my painting look good.

I admired the wide scroll frame with its gold-flecked accents on the corners and the raised carvings. Finally, I existed in a place I understood.

I tilted my head.

Yet somehow something was different about it, something slightly repellent, and I didn't get it.

"You will." Bailey's voice made me jump.

I turned towards its sound. The three orbs floated above Kingdom of Flesh's top fat pancake with the crown on it. "Were you there all the time?" I asked.

"We arrived with you, yes," Bailey replied.

"It's hard to explain," Blair added. "Wrath changes its form as you transit through it. It shows itself in different ways."

I frowned. I didn't get that either.

"Observe the painting," Bailey said. "Why did you buy it?"

"To go with my living room's new paint job. I'd bought the house with my own earnings. I renovated it. I, and I alone, designed every room. I left at quitting time on the dot eager to work out the details.

I spent hours in the paint store, deciding on the precise shades I liked." I paused as I drank in the living room's colour. Taupe. An eighties colour, yet one I'd liked until the day I'd—

"Human-killer," Kingdom of Flesh bellowed as it swept up an armful of coins then let them clatter and clink to the ground.

I stared at the coins swivelling on their edges, collapsing against each other. The gold sounded wrong. *Does gold have a smell?*

I lifted my eyes to the wall. The taupe colour looked wrong.

"I don't get it," I said.

"Why did you buy the painting?"

I shifted my gaze back to the landscape, and confusion tightened my face.

"To go with my walls?" I hesitated then stated, "I liked it."

"No, really, why did you really buy it?"

I dragged my gaze away from the painting to Bailey and stared. "What do you mean?"

"We all have surface reasons and deeper reasons. Your surface reason was about your material world. The deeper reason was about you. What was your deeper reason?"

Anger spurted venom into my voice. "I have no deeper reason. I died. End of me."

"Yet you existed and still exist. Right now. Here with us. What's wrong with the picture you're looking at?"

"It's incomplete," I blurted and clapped my hand over my mouth. *Where had that come from?*

"Innate knowledge," Blake drolled.

Bailey floated towards me, obscuring Kingdom of Flesh's head and crown from me. "Is there really only the material world?"

I recalled what I'd said only moments ago in front of that hideous thing: *I wanted to live.*

I didn't remember thinking that before. My vocabulary hadn't contained that phrase before. My whole being had focused on ending my pain and suffering for so long that I couldn't remember a time I'd wanted to live.

Here I am, still existing.

My mind swirled like a drain swallowing overflowing water. I shook my head. *No!*

"Yes, you still exist. You still exist because you're more than material."

No! I will not countenance it. Material is real. I can feel, touch, see, hear, smell the material world. The squishy sound of paint rolling onto the wall, the machine riffling through a stack of twenties, the frying of an egg as fat spits and bubbles the whites. The soothing taupe on the wall, the landscape that seemed to add colour nuances to the taupe, the whites on the computer screen and icon colours of oranges and reds and blues.

"Have you not heard or seen things here, too? Haven't you smelled the fragrance of roses or the smell of pseudo gold in Wrath's hands here, now? Don't you find these more vivid, more real, than what you're familiar with?"

No! I clapped my hands over my ears. "Human-killer!" shouted Kingdom of Flesh in the silence between Bailey's words that allowed me to hear its voice. "Destroyer of realms, where are you going?!" Thoughts clashed in my head like crescendoing drums. Want. Live. Exist. Dead. End. Consciousness continues. I gasped and dropped my hands.

Consciousness continues?

"Yes," Bailey said. "Consciousness continues. You still exist."

"Where are you coming from human-killer! Where are you going destroyer of realms?!" yelled Kingdom of Flesh as Bailey allowed silence to stretch for me to hear its question. Really hear it, I realized. Volcanic anger spread throughout me: *I'm dead! I really am! I don't want death!* I'd wanted my pain to end and had thought Dr. V's cure was the only way. I'd believed the Dying with Dignity Suite provided a dignified end to my endless tossing nights, my heart squeezing in misery, and my early mornings waking up in mind-lancing pain that followed me as I'd hustle into my running gear and race out my front door, the exertion killing off the pain while I ran through the tranquil city streets. *Had Dr. V's dogma deceived me?*

I had killed my material self, yet I still lived. Lived. I rolled the word around in my mind, recognizing I'd subconsciously sought revenge on myself. I fisted my hands, threw back my head, and screamed, "Noooo!" to the dull white ceiling.

"It's okay," Bailey said over my wail. "You knew only the material world. No one taught you about the rest of yourself. You bricked your emotions up to protect yourself as a child, and no one helped you to free yourself, so how could you know what you were feeling?"

Had Dr. V?

I stopped screaming. I dropped my vision to Bailey and allowed their words to find purchase in me. *Why had Dr. V desired to lead me to end myself? He believed nothing lay beyond death.* I relived those minutes in his office, the eagerness with which he explained how science was certain about death, about how science deftly explained near-death experiences with our modern knowledge of oxygen deprivation, loss of blood flow, how the brain tricks the mind. I relived him leaning towards me in his earnestness, his need for me to believe him, to entertain no doubts that his method would bring an end, that the Dying with Dignity Suite was the best and only answer for my excruciating, endless heart pain.

Why had he advocated for death? No thought of second chance had entered my mind, so zealous were his beliefs. Why so zealous for my death? *He listened to me; he heard me only because he admired death as a cure. Zeal for Death?* Understanding flashed across my mindscape. I hadn't been different, either. I'd been just as zealous as him for his cure.

A cure one can't come back from, I thought sourly. *Any second chance at life is gone now.*

"He didn't triumph, you know," Blake dropped into my thoughts.

I lifted my gaze to take them all in. The pancake-stack-being, whose mouth was moving in its repeating silenced questions; the soul family beholding me, accompanying me, nurturing me. Wherever I went, there they were. *There they are.* Yes, they'd meant it.

"Why did you buy the painting?" Bailey asked.

"It went with my house. I'd bought my house with my own earnings to get away from Mom and Sally. I wanted something substantial I called my own and no one could take from me. I escaped Mom's love by buying the house and getting away from her. I paid off my mortgage with accelerated payments then decorated it to show I had power and control over my world. I created the best world for myself that I could and treated myself to everything I wanted."

"Your material world. Your material self."

"Yes," I acknowledged. "My material world." I paused, and the realization stunned me. I'd only had control over my material world and had focused only on my material self. The rest of me, though...

There's something off about this place. I circled the room, studying the walls, the painting, the coins. *It's a facsimile of my material life! But I've seen beyond now!* I said, "It's repellent because Kingdom of Flesh hasn't been able to reproduce it exactly and because material no longer satisfies me." I expanded my chest and relaxed my being. "I accept I killed myself," I said to the mountainous creature with its coins and crown. "My material self. I think you created here," I gestured to Kingdom of Flesh manifesting as my living room, "what I created in my wrath. I focused on my material self because that's all I knew. And...." I sucked air in or what passed for air in this strange place. "I felt safer believing that's all I was, a material being in full control of herself and how she existed. I believed only I had choice over my existence."

I paused as I ran from the revelation of the deception. My mind drained itself of all thoughts and emotions. I shrugged my shoulders. "There's still no second chance at life, though."

"Where are you coming from human-killer? Where are you going destroyer of realms?"

Its words plunked into my mind like shotputs of dirt. I spoke automatically, "Earth. I don't know where I'm going. But not here."

Chapter Twenty-One

WRATH'S MORPHING FORMS

A green hill trundled into my house, imposed itself over the pancake-stack-being, widened itself, gobbling up my house. *Foolish Wisdom of the Flesh!* I recalled its deception. I pedalled my feet backwards, and needles thrust upwards to prick my feet and stab my ankles. I frog-marched and tippy toed and pumped my torso upwards, trying to escape the needled ground. In this strange place with floating orbs floating, why couldn't I float, too? "I'm not believing you!" I yelled at it.

"Where are you coming from human-killer?"

I turned my back to it, and the ground whizzed me back round to face it and its glaring fluorescence. That faint light, its rays shining towards me, faded in behind the green hill. It held me. And for the first time, I looked straight at it. Nuances of fresh-grass green flickered in and out of its rays. Beauty shone delight. The fluorescent green hill stretched up its peak to cover the light and expanded its base towards me, enticing me to climb it.

"No!" I flung myself backwards and slammed into energy pockets that sparked my outer skin like firecrackers.

"Hey!" Blake objected into my ear.

I twisted my head. I'd hit the soul family. "Sorry, I'm so sorry," I said, raising my right hand, palm facing them.

Furry green grass tickled my ankles as the ground rose underneath my feet. I whipped my head back; the deceiving hill had moved towards me. "No," I told it. "You can't deceive me. I won't let you slide me down into that strange place with all those people. I don't believe you. I know where I'm going this time."

"Do you, destroyer of realms?" it purred.

Yes, I thought. I vowed not to doubt.

Blake chirped behind me, "You go, Charlotte Elisabeth. You tell Wrath what's what!"

Wrath? "I know where you'll take me, you deceiving hill."

"It's the Foolish Wisdom of the Flesh."

"Whatever that is," I said. "I'm not believing it."

The hill roared. Its artificial furry grass jiggled as if made of extruded green jelly. "You don't believe me? Hahahaha! People don't believe you because you're so old!" Its words triggered a fight within me, of men ignoring my expert knowledge and women dismissing me in favour of younger accountants, who, they asserted, were up to date. It didn't matter that I'd kept up to date; my schooling and matriculation date designated me ancient and taking up space. "Your generation can't possibly know what's current," some clients declared after meeting me in person and seeing my face with its wrinkles and jawline sags. I shook my head free of those thoughts.

"You can't believe what you don't know. You are like me."

"No," I retorted. My anger's fire tamped down. I pushed down on my diaphragm with my breath and sucked in my lips until pain like lancing electrocution zigged-zagged throughout my face. "No!" I shouted. "You Foolish Wisdom of the Flesh deceive. You are like those people who make up lies about me and then insist they're the truth. I won't listen to you, either. You can't affect me!"

"That's it, Charlotte Elisabeth. You're starting to see."

I stomped my right foot, ignoring the artificial grass's electrical fire cutting my calves. The light behind the hill flared towards me. I didn't understand it. I wanted out of this place. *Now!*

The garish green vanished. The light remained in the same upper right, pink edging its rays. Clothes of pink and violet and hues of red appeared to my left; bowls of chocolate and burnt marshmallow and fresh strawberry ice cream to my right; grey hearts patterned the hard surface beneath my feet and stickered the surrounding walls. A cake waited on a table draped in cream and white lace. Candles stuck in the cake flickered flames in heart shapes. *Love?*

The clothes and cake and ice cream, the floor and walls, spoke. "All that you seek is here, for you destroyer of realms. You don't need to go anywhere else."

I stepped forward into this magical place, with everything I'd accumulated waiting for me. I tried to ignore the cake. It alone mocked me. *But that ice cream...or maybe those dresses with their A-line skirts...which should I approach first?*

"Don't be deceived, Charlotte Elisabeth," Bailey said from behind me.

"This is not Wrath," I said. "This is beauty and pretty. It's the things I accumulated in my life." I fingered the clothes, and the floor's hardness ached my calves. I let my mind drift: *such pretty dresses in polyester silk, my favourite fabric.* I'd had the money to pay for dresses made just for me out of that fabric.

"And looked where that expenditure lead you."

"Don't listen to them. They don't know what they want. You do. Tell me where you're going destroyer of realms," purred Foolish Wisdom of the Flesh.

I grasped a skirt to rub its silky softness between my fingers. Roughness scraped my fingertips. The fabric sandpapered off a layer of my skin. "Ouch!" I let go and shook my hand free of the pain.

"What the—," I exclaimed before I could stop myself. I turned my head towards Bailey.

"Wrath deceives, remember?"

I surveyed this space. The clothes moved towards me. The birthday cake zipped over to me on the other side, its glittering candle flames rising higher and higher into giant hearts that waved in laughter. The red dress lifted its skirt up to my left arm and scratched me. I leapt backwards, and ice cream splotched shards of coldness down my back. "What are you doing?"

"You answer my question! Stay here where I'll feed you what you want."

"I don't want this!"

"You spent all your money for this!" The clothes and ice cream cackled at me in front of and behind me, and rage tinged their auditory assault.

I was dead, so why did my assets and drained bank account matter, anyway? It's not like I could take my savings with me. So why not deplete them to surround myself with what gave me pleasure?

"Did it, though?" Bailey asked me, silencing the mocking.

"Yes, it did!" I defended my choices. "Money makes you happy. Having fine things makes you comfortable. People are fickle. They tell you lies, but stuff doesn't."

"So where's your stuff?"

My stuff banged into me and smothered me in their pink and violet and red, stroking my cheeks like a facial sandstorm. *I don't like those colours, anyway*, I huffed to myself, *I preferr mustard and browns and greys*. I hauled at the violent clothes, trying to pull them off me, and blackness swirled into my mind as if I was suffocating. *But there's no air here.*

"You're right, Charlotte Elisabeth. You don't need to breathe to live here. You exist no matter what Wrath does to you."

"You want to stay here with me!" declared the clothes and ice cream crawling up my back on drops of frozen cream.

"No!" I shouted.

The cold cream and the sandstorm clothes vanished.

Ignorance thumped and clunked in circles around me. I blinked. *What's happening? Ignorance's wheels are my height.* They reminded me of loonies with red paint worn off. The light in the upper right expanded, and its core shone gold, its rays hues of emerald and turquoise, rose pink and sunset purples. The light hypnotized me. I wanted to understand it.

Smack!

My face throbbed as my feet spun and my body fell into a two-dimensional wheel clunking on its angles as it circled me.

"You're old. You don't know anything anymore. You don't know where you're coming from human-killer." A second wheel spun on its axis and smacked me on the other side of my face. I stumbled to the opposite side of the circle.

"We're here Charlotte Elisabeth," Blake called out, bouncing up and down on the other side of the circle.

What good are they over there? I thought.

"Listen to our voices. You'll gain strength from our voices!" Bailey hollered through Wrath's Ignorance Form.

"Sounds like therapy," I retorted as a third wheel slammed me from behind, flinging me forwards into the one thudding on its angles round and round me in the circle queue. I ricocheted, the third wheel smacking me downwards, and I landed on my hands and knees on the unyielding surface, its reddishness searing my vision, and I saw red spots. I squeezed my eyes shut and tried to take a breather. But a wheel kicked me from behind. I flew forwards and landed spreadeagled, my face smooshed into the surface.

"Where is your family now?"

"They're nowhere," I spoke into the artificial ground. I was unfamiliar with its material; I'd have preferred eating a mouthful of natural turf and earth. It snarled into my mouth, "You are alone." Its words echoed what I'd known since my father and Mom had left me alone in my crib in my white bedroom.

"I had to get away from them. They only wanted to destroy me."

"Is that where you came from human-killer? You killed your family then yourself?"

"No," I moaned. Thump. Thud. Clunk. Clang. The noise of the wheels circling on their angles crescendoed. Their clashing reverberated into the ground as if they were one with the surface. My being convulsed; my atoms vibrated out of their places. "Let me go," I moaned.

"You have the power to leave them, Charlotte Elisabeth." Bailey's voice sounded distant. *How?!* When I tried, Ignorance—

"We are Wrath! We are the third power of Wrath: Ignorance. Do not confuse us with the Third Power Ignorance."

What? What's the difference?

"Third Power Ignorance are straight up ignorance. Wrath ignites our ignorance to capture and ensnare you. We will avenge ourselves upon you if you don't answer our question even if it means our destruction. We will bend you to our will by any means possible. Our power of wrath will force you to answer our question."

Their anger ignited mine. *Forget it!* I leapt up. I marched towards the nearest one circling past me. None broke formation as I closed in. I straightened my arms, fisted my hands, powered my legs, and stormed right into them...

...and squeaked to a halt in a black-and-white courtroom.

Now what?

Chapter Twenty-Two

WRATH'S WISDOM

A judge perched behind the towering court bench. I stared, straining to make out what was wrong with what I was seeing. Ephemeral criss-crossed black and white stripes marked the bench like a chessboard, yet I couldn't discern the striping. The bench's material was neither wood nor any known natural or artificial material. It's artificiality struck a harsh note, and way up above me, behind the bench, the chalk-white-faced judge sat in white robes with a black wig on its head. Its white hand gripped a black gavel. I surveyed the scene covertly as I stood before the bench and beside the floor-level witness box attached to the bench on my right, its artificial material shrinking into itself, like liquid plastic forever melting down. Yet the distorting plastic disguised the witness inside the box. Black and white diamonds stretched into infinity under my feet; the walls receded into white noise. I raised my hands to my face to check if they'd transformed into white and black, too. No, they remained transparent, and I saw the tiles through them. I dropped my hands to my side.

Why am I here? Where is here?

"You are in the judgement seat of the Wisdom of the Wrathful Person. You dare to resist Wrath? This form will defeat you, destroyer of realms," intoned the judge from above me.

Weariness washed over me like a tidal wave. Strange words, incomprehensible questions, places that spoke, and beings that were places, and everywhere I go, three orbs follow me as if this is perfectly normal. *When will this end? This can't be reality.*

"It is." Bailey spoke from behind me. *Always behind me!* I groused to myself. "We followed you in, that's why we're behind you. But," the three moved to my side as Bailey said, "we'll stand beside you."

"Where are you coming from human-killer? What say you to the first question?" demanded the black-wigged, white-skinned judge as Wisdom bent its head, and the bench leaned forward towards me. I flapped a helpless hand and let it drop again.

Bang!

Wisdom of the Wrathful Person whacked the gavel against the hidden top of its bench. Its power chattered my teeth, scattered shards of pain into my head, and juddered my magnetic field, threatening my atoms to leak and me to disintegrate.

"I'm dead," I said monotonously through my gritted teeth, regaining control over my being, refusing to wonder how transparent teeth chatter. "I have no teeth. No head. No body. No hands. I'm a figment of my imagination. And I'm alone in this."

"You're not, Charlotte Elisabeth," Bailey reassured me. Soft pink light washed over me, soothing my jangled atoms. I turned my head to stare at the three. My soul family, they'd said. "I am alone," I asserted. "I go through these...what do you call them?"

"We're Distortans. We're distorted forms created by you humans as you transited between Earth and Heaven. Your souls, filled with decay and deceit, with light and love, created us on Earth, and we live in this Earth-Heaven Interdimensional Expanse. We exert our powers from here to down there, but you didn't defeat us on Earth.

We have power over you now because you never resisted us. You avoided learning about us. And became our willing pawn. Now you're here in our courtroom. We have you."

"Courts are places of justice," I declared. "As science understands death, so courts understand justice."

Blake choked back a laugh beside me.

"What's funny?" I asked.

Blake swivelled back and forth in the air that wasn't air. "Nothing." Silver laughter bubbled behind the blue jet streams.

"Explain. What's wrong with what I said? I'm tired of this. Tired of not understanding."

Blake broke off laughing. "That's progress."

"Progress! I'm in a court, but I'm innocent. Innocent people don't go to court."

The three's silence weighed like an anchor on me.

"What?" I demanded, resisting their silent censure.

"We're not criticizing you," Bailey said. "We want you to think and not react."

"Face me!" Wrathful Wisdom commanded.

I obeyed. "Answer this court. Where are you coming from human-killer?"

"Earth."

"That is not an answer. Legal language rules for answering questions don't apply here. You must give a full answer, even to the questions I don't ask. We do not tolerate lawyer speak in this judgement power. Wrath has the ultimate authority here!"

"I killed my body."

"Yes, you did. Why? It's God who decides it's over when their plan for you on Earth is done, when the end time arrives—"

End time?

"—kill your body before God finished your Soul Track?"

"Because my heart was failing. I was dying. The doctors gave me medications, but I was tired of medications. Every morning, one pill. Every pain, another pill. Don't fall down. Fear falling down. Exercise and eat the way we tell you. But I didn't escape Mom's home to have another authoritarian know-it-all tell me what to eat or do. My house is my sanctuary, where I do what I desire."

"You killed your body by not obeying the doctors?"

"I obeyed the doctor who counted. I obeyed the one who listened to me. The cardiologists only told me what to do, not caring what mattered to me." *I wanted to live*, the unbidden thought rushed in. My right hand brushed that betraying thought away, as my left hand scrubbed my face to erase the pain building up in it. "That's no way to live. I was angry!"

The judge nodded. Its black wig slipped down over its white face, then suddenly, it winked out and reappeared on top of its head. I jerked, yet wondered why that startled me after seeing so many strange things: talking hills, wheels that body-slammed me, an alive blob of jelly. Shaking myself free of those thoughts, I asserted, "I wanted to live on my own terms, and since I couldn't, I ended it. No one decides for me what to do."

The black-wigged judge, the chessboard bench, the melting witness box, and the black-and-white diamonds underneath my feet hooted and howled. Their roaring laughter vibrated up through my feet, my calves; like a rippling earthquake, it shook my knees into their components as they split from each other, releasing my thighs, which flung up as my hips slammed down and my torso ripped backwards, and my head flew forwards. My arms and hands pin-wheeled as I sought purchase to regain my balance and put myself back together. Their cachinnation crescendoed like a thunderous cloud driven towards me by a deafening wind, ever thundering, ever shaking the ground.

"It's okay, Charlotte Elisabeth," shouted Bailey over the maelstrom. "Wrath is laughing at your hubris. But we understand it. Humans think they can live only with full control, and they always have full control. But reality doesn't work like that. Did no one tell you?"

"No, no one told her, Bailey. Kind of obvious," Blake shouted back. "Why does everyone think they have full control?"

"And need it to live a good life?" Blair bellowed, ending Blake's sentence.

"We all did," Bailey stated baldly. Somehow, through my shaken-apart, quaking being, I heard their words clear as pure bells. Bailey continued, "We all grew up with that hubris. Remember how we learned to let go and to understand we were created to sway with the winds of life, that we could thrive while not having control, that death was a process just like birth was and infancy and childhood and adolescence and adulting?"

"I hate that word," Blake interrupted. "It sounds so immature."

"We adopt new words as English evolves," Bailey retorted. "English is like us. If it remains static and always in control, it grows stale and useless."

I screamed, "What has that got to do with me?"

Suddenly, the shaking and thundering stopped. The bench and surfaces stilled, and my parts snapped back into place. The judge intoned, "You should not have killed yourself. For that, you must pay. But worse, you destroyed the realms up to this one. We will have to determine your judgement."

"What realms," I asked, exasperation overcoming my instinct to dive into myself and hide out there. I was thinking and asking questions in an unfamiliar way, yet I didn't seem to care or fear it. I shoved that revelation to the side because right now I needed answers and to stop being shoved helter-skelter. I hadn't earned and saved to buy my own place, to escape Mom and Sally when I could, for another authority to take their place and oppress me.

"The Distortans are the realms. Our powers are the realms. Dark, Desire, Ignorance, Wrath. I'm the seventh form of Wrath. Wrath comes in seven forms: darkness, desire, ignorance, zeal for death, kingdom of flesh, foolish wisdom of flesh, and last, where you're standing, wisdom of the wrathful person. Wrath sees reality as it is. Life is black and white. Reality is black and white. There is only with us or against us, and you've proven yourself against us. We won't tolerate this."

"What does that mean?"

"Where are you going destroyer of realms?"

"I'm going to the end of my existence. Dr. V offered me a restful end to my pain, and I took it. There was nothing wrong with that. I'm alone in this world, and I need to look out for me because no one else has or will."

"God is. We have," Blake murmured, hurt edging into me from the three.

I marched away from them, and keeping my eyes on the judge, I yelled at them, "What is this God? I've known of no God in my life. I've seen no God. Spoken to no God. Worked with no God. You say you're my soul family, you say you're with me. But how do I know? I've hardly known you. I only met you here, in Distortans territory. You're like others. You come along, say nice things, and leave. People leave. They always do. And if they don't leave, they control you. You're trying to control me. You all are. I won't stand for it!" I raised my right knee up and stamped my right foot down on the ground. I ignored the dull pain that shot up my leg. I fisted my hands and slammed them both against the black-and-white chessboard bench. With each hit, bruising pain expanded into my hands, my forearms, my elbows, my shoulders, my head. I welcomed the pain if it meant taking down this bench and dispatching the soul family.

"Wisdom," I yelled to punctuate my slamming fists. "You want to know what wisdom is? I'll tell you what it is! It's understanding that we're ultimately alone in this world! Wisdom accepts you can't stop people from hurting you, but you can protect yourself from them. Wisdom is skeptically viewing every offer of help because help always comes with strings attached. Wisdom is knowing no good deed goes unpunished. Wisdom is getting them before they get you. Wisdom is that love comes with conditions. Wisdom is that money keeps you safe. Money makes the world go round—"

"Relationships make the world go round," Bailey said.

"—if you don't earn your own money, people will make you pay. They'll shun you and judge you. So you'd better work and work hard. I worked hard for my money. I worked hard for my stuff. My stuff was the only good thing. It didn't leave me. My material stuff didn't judge me or mock me. So my heart began failing? Was that my fault? Was—"

"Actually, it kind of was," Blake tried to speak through my rant.

"—that a reason to not listen to me? That was my cue to end it. I wanted to end it. Wisdom is that there are no second chances, you're forced to end the pain. If I destroyed your powers, I don't care. All I care about is what Dr. V offered me and I grabbed: death. Why am I not dead yet?" I screeched as I slammed my entire body into the bench and landed face down in steaming garbage. I lifted my head as I braced my hands against slippery plastic bags, poking broken wooden chopsticks, squishy rotting mangoes, and things I'd rather not identify.

"Welcome to Hell Track," said the computer monitor in front of me.

Chapter Twenty-Three

HELL'S RED ROBES

I scurried backwards from that awful monitor I'd forgotten about. It's irritating chiming welcome to the garbage dump slithered through me like a spiky snake. "Ouch!" I yelped as a sharp needle poked me. I twisted to investigate as I froze in crab position. A syringe looked up at me as the monitor said, "Welcome to Hell Track." The needle seemed to say it, too.

"No, no, no," I moaned. *I can't do this again!*

I flipped myself over and the syringe jabbed me through my hand. *So careless, Charlotte Elisabeth!* I remonstrated myself. "You're always so careless!"

I lifted my hand, and the syringe fell out of my palm, and the dump absorbed it. *I got myself off this dump before, and I'll do it again.* I scrabbled onto my knees, my back to that hellish monitor, and scanned the dump for its edge. But all I saw were piles of plastic bags; grey smoke or gases drifting out of thin crevasses in a regular, familiar pattern; mounds of rotting paper; crumpled metal; torn fabrics in reds and yellows and greens, like colourful punctuation marks in the sea of slippery white and tarnished chrome. Far in the distance, red stuck out. I squinted. Red Robes. The Red Robes were sitting in a circle.

Why were they on the garbage dump? Never mind. I stood and immediately sank to my knees, needles stabbing me, plastic sliding me downwards, dehydrated apple cores scratching me. I lurched forward and landed on my palms. I flattened myself and crept out of the sinking hole. My torso emerged, then my hips, then my legs. At last my feet found purchase, and I wriggled towards the Red Robes. *This will take forever*, I groused to myself.

Suddenly, they materialized before me, sitting in their circle, a little distance apart from each other, like they feared touching each other. Their tomes sat open in a haphazard pile in the centre of their circle. As usual, they were debating each other. I stopped creeping forward and raised myself up on my hands and knees. When I felt safe, I sat back carefully on my knees, my palms on my thighs. I rested. Exhaustion overwhelmed me. As did manure. Pig manure. I tried to habituate myself to the ammonia smell—I didn't know how the Red Robes could stand it—they must be habituation experts. I was failing at it. Flashbacks cycloned in. Showing Mom my marks; Mom remonstrating how I always failed her, and that's why Father left, but she couldn't leave and—

I smacked my head hard with my right hand.

The Red Robes stopped talking. One of them, with his right side to me, turned his head towards me and glowered. "Yes?" he asked.

"Did you notice what you're sitting on?"

"What do you mean?"

"The manure."

Red Robe Two, their left side to me, turned their head towards me and frowned. "What manure?"

I pointed to the pile underneath them and blinked. What I saw didn't jibe with what I smelled. I stared at the white plastic underneath them, cushioning them like a straw mattress in a bier. I made out the shapes. Tubes. The white plastic tubes resembled the ones Dr. V used to plunge his deadly drugs into me. Little glass vials littered the area, their necks broken like when doctors prepare sleeping drugs or any medication for injection. And syringe needles glinted higgledy-piggledy, pointing upward in crowns all around the Red Robes.

"Don't they hurt?" I asked.

Two Red Robes frowned at me, the two beside them turned towards me, confusion wreathing their faces. They turned towards each other and whispered, "What is she talking about?"

One of them shrugged.

"Can't you smell it?"

"Yes, it's a fresh smell. A hygienic smell," the one who first spoke to me said. The other three nodded as a nearby crevasse spewed acrid gases.

A scream penetrated the gaseous eruptions. I pivoted, my attention galvanized. "What was that?" I heard more screams. I searched for the source and then remembered people running away from giant gates outside the dump area.

"Help me!"

"Help me, I need help!"

"Don't let the Gates get me. Help!"

My heart constricted and I wrenched from the pain and desperation zinging towards me. "Those cries!" I ejaculated, raising myself and entreating the Red Robes with outstretched hands. They reared back from me as if I smelled. I flopped back down on my knees, my hands slapping into the tubes.

They relaxed back into their circle as they eyed me. "We hear no cries," said Red Robe Four.

How can you not hear those cries? I wondered.

The four observed me, and I squirmed under their stony gaze. *Something is wrong.*

"Well?" asked Red Robe Three from the circle's far side. "Why are you here?"

Why am I here? I couldn't remember. I looked around me. *Oh yes, I wanted off the dump.* I smiled at them, hopeful, waiting for their instructions. They stared back at me. *Why didn't they answer my question?*

"We're over here," a voice like pink noise susurrated from far away, and I cocked my head. "You're—"

"Help me!"

"Help me!"

"Help me, please!"

The cries interrupted the pink voice.

"Well?!" demanded Red Robe One, whipping my attention back to the four. "We have spoken to you. When we speak, you answer."

"Uh..."

"We don't have all day!"

I frowned at them. "Didn't you hear my question?"

"How could we have heard it when you didn't speak?"

"But everyone here speaks through thoughts."

One of the Red Robes at the back waved a dismissive hand. "That's for them. We are consumed with our learned deliberations. We cannot allow ourselves to be interrupted."

"Learned? What are you learning?"

"Learn-ed," condescended the same Red Robe at the back.

Oh-kay, sorr-ry, I thought, resorting to my adolescent ways. I chided myself. *I'm sixty-one years old. Have some dignity.*

"I'd like to know how to get off this garbage dump," I asked out loud.

"What garbage dump?" Red Robe One asked me.

"The one we're sitting on."

They studied me. Red Robe Two said, "We'd know if we were sitting on a garbage dump. We're in our deliberation hall. We find sitting in a white room enables our intellectual rigour."

The sweet-sour smell of dead blood assailed me.

At that moment, the men I'd seen before with them came sloshing towards them, raising clouds of micro-plastics, mould, and paper detritus in front of them. Diesel exhaust accompanied them and mixed revoltingly with the acrid pig manure. I gasped as memory hit. I knew where I'd smelled that acrid manure before: a factory farm I'd passed on one of my drives to a rural client. I'd arrived with my handkerchief to my nose, and she'd told me they kept pigs so closely penned together that the manure they excreted created toxic clouds of ammonia, requiring them to keep their pens sterile and farmers in Hazmat suits so the pigs wouldn't get sick. The pigs' imprisoned living conditions weakened their immune systems. I'd stopped eating pork after that. I despised political movements, but that place had put me off.

The men neared the Red Robes, and the Red Robes raised their hands like stop signs. The men stopped out of touching distance. The Red Robes remained seated, legs crossed underneath their draped cloaks, and the men crouched. It reminded me of an ancient court.

"Our arguments held no traction," the one with the thick, black, wavy hair said.

"I backed him up," said the pompous one with the slicked-back blonde hair. "I spoke plainly. But they didn't buy it. I'm fair. I don't lie."

"I don't either," said the black-haired man, side-eyeing the blonde. "We understand the difficulty these people have. We want to help everyone. But they won't let us through the mist at the top of the ramp. We felt at home here for a time, but now..." He fell silent for a moment. "Well, now we need a better reason so they'll let us return to Earth where we can lead."

The four Red Robes nodded. "We've been deliberating on these matters further. We don't understand why you want to leave this place. Don't you find it comfortable?"

"Well, to be honest—and I'm a forthright man—I speak plainly so folks can understand me. I don't stand on ceremony. I say what I say and mean what I say."

The Red Robes nodded sage-like.

"I don't," the black-haired man said. "I'm finding the cries for help uncomfortable. Your judgements kept them at bay for awhile. I couldn't hear them, but now they've grown louder. I have to respond to what the public wants. 'I hear you,' I tell them, 'I hear you,' but here they don't believe me. I must return to Earth where my citizens believe me."

The Red Robes nodded in unison. "No, we understand. Some people don't recognize rights and our wisdom for what it is. We've seen the public understand our judgements as good."

The men nodded. "We did, too. The public was onside with us. As those in charge, we gave them what they wanted, what we all understood to be humane."

"We'll put our clerks to the books and investigate solutions for us."

The blonde man began, "I hate to break this to you—because I know you're good people—and good people and you wise Red Robes know what's what—and I'm telling you what's what but—"

"You don't have clerks," interrupted the black-haired man, his face shining palely through a sudden gust of gas. His long nose didn't twitch. The other men had remained quiescent, but the flimsy-red-haired one clapped him on his left shoulder. "Let me take a crack at it. I speak to the public what they want to hear. They'll believe me. They always do." He grinned, straightened up, and marched off, arms dragging down in front of him, his head leading the way like an albatross.

The Red Robes watched, agape. Red Robe One whined, "But we always have clerks to do our work for us. How will we get anything done?"

Red Robe Two responded. "Well, we'll have to make do. We'll refer to precedents." They gestured to the open tomes in the middle of their circle. "Leave us to it. The public applauded our cogent arguments for seeking death. When people are dying, why wouldn't they prefer to die on their own terms?"

Yes! They get it. Why can't soul family and the Distortans get that?

"And the disabled. That's no way to live. We must alleviate people from their suffering. We gave them that right."

They did? They gave me the right to control my own end? The news stunned me. *Had I heard that before?* I sought an answer as I gazed sightlessly beyond their circle.

All the attending men nodded. The black-haired man said, "I hear them. I've given them what they wanted. I spoke privately to you, you remember. We expanded on your judgements. We understood what the public desired."

He did? He allowed Dr. V to help me? He's the one who made it possible for me to be heard?

"We can't spend money like it was going out of style. People work hard for their money," said the blonde.

I nodded along with the Red Robes at that, too.

"People tell me they work hard for their money. They resent seeing it going to freeloaders."

We hummed to each other.

The black-haired man responded, "Citizens recognize, like I recognize, that hardship isn't a right. Controlling your own death is. Who would want to live in suffering? No one, of course. We all know that the disabled, the depressed, the ones with mental challenges, don't want to live like that. None of us can imagine living like that. I gave them a dignified way out. I listened to the progressive movement, the first genuine leader to do so, and I gave them dignity. And the public adulates me for it. We've brought equity and inclusivity to our citizens. Why don't the mist-keepers understand that." His whine screeched like an old microphone, yet the screech didn't make me cringe. I liked it. I liked him.

"He," the blonde gestured to the black-haired man, "and I are on the same page. Yeah, we come at it differently—he speaks about ideas, me, I'm a plain man. But these folks here, who keep us in this place, they just don't understand. They said we belong here."

"Well, it's a nice place," said Red Robe Three at the back. "We don't understand why you want to leave it."

"I gotta tell you, those screams are getting to me."

"I tell them I hear them and we're pulling out all the stops—"

"My words," the blonde concurred.

"—but they won't stop screaming 'Help'," finished the black-haired man.

I turned to look towards the dump's far-off edge from where the endless screams emanated—sitting with the Red Robes had muted them, leaving my mind free to hear wisdom words. I spoke up, "Stay here with the Red Robes. We can't hear them here."

The two men ignored me. They shifted positions on their haunches.

Red Robe One said, "People don't always appreciate the wisdom of our intellectual reason. We deliberate months on these issues. We don't take them lightly. We peruse rights and freedoms, study precedents, interpret the words of our learned forebears, spend hours poring over the books our clerks have earmarked from the law library, yet the public rejects our wisdom. What can we do?"

"They don't all reject your wisdom. So many understand we're helping them by expanding the laws to be inclusive. But they don't accept that here. They call it Hell Track. That monitor keeps chiming 'Welcome to Hell Track' whenever we come close to it."

Phew! It's not only me who hears that irritating monitor. I sank further into my knees and settled into a bunched-up stack of bubble pack. No pops, though. Someone had popped all the bubbles.

"They tell us that God's wisdom reigns here, not the Wisdom of the Wrathful Person nor the Foolish Wisdom of the Flesh."

"God's wisdom," snarled Red Robe Three.

"We are not foolish!" Red Robe One bridled as they straightened their neck and glared at the black-haired man. "We are enlightened enough to know that God has nothing to do with rights and freedoms. Church and state are separated for a reason. Reason holds sway over people's lives, not foolish old texts."

The two men raised their hands, palms towards the Red Robes. "Hey," said the blonde, "He's only repeating what the mist-keepers tell him. We speak plainly—and as I say, I don't lie—we tell the mist-keepers, we hear the folks—"

"We have to get past the mist-keepers through that mist. Back to our lives. Our time on Earth ended too soon," the black-haired man interjected.

"Yes, you're healthy. We asserted your right to live. There was no reason that we could judge for you to die."

"It was a heart attack for me. Too soon. I had more to give the folks."

"Cancer ate at me. I lived healthily and didn't deserve to have cancer."

The blonde chuckled, "Better my heart attack than your anal cancer."

The black-haired man smacked him, and the blonde grinned back. "I was just speaking plain."

Red Robe One signalled them. "Away with you both. We must deliberate. Our wisdom is the highest in the land. We understand what's right and what freedom means. No god infects our deliberations. We're the ultimate judges, and no scripture, no religion, no dogma, no church can change that."

I nodded as I reflected on how they laid the path for Dr. V to help me. *I hadn't thought about it before at all,* I was forced to admit. When Dr. V had offered me a dignified end, one under my control, I assumed doctors had always been able to. I didn't know it was new. Or new-ish. I wondered when these Red Robes had changed the law. *Does it matter?* I asked myself. *No,* I grinned. *It doesn't.* I couldn't smell the acrid manure or the diesel exhaust anymore. *Why had I plugged my senses from the smell? They were right. It smelled hygienic and reminded me of the Dying with Dignity Suite.* I nestled into the bent and crushed plastic tubes, the nest of syringes and red-stained gauze, to learn more from these wise intellectual giants who'd saved my health.

Chapter Twenty-Four

HELL SEDUCES

I sat contentedly near the Red Robes. Their wisdom comforted me. Knowing their intellect and judgement made my end possible filled me with hope. *Where they exist, I exist. They'd given me choice on Earth, so they'll do that here, too. They'll find a way. Maybe this is my second chance?* I idly stroked my hands through cracked and bent tubes, whitened opaquely where damaged. Like me.

Pink noise billowed towards me. It caressed my right side—my right cheek, right shoulder, right hip, right thigh, and right knee. I stilled myself, safe near the Red Robes.

'What is she doing?" Blake whispered to Bailey.

"She's hiding," Blair said.

"She's retreated to her place of safety," Bailey replied.

"What do we do?"

"We attended that workshop on dissociative stress response. This is classic."

"You paid attention?" Blake asked, surprised.

"Yes," Blair said, biting her word off. "We both did. We had to if we wanted to help her."

"We have to figure out a way to get her out of that state," Bailey mused.

"Well, what did the educated guy at the workshop suggest?"

"He didn't," Blair said, irritation creeping into their thoughts.

"'Only when you meet your newest family member and get to know them will you know what to do. I can teach you about the stress response and some fundamentals, but only you will discover what will work to help your family member through the Barrier.' End quote," Bailey intoned.

"Well, that's not helpful," Blake retorted.

"It isn't," Blair agreed.

"Whether helpful or not, we have to figure it out. We won't leave her here with those four."

A cloud of micro-plastics snatched my attention. I slanted my transparent eyeballs towards the cloud and saw the men returning. I watched their progress towards the Red Robes.

"Well, those caught her attention," Blake noted.

"Yes," Bailey mused.

"Why?"

"They return in a cycle. Perhaps she hasn't seen that yet?"

"Yeah, let's watch," Blake said.

The men reached the Red Robes.

"Do you have a reason yet?"

"We've considered the petition, and we have a response," said Red Robe One. They handed the men a sheet with black-inked lines scribbled across both sides. The black-haired man held both edges with the fingertips of both of his hands, and the blonde one leaned over his upper arm to read it. The other men tip-toed up to read it. They grinned and nodded at each other. The black-haired man released one edge and slapped it with the back of his fingers. "Perfect."

They pirouetted as one and left the way they came.

Blake rotated as if she was facing the Red Robes. *Well, that was enlightening!* The thought gunned from Blake like a backfiring engine. The edges of the Red Robes closest to Blake rippled as if rough waves had pushed their skins in and out. I goggled. The Red Robes furthest away reared back. "Who touched you?" screamed Red Robe Three as Bailey said, "You know not to do that here Blake."

Blake rotated back, saying, "Pfft. They deserved it."

"Nothing changes with them," Blair noted. "They think only in physical terms, as if they're still on Earth in the material world."

"Yeah," Blake drawled. "They think only their thoughts are important. Our thoughts can't have any effect on them." She snorted.

Red Robes One and Two patted themselves as if trying to stop their skin and cloaks from rippling. Red Robes Three and Four pawed the air near them. Bailey rotated, and it was as if I could see her thoughts taking the physical form of gently lapping waves. *Your skin is intact. You are whole in form.* Their shapes returned to baseline.

Bailey rotated back as I tried to compute what had happened. She said, "Enough about them. We must help Charlotte Elisabeth."

"Why don't we try prodding her?" Blake suggested.

"That won't work," Bailey replied. "Remember what the dissociative stress workshop said: if we threaten, they will retreat further in."

"We will cajole," Blair said.

"No," Bailey replied. "Charlotte Elisabeth views love with suspicion. Life taught her a distorted version of love."

"She does have a skewed way of looking at it, like it's bad or something," Blake said.

"So if we can't threaten—"

"And we can't prod—"

"And we can't cajole, what do we do, Bailey?"

"I don't know. She's as buried within herself as the earliest Caribou skins in the bottom of this dump from when humans first created this suffering waste."

The dump hushed, and the Red Robes' intellectual chatter became clearer to me. As I listened in, Blake blurted, "Well, there's a colouring book and crayons over there. While you two figure it out, I'm going to go colour."

Blake crossed my line of vision between the Red Robes and me. A colouring book and a box of crayons, its lid ripped, and some crayons broken and bent, glided towards where Blake hovered. Their bright colours stuck out from the lake of whitened plastic and syringes, glinting chrome and steel of needles that pooled all around me, and the vivid Red Robes. The crayons' vibrant reds reflected the Red Robes; their iridescent greens highlighted their robes. I watched the crayons follow underneath Blake towards me as if she was a helicopter pulling a dangling basket. Blake halted, and the colouring book and box of crayons flopped next to my crossed legs on my left side. Blake floated slightly above the surface, facing the colouring book, and it fluttered open.

This telekinetic ability fascinated me.

I leaned to my left for a gander.

A red crayon, labelled crimson, slid out from the box, angled itself upward, then lowered itself to the colouring book. The book's pages flipped one, two, three, until two pages with black-line drawings faced me. The crimson crayon lowered itself more and touched the outline of a hat. *A toque*, I thought. Crimson filled the toque as the crayon scratched its blunt tip back and forth on the paper.

Micro-plastics showered me, and I hunched, hands over my head, and peeked up. The men were storming towards the Red Robes. The Red Robes paused in their animated discussion and looked towards the men.

"They didn't accept your arguments!" The black-haired man threw back his wavy hair and flung the paper they'd taken eagerly only a moment earlier. The paper fluttered into the middle of the Red Robes circle. Red Robe Two reached forward and picked it up. They scanned it and nodded. "This was a most reasoned judgement. Why did the mist-keepers reject it?"

"They said it doesn't conform to God's wisdom."

"What does God's wisdom have to do with the right of egress? You have the right to exit to Earth, just as we have affirmed the rights of people to exit from Earth," lectured Red Robe One.

"We'll return to receive your newest reasoned judgement."

"Do that," snapped Red Robe Three at the back of the circle. "We will have it ready for you."

The men swivelled on their heels and stomped off, the force of their feet stirring clouds of paper and plastic, detritus galore, up and all around them, their motes reflecting the blue light from the overhead arch.

A crayon fell beside my idle hand. Blue. Light blue like the arch overhead. I picked it up and studied it. The paper encircling it whispered familiar sensations through my fingertips. I contemplated the blue crayon. Its label said "Sky Blue." A small tear decorated its edge near the tip of the crayon, yet its tip had that new-crayon point as if sharpened by a well-tuned machine. I dropped my gaze to the colouring book. The perfect page lay underneath my hand that held the crayon, inviting me to draw, and I obeyed, scribbling blue arching lines across the top of the page, back and forth, back and forth, lower and lower down the page. The hypnotic effect soothed me, and I leaned leftwards to reach further towards the spine of the page. Having filled the whole top half with sky blue, even across the outlines of a drawing, I paused and considered my efforts. A pretty blue. I raised my eyes, bent my neck backwards, and let myself drown in the blue overhead. *I've drawn the sky*, I thought.

I straightened my neck, dropped my eyes, and spotted a yellow crayon half out of its box. Its sun-golden colour appealed to me, and I slid it out with my right hand and read the text on its partially torn-off label. Goldenrod. I remembered goldenrod invading the neighbour's garden, their tall stems top heavy with tiny yellow flowers, flocked together like sneezy clouds. Mom always ripped them out while the neighbour was shopping then denied it when confronted. I clenched my fingers, and the crayon snapped in half. I dropped both crayons.

The cloud of microplastics reappeared, heralding the men's return. I watched the Red Robes offer them a sheet of paper covered in lines of black calligraphic ink, identical to their previous offering. The men's glowering visages changed to nods and high-fives, and they hurried off in eagerness to the dump's edge and the mist-keepers. This time I noticed women appearing with their hands on the mens' backs as they scurried towards the ramp.

Movement caught my eye to my left. Blake was levitating a green crayon. It reminded me of the colours of green olives. Saltiness invaded my taste memories, and my mouth curved upward in remembered pleasure. The olive-green crayon touched my left hand as the colouring book fluttered its pages to reveal two blank pages. I picked up the crayon, almost without thinking, and drew an olive. It needed pimento red. I glanced over at the crayon box, and a red crayon was lying on top of it. I grabbed it and read its label. *Hey*, I thought. *It's pimento red!* I grinned and coloured the red in at the top of the olive. *The olive needs accompaniments.* I leaned into my drawing as Blake drew cheese and waffles on the facing page to my left.

Micro-plastics blew up around me. Unintelligible yells flung themselves into my ears. But I kept drawing my tabletop tableau of olives in a jar, olives in a wooden creche, olives scattered in a bowl of almonds.

"I don't like spicy things," I said to Blake, looking up at her. "But Sincerity introduced me to olives and almonds to snack on before a meal. You know, when you're a bit hungry but it's not dinner time yet."

"I know," Blake smiled.

A dull ache made itself known underneath my right butt cheek. I twisted my head around to look behind me. Needles pointed upwards all around me; their sharpness was piercing my hip and my calves where they lay in the plastics. I leapt up. "Ouch! Where'd they come from?"

"You've been sitting in them," Blake drawled.

"But I didn't feel them."

"We stop feeling what we get used to," Bailey explained neutrally.

"I guess so," I muttered. I looked into the far distance. A cloud erupted near the dump's edge. "I was on my way towards the edge," I said wonderingly. "I forgot?"

"It's okay," Bailey said. "We all get distracted. We can show you the way to the edge, if you like?"

I nodded. *Yes*, I thought. I wanted to get away from the endless cycle of men returning to the Red Robes' for arguments that failed to satisfy the mist-keepers. *Why can't they satisfy?*

"They don't understand that the wisdom of God rules over all."

"Why?"

"Think about your drawing. You created it."

"Yes," I replied, thinking that was obvious.

"It's obvious to us when we create something that it's obvious we created it. But it's harder to think that we're the creation of another mind, a mind greater than we can contemplate. We call that mind, that consciousness God. And just as your drawing doesn't understand your intent and can't see the complete picture nor understand your plans, neither can we God's."

"But how does that make...God? God is the name?"

"Yes, God. That's the right name."

"How does that make God wiser than the Red Robes?"

"Do you see their futility? The futility of the male leaders who confer with the ones you call the Red Robes? If they understood their own creation as well as their author does, then they'd be able to design reasons that'd convince the mist-keepers to allow the men to return to Earth. Their efforts are like your olives making up their own laws about how they should be drawn and interact and expect their laws to be stronger than your creating mind."

I barked and clapped my hand over my mouth. I hadn't heard myself laugh, even in derision in years and decades. The sound horrified me. *I wonder what the women at their backs want?* I let the question float away. The men neared enough for me to hear their yelling and see their arms flailing in the air. I suddenly hated it and didn't want to participate, even as an observer, in such mindless recycling behaviour. I wanted out.

"Come on," Blake said, bouncing forward. "Let's get out of here."

"Wait. I want to take my drawing." I sank to my haunches and began to rip it out from the colouring book.

"You don't think you can take that with you, do you?" Blake giggled.

"Hush, Blake!" Bailey remonstrated.

I stared at my drawing. *Why couldn't I take it? Maybe I'll—*

"Remember the woman with the purse," Bailey murmured. I thought back and slowly nodded.

"Yes. She couldn't take her purse with her."

"That's because the dump doesn't know her."

"And it doesn't know me?"

"No, it doesn't, because you don't belong to it."

"Who do I belong to?"

"You belong to us."

I stood up. *Yes*, I thought, marvelling at the feeling of safety that expanded outward from my heart. *I do.*

"Yes, you do," Bailey, Blair, and Blake chorused, gladness tinging their voices with singing harmonies of pink, yellow, and silver.

The three guided me over mounds of plastics, hills of shredded paper, sharp-edged piles of crumpled metals, ripped and torn fabrics. I struggled to stay on top of the garbage, raising my feet high and putting them down as gently as I could so I wouldn't sink down to my knees. The journey went on and on. We came to a group of women. I stopped to rest. Their blonde hair waved down their backs and fronts. I lifted my hand subconsciously to touch my own blonde hair. A brunette stood out; her hair, with its grey streaks, curled and waved and stuck out around her face, its colour leached out by the blue arch above.

"The men will get the right answer this time," asserted one woman.

"They haven't lead us astray yet."

"We're lucky to be with the first feminist leader."

"Isn't his black hair amazing? I love how it waves," another gushed.

"Who cares. What matters is he recognizes we're equal."

"I wonder if they'll come back with reasons good enough to let the mist-keepers through this time?"

"We can't go wrong following them. With their understanding that women are powerful, we'll exit with them."

I rolled my eyes and resumed my struggling walk to the edge. I passed them by.

I spotted the edge beyond Bailey, Blair, and Blake and picked up my pace, but not quickly enough. The men's shouts closed in from behind me. Women's voices joined them in triumph. The men raced past me, their hustling feet churning up clouds of metal fragments glinting wickedly as they flew backwards towards the women whose hands were seemingly glued to their men's backs. I ducked my head and averted my eyes. When the crowd had all passed me, I lifted my head up again. They leaped off the edge, the black-haired man leading the way, waving papers triumphantly in his hand. Gleeful shouts disappeared into the distance as they mixed with the never-ending, never-diminishing screams of "Help me!" sliding towards the Gates while they ran onto the ramp towards the mist and the mist-keepers. *They'll be back.*

I waited for the paper they clutched to disintegrate and return to the dump in a stream of pixels. It didn't.

I hastened to stand on the edge of the dump. *How can the paper remain intact in his hand?*

"Like with the Red Robes' law tomes," I whispered, remembering.

Bailey said, "The garbage knows its own."

Chapter Twenty-Five

HELL GATES

I jumped down and somersaulted onto the cobblestones. I sprang back up and scanned my surroundings. No longer awash with mud and raging water, the dry cobblestones' chips and cracks were visible, worn and stained from millions of feet scuffing them, I assumed. I lifted my head and drank in the blue sky. *Will a vortex appear?* I looked left; I looked right.

An older man, grey of hair, elegant in bearing, vaulted off the edge of the dump, and the surrounding molecules shivered. Anxiety crawled like itchy spiders through my mind.

What tableau will appear?

Hell Track answered with a driveway. A Volvo SUV. Black. Its four doors closed. The molecules gathered around the vaulter, shaking and shaking until he rocketed towards the SUV, thudding onto grass edging a flagstone driveway the SUV was parked on.

What's the error here? The molecules whirled into a vortex, and the SUV tableau vanished around its radius.

I waited.

In slow motion, the tableau reappeared; the rear wheels sat on a concrete sidewalk beyond the flagstone driveway's end, the SUV's back end extending beyond, consuming one-third of the sidewalk's width, leaving only the sloped curb for pedestrians to walk on.

A tiny woman pushing a stroller shimmered into view. She was leaning down over the stroller, its hood up, as she walked on the sidewalk towards the SUV. The SUV's elegant grey-haired driver marched towards the back of the SUV as the stroller hit the vehicle's rear. The woman's head startled up; the man's glass-grey eyes stared through her. They vanished round the bend as the woman asked, "Why park on..."

The vortex cruised towards the Gates, and the tableau reappeared in slow motion, a teenager having replaced the woman. The teenager was leaning on a cane and glaring at the driveway slope. "Hey! The sidewalk ain't your driveway."

The grey-eyed SUV driver regarded him.

The teenager shook his cane at the driver. "You can't be telling people to walk on a slope. You think I can walk on this here slope?!"

The tableau whizzed out of sight. The vortex slid into the space between cobblestones and followed its path towards the Gates.

As the tableau reappeared, a young woman, anxiety writ on her face, ran from behind the grey-eyed driver as he stared at a tall woman glaring at him from the road. "Get your fucking SUV off the sidewalk!"

The young woman, her blonde hair shining, her eyes framed with smudge-proof mascara, her lips shimmering pink, her fair skin glowing, rushed towards the tall woman. The grey-eyed man's wife, I somehow knew. "I'm so sorry, I'm so sorry."

A car materialized; grazed the tall woman's back; and she lurched forward. "For fuck's sake!" Her arms flung outwards to rebalance herself.

"I'm sorry. I'm sorry," the young woman stretched her hands out towards the tall woman as the grey-eyed man arched his eyebrows. "The garden's in the way...that wall...I'll try harder to park it closer to the garden...," she babbled.

The blue sky yanked the vortex up.

It vanished.

"Help me!"

I whipped my head around towards the ramp. I squinted at it and at the people hustling towards the mist at the ramp's upper end. Yet some were leaning backwards as they slid upwards. An elder was weeping, hands covering her face, a man stooping over her as if consoling her. As she slid inexorably towards the mist, he crouch-walked beside her. The mist was the gateway to and from Earth. Except for her, the people entering were dead like me yet eager to walk through the mist. *Why are those people scrambling towards the mist? What's so great about Earth?*

"Not quite like you," Bailey said. "Some want to remain here only after they arrive, like that old woman."

"She doesn't want to go back," observed Blair. "He's persuading her she'll like it."

"Jesus is so rude, always thrusting people out when they don't want to go!"

"Blake!"

"Well, it's true! That man softens it for them. He's nice," Blake sighed.

"Who's nice?" I asked.

"The man consoling her. He's a fixture," Bailey replied. "Searching for his father since he arrived here from Heaven. No one knows how he managed to re-enter Hell Track, but since he came, he helps those on the ramp return to Earth when they don't want to go."

"And persuading those who want to leave, to stay and head to the Gates," Blair added.

I regarded him. The elder vanished; the man loped back down the ramp through the crowd fighting to return to Earth, speeding past the crowd resisting the mist.

"They're not quite like you," Bailey repeated.

I turned towards my soul family. "What do you mean?"

"These dead entering Hell Track have travelled their Soul Track on Earth, while you weren't given a chance. You were forced to endure a short, aggressive form."

"That's what happens when humans after death bring all their unprocessed detritus with them and don't know how to make it through. They distorted the Soul Track on Earth and created the Distortans in the Earth-Heaven Interdimensional Expanse."

"Why?"

"That's a long story," Bailey replied.

That's what you say when you're lying, I thought.

"No, I'm not," Bailey replied evenly. "It really is a long story. And you will hear it, but right now you need to figure out how to get out of here. One step at a time."

I raised my eyebrows, not reassured. The three orbs blandly returned my gaze, and I dropped my shoulders and brows and sighed. For some reason, I felt she was telling the truth. *She? Hmmm, when did I start thinking of her as she?*

Silvery giggles shivered Blake. Her blue energy orb streams angled upwards like they were smiling. I smiled back. My cheeks hurt. I straightened my mouth. I raised my shoulders and turned away from them to look across the expansive cobblestones towards the ramp.

"Help me!" Hands grabbed my front and pulled me down. By reflex, I grabbed those grabbing hands and yanked. "You must help me!" cried the woman, whose face distorted as if a wind blew across it towards the enormous Gates opposite to the mist. I choked. *I can't*, I thought, straining to pull her hands off me.

"Yes, you can!" she cried, her hands stretching downwards under gravity's force—or Hell Track's version—while she kept her grasp on me.

"I don't know how!" I cried. Tears flooded my cheeks; my internal bricks cracked apart and tumbled down. I pulled her hands off of me, and she slipped down and away, towards the Gates as she cried, "I'm sorry! I'm sorry!" I tracked her slipping and sliding progress until she splattered against the Gates. She fell onto her left side, her arms flung above her head, her feet angling towards the space underneath the Gates. She scrabbled for purchase on the dry cobblestones, yet couldn't seem to catch a finger in any of the stones' cracks. *How can I see so clearly what she's doing when she's a speck?*

"It's the nature of this place," Bailey replied. My vision shifted to her. "It's the nature of existence after Earth life. You can see clearer because you're seeing with your mind, your consciousness. No more do you have to rely on imperfect physical systems that have limitations we're not aware of until our physical bodies die. You can see what you're looking at. You can see its size in terms of distance from you in space-time, and you can see every detail and colour of it. Including her." Bailey gestured towards the Gates, and I followed her gesture. The woman was halfway underneath the right Gate, her fingernails carving grooves into the cobblestones, chips flying up into her face. The Gates ate her: her torso, her shoulders, her neck, her head, and lastly forced her fingers to release their desperate scrabbling just before she vanished completely.

Silence descended around me.

My tears dried, and I about-faced to watch the people running and stumbling up the ramp to the mist, their screams and shoving echoing off the blue arch overhead. Cacophony once again burst around me. I thought about Bailey's explanation of vision and experimented with it by staring at the ramp. Strange creatures guarded the mist. Some grasped the collars of people far away from them and hauled them forward, throwing them through the mist, as their frenzied screams pitched to relief. Some creatures shoved and flung other people towards the Gates; the resisters bent their bodies in a v-shape against the Gates's vacuuming and aimed their sliding steps back towards the ramp, trying again and again to return to Earth.

"I'm not going back to Earth, am I?" I asked, fear quavering my voice.

"No," Bailey said.

"Then it's to the Gates I go because I'm not staying here. Futility lies in this place. What lies behind them?"

"You'll have to find out on your own. We can only accompany you. And we won't leave you. Where you go, we go."

"Even here in hell," I stated.

"Yes."

"What is Hell Track?"

"It's one of the three tracks in the Earth-Heaven Interdimensional Expanse."

"Why does everyone want to leave except the Red Robes, those posturing men, and their imbecilic women followers?"

Blair chuckled. Soon all three were bouncing like laughter in motion.

"What's so funny?" I frowned.

"You spoke truth in a way that tickled our funny bone. Sometimes truth is just funny," Blake gasped. "And no one dares speak truth in this place."

"Oh-kay," I drawled out. I puckered my brow and stared at the three of them. "Why does no one dare to speak truth here?"

"Because lies birthed this place," Blair said, the first to stop laughing. "Only those comfortable with lies belong here and want to stay here. The rest aren't, but they can't perceive truth."

Remorse caught me unaware. I was sorry I'd listened to and believed the Red Robes.

I swallowed and shifted my body until I faced the Gates. Wind whistled behind me. I looked up. Clouds gathered grey against the edges of the blue. *Not this again*, I thought.

The three hovered in front of me, almost as if holding their breath.

"Since I don't want to return to Earth, I'm going to the Gates. That woman stopped fighting them once her head was under. What did she see?"

The three said and thought nothing. I realized they'd blanked their minds to force me to figure it out on my own. I gazed around Hell Track and spotted that dump again.

A woman, her blonde hair in waves, her enormous eyes glittering green, leaped off the dump, and molecules shivered. Their shivering grew into shaking back and forth until they dislodged her footing and launched her into a green Jeep Cherokee Sport with its wheels covering much of a concrete sidewalk, landing her neatly into the driver's seat. *Haven't I seen this before?* The Jeep's heavy steel door slammed shut; its surrounding molecules whipped themselves into a vortex, rising the Jeep higher and higher as the woman cranked her window down. She yelled at the small woman she'd forced onto the asphalt road, "I'm dealing with something!" the blonde growled at her as the tableau whirled out of view.

Why is this tableau repeating itself? The Jeep's driver wants to park where she wants to park. Why is she the lyric on a stuck record? Is this her Soul Track? I groaned. *I don't want to see this again!*

The Jeep, with the blonde woman gripping the steering wheel, her head facing the window, reappeared; the vortex slowed its circular motion.

"...there's room for you, you bitch!" the green-eyed blonde yelled at a slender man hanging on to the harness of a guide dog.

He said, "Not for me. You hear about accessibility? And, by the way, I'm not a bitch. But my dog is!"

I shut my vision. *Do I have to see this over and over again?*

The vortex flung itself towards the Gates, and I turned my back to it and focused on the cobblestones below, not the blue sky above. *Hell Track vortex dooms her to relive her rage ad infinitum, screaming her blue language, wanting to do what she wanted to do.* I heard an upward sucking. *Will this vortex drop her if she one-eighties her attitude towards considering these people she's forced onto the road into the deadly paths of similar thoughtless drivers? I don't want to stay here, repeating my mistakes.*

The vortex with the couple using the sidewalk as their driveway slid past me, their rage, entitlement, and pseudo-apologies dragging spidery fingers across my mind, quaking my being. *Hadn't it vanished? Why is it back?*

Wind blew me forward and swivelled me around until I was facing the cadre of men and their following women. They were standing in a ragged circle, the women on the outside. Papers and cobblestone dust blew around them; their arms gesticulated upwards, driving the wind as thunder cracked above them, not interrupting their single-minded goal with the Red Robes yet halting the ramp people who grasped each other's arms, wary eyes on the gathering storm, some eyeballing the thundering clouds, some the men and women creating the frenzied whirling wind.

I whirled myself and ran towards the enormous Gates, tears of regret cracking my vision. The roar of an approaching tornado chased me as I ran. Bailey, Blair, and Blake flew next to me, keeping pace with me. Rain prickled my back then blasted me with peppering hail. Pain like shards demanded I stop and fling myself down to find cover next to the garbage dump, but I didn't slow. I gritted my teeth and set my jaw against the pain. I'd lived with pain for sixty-one years: what's one race to the Gates in contrast to that?

A stone clobbered the back of my head. *How can it?* I thought as harmonies of mind-numbing songs rung my mind. I couldn't see; I raised my arms, hands and fingers extending, searching for, reaching for the Gates.

My fingers crumpled into their joints, my elbows bending, my shoulders smacking, my face slamming into the Gates. I forced open my vision into the reddish iron glow. I grasped the verticals and shook them hard. The Gates didn't budge.

"You must admit to the truth," Blair said.

"Hush. She must figure this out herself," Bailey remonstrated.

"At least she's not stuck in a vortex—"

"She didn't harm others," Bailey interjected.

Blair kept talking, "—unable to face the truth of endangering others through thoughtlessness. Forever whirled until they change their thoughts to consider those they harmed."

"No vortex when you only harm yourself!" Blake chimed. "We'll stay here forever if you don't just admit the truth."

Truth? What are they talking about? I didn't dare turn around and face the maelstrom behind me. Hail and mud flung their hatred against my back. I buried my face in the verticals, my hands holding on for my life. *Life? Is this about my life? My thoughts about my life? I don't want to live. And then I remembered the wretched words I'd blurted out to...to...whom? I couldn't recall. Does it matter?*

"It all matters," Blair stated.

I want to live, I thought, despair at this unwelcome truth weighing my shoulders. My hands let go of the verticals. Suddenly, a great force tugged at my feet. I slipped. "Nooo," I cried and tried to grab the verticals again. But the force dragged my feet forward, and my arms flew straight out.

Whump!

I landed on my back like a fish flung onto the land. Rain drilled my face. I closed my eyes and let go as the Gates vacuumed me under them.

Noise crackled around me. I opened my vision and squinted against the pure bright whiteness that greeted me. It buzzed like white noise, and I hurled myself away from the sight. I spotted pink. A glowing rose pink of the sweetest perfume. I turned my body onto my right side and wormed towards it until I could raise myself up on to my hands. I twisted my hips and legs around and used my toes to help lift me up. I unfolded myself and swayed on my feet against the buzzing white noise light on my left, concentrating on that far-off pink. I staggered towards it.

Chapter Twenty-Six

FLOWER POWER POSTCARDS

I turned a corner, away from the blaring, glaring white noise, and pinkness greeted me—roses in rose, salmon, coral, scarlet; fuchsias of brightest pink and palest pink; tulips in claret, rouge, pink-blushed red; azaleas in cerise, blush, ruby, cherry. Fields and fields of flower buds opened their petals to greet me. I braked. *They're greeting me? Why?* Thoughts fled into their cavern; emotions bricked themselves up.

"It's okay," Bailey said, leading me into the pink blooms, their grey-green leaves softened with delicate hairs, their centres blushing light that shaded their environment a happy golden pink. I took a hesitant step forward to follow Bailey, and the leaves leaned forward to caress my ankles. Warmth flowed up into me: acceptance, greeting, joy, and a mental state my mind skittered from. The blue overhead arched itself like a cat waking up after a pleasant nap. I dropped my vision back down to the field in front of me as we wandered through it, away from the Barrier, the roses and tulips and fuchsia springing back upright as we flattened them in our walk. In the distance, a golden speck wagged its way towards us. The Golden Lab!

Does this dog live here? And why is there a dog in this place?

"Call Flower Power Track's dog Greeter. Dogs make the best greeters, don't you think?" Blake chimed.

I didn't know. I'd never had a dog.

Postcards appeared. They zipped themselves around in a one-eighty and zig-zagged their way towards me. I leaned backward and back-pedalled as quickly as I could. I didn't want to go into those again! But they sped up. Closer and closer, they came towards me. I tried to turn and run.

"It's okay," Bailey said.

No, it's not okay! I thought. Any time I hear her say those words, it's—

I STOOD IN my birth home's living room. Mom was rushing about, moving the furniture, and I—the historical child me in the post-card—was standing in the corner. I didn't remember this scene. *Where am I?*

"You're in your home, shortly after your father drove away," Bailey said into my right ear as I stood apart from the scene and watched my three-year-old self and Mom. *Are Sally and Sincerity here?*

"Yes," Bailey said. "Look around."

I swivelled and saw Sally huddled in the couch's corner, and Sincerity hovering in the doorway, sucking on her fingers jammed into her mouth. Fear emanated from Sally. Fear and...*What's she feeling?* I wondered.

"Focus on her, and you'll recognize the emotion," Bailey advised. "You're finding it difficult because this is the next time you further pushed your emotions away. When you shut things down, you can't identify them easily enough. But it's okay because that was then, and you're learning now, exploring what made you, you."

I raised my left shoulder and averted my gaze to avoid the scene. But Mom's words slapped around the room in her agitation...*Agitated?*

"Why is she agitated," I wondered out loud. I glanced at my three-your-old self and noticed my cheeks sported dried rivulets of salt water. Bunches of my black hair stood erect on my crown and loose bits lay messily over my shoulders. Watchfulness emanated from child-me. Watchfulness...and sadness...and an intense desire to see Father again. Confusion like a miasma infiltrated the scene. I heard the questions cycling from child-me's consciousness to Sally's to Sincerity's to child-me's, round and round: *Why did Daddy leave?*

Daddy? I interrupted my absorption of her thoughts and emotions. *I'd called Father, "Daddy?"*

I asked Bailey, "When did that happen?"

Bailey replied, "You always called your father Daddy until the day you stopped."

"But I heard Dad in the baby life review."

"It's what your mom named him to you. Watch."

I didn't want to, but it seemed I was stuck here. These postcards swallowed me up and forced me to relive moments I'd rather forget. "Or I had forgotten," I whispered to myself, astonished at the realization.

I refocused on my three-year-old self sidling towards the corner. "Why did Daddy leave? What is Mom doing?" The questions circled each other over and over like two stars in child-me's mind while fear splashed out of Sally sitting motionless in the couch's corner, her knees up to her chest, deep grief tearing at her. *Grief?* She was missing my father. I recoiled, shocked that she, the one who had mocked me for driving him away and claiming it was the best thing that had ever happened to her, while also blaming me every week for us not having a Dad—she actually missed him?

"Yes," Bailey said softly into my hearing.

I shifted my vision to Sincerity and concentrated on sifting out Mom's rampage.

Crash!

Mom had ripped a painting down off the wall and chucked it to the floor.

I lasered my focus on Sincerity. Confusion emanated from her and fear at Mom's furor. A question revolved in her mind—"How do I make Mom feel better?"—and her mind gave no answer. Sincerity, I realized, had always wanted to make people feel better. She must've been born like that. She, alone of the three of us, was the only one thinking about how to approach Mom. Sally and me were hiding from her within ourselves.

"Sincerity is braver than me," I said under my breath.

"Courage is not a hard definition," Blair stated.

"What is Mom doing?"

Mom stormed out of the room, brushing Sincerity and knocking her into the door frame. Sincerity, unfazed, continued to revolve her question and sucked harder on her fingers, trying to figure out this problem, as she stood in the doorway following Mom's noisy tumult down the hall. The rage and self-satisfaction that filled the room dissipated the longer Mom was gone. But none of us stirred.

Sincerity squeezed herself against the door frame. Rage barged into the room, followed by Mom carrying—

My heart stopped. I couldn't breathe. *Get me out of here!* was my singular thought.

"You're not alone," the three chorused as they surrounded me, their energy holding me.

Mom's rage engulfed me. Her self-satisfaction and revenge pummelled me. Fear erupted from out of my three-year-old self.

A scream!

"Stop that!" Mom yelled. My three-year-old self kept screaming and screaming.

Mom placed her load down on the floor gently; stomped over to me; and smacked my three-year-old face hard with her right hand across my left cheek. My head spun to the right, and I tumbled into the corner. My screaming stopped. Child-me curled up in the corner, wrapping my arms around my calves, trying to disappear into the walls. Mom smiled. But underneath her smile, I sensed fear screaming. She suffocated her fear with her controlling need, relief at seeing me cower, knowing nothing bad could happen as long as she controlled us girls.

"That doesn't make sense," I said to Bailey.

"Your mom is a complex creature," she replied.

Mom walked back to her load, stooped, and lifted it up. She stared into its dead life-like eyes, daring herself to be afraid and repulsed, feelings I didn't remember seeing. She swallowed her feelings as she breathed to it, "Greg wouldn't let me display this, my greatest achievement Dad and I did. But he's gone. Greg dared to leave me, so I can put this up. Every time I look at it, I'll know Greg can't rule me." She affixed it to the wall. "Sally come here," she commanded. Sally had buried her head in her knees, muffling her sobs. She brushed her cheeks against her knees, drying her grief into a small pile of ashes, then burying them under a frosting of hard diamonds.

"Yes, Mom," she whispered over her knees.

"I said, come here," Mom commanded as she stared into the golden eyes of her new display, her right forefinger pointing to the bare wooden floor covered in torn cushions, their stuffing strewn under the crashed painting. She lifted her right foot and deliberately placed it in the middle of the painting. She glared at her foot and the painting a minute, two minutes, and lifted her foot and slammed it down; again and again, she stamped until the painting's shreds mingled with the cushion's stuffing.

I fought the fear strangling me, for I needed to understand her. My need diminished the fear. "Why does she hate the painting?"

"Listen to her thoughts," Bailey said.

I hate Greg! He shouldn't have left! Crush him! Crush his painting! He thinks he's an artist, displaying his pathetic efforts over Dad and me's triumph.

I thought the painting seemed familiar, yet how could I know it? I never saw it growing up.

"But you did."

I stared hard and suddenly saw it on the wall.

"Where is Sally? What's keeping that child?" Fear blazed out at Sally because Mom couldn't tolerate Sally reflecting her own buried truth. This, on the wall, was her triumph. This was her moment with Dad. No one, no kid, was going to ignore her triumph. *Sally will believe I won!* Mom thought.

"Sally," Mom growled.

Sally uncurled herself and crawled off the couch to stand beside Mom. Her body shook, and she shoved her hands deep into her pockets.

"Look up at this magnificence," Mom said to Sally. Sally raised her eyes with trepidation, keeping her head straight. Mom grabbed Sally's hair—she would have absolute control and dominance. Emotions were threatening to flatten her, and only control could keep her upright. She yanked Sally's head up. "Look!"

The tableau slowed for interminable minutes as Sally's body quaked, then the quaking diminished to trembles as she decided she wasn't afraid. *I'm like Mom,* Sally thought. *This is Mom's win. Dad ran away, but Mom stayed. He wasn't Dad. He was Greg, and he ran cuz he knows he doesn't belong with us.*

Emotions had vanished from my three-year-old self. I'd retreated so far into myself, nothing came out. Sincerity thought, staring at the new wall display, *Yuck, but Mom feels better.*

"You know how I came to have this?" Mom asked the room.

Sincerity removed her fingers from her mouth. "How?" Sincerity replied as she pressed herself into the doorway.

Mom let go of Sally's hair, and Sally stayed in place, not daring to move, battling her fear, forcing herself to feel proud of Mom and her triumph.

"Dad took me on my first safari. He'd taught me how to use guns. In Africa, he had me practice with his long gun, his pride. He cleaned and protected it for years, never letting me touch it. But once at our Safari lodge, he opened its case, lifted it out, and handed it to me. 'This will be your first kill, and you've earned the right to use the finest weapon,' he said to me. I was so proud. I took it from his hands with both of mine, reverently as the moment demanded. For days, he'd set up special targets for me to practice shooting with. My father was wealthy and we had all the time in the world. Not like Greg," she added disparagingly. She shoved pride into her voice and continued. "Finally the day came. He explained to me that lions are predators and villagers need our protection. That's why we came all the way from North America to help them. They'd be hunted, their cows and goats killed, without us and our prowess. He had our local driver take us out to where the pride was. He said he'd been scouting out the terrain and knew where I had the best chance of taking down the head of the pride. The one with the biggest mane. He told me, it's good to kill these beasts, especially the older ones. The old male lions were past their prime. Culling was a time-honoured way of keeping the wild in check, humans safe, and their domesticated animals safe for human consumption when they'd matured enough."

Mom sighed happily.

I frowned at her sigh because she'd made it happy. Her thoughts were instructing her she was happy. So confusing. *Nothing but confusion since Dr. V killed me*, I thought resentfully.

Mom's voice punctured my thoughts. "I got in position. I was only twelve, but my father was an excellent teacher, and I his best student. Remember that, girls." Mom raised her voice. "We are students in this family who excel. We do what our parents tell us."

Sincerity replied, "Yes, Mom."

Sally said nothing. I looked over at my three-year-old self. She didn't so much as twitch; her thoughts and emotions buried too deep for me to feel. I didn't remember this scene at all, so I couldn't remember what I was thinking or feeling.

"When I shot him, I got him in one. Father was so proud of me—"

Father? Hadn't she called him Dad?

"—had me cut off its head, and I posed with it for photos. Then he sent it off to be stuffed, and he displayed it in pride of place over our fireplace for years. It was just me and him, and we did this together." Grief choked her, but she mastered it so that not a speck manifested in her voice. I caught her thought before she smacked it down: *This was the only thing Father and I did together, and the last time he spent with me.*

The lion's head, with its ratty mane, roared out from its place on the wall. I jerked and landed on the ceiling.

Bailey said, "Don't fear. You'll learn after you pass through the Barrier why you heard the roar."

"You'll brush that mane weekly, Sally, until it shines," Mom instructed.

Revulsion burned Sally's throat, but she squawked, "Yes, Mom." Determination to obey and show Mom she was onside so that she, too, wouldn't leave, quelled her revulsion a bit. "I'll show you where the special brush is," Mom said, leading Sally out of the room, who hustled to follow.

Rage left with them, but fear remained.

Sincerity leaned into the hallway, cranking her head around the doorframe, then walked over to me. She stroked my tucked-in head. "It's okay, Charlotte, it's okay. Mom's gone. Let's go play." My three-year-old self uncurled. Sincerity, a year older than me, took my hand and helped me stand. Then she led me out.

I held my breath as the room, emptied of all human emotions, lay silent except for the one thing that had kept me out of the living room as much as possible my entire life and now held me. I tried to turn to Bailey to ask her what was going on, but the lion's roar fixated my gaze. "What is that feeling in the room," I whispered.

"That's complicated," Bailey said.

Anger spurted. Really? You bring me here and give me that therapist-style non-answer?

"We didn't bring you into your life review. You journeyed through the Distortans and figured out how to leave Hell Track. You did that. We feel so privileged to be with you on your journey, but it really is hard to explain the feeling you picked up on. It's not a feeling; it's a presence."

"Presences," Blake clipped. "If you want to get accurate."

Presences? My eyebrows lifted into my forehead, and I narrowed my vision as I scanned the room. I saw nothing but what Mom had thrown onto the floor, the furniture haphazardly moved around, and that poor, tragic creature screwed into the wall as if killing it was the best thing humanity could do. *Triumph and power lie in being able to kill?*

I waved the thought away.

"Don't wave it away," Bailey said. "These revelations are part of your Soul Track."

"I don't know what to make of it all," I said. "It's tiring. Mom was always in control. She never showed fear or anger."

Blake choked back a bark of laughter.

I glared at her. "Never!" I asserted.

"Okay," she smiled back.

How can I see an orb smile? No! I won't think about it. It's irrelevant. The relevant question is why am I still here?

"Open yourself up and tell me what you sense. You're safe now. Nothing can hurt you," Bailey tried to reassure me.

Safe? What is safe? Emotions are not safe, never have been. I fluttered my hands. *I must leave this place.* I clenched my hands and closed my eyes against this thought and tried to obey Bailey.

"It's okay. You're doing fine for someone who has worked most of her life to shut down her senses, to bury your feelings, and shut out questions. Just stretch your mind out into the room."

I regarded Bailey, decided to trust, and tried.

Anger—righteous anger, vengeance, and outrage at such a thing being done to an elder—flooded me. I gawked at the lion's head, and its eyes burned golden orbs into my mind. Determination not to rest until respect and justice are done.

WE LANDED IN Flower Track's pink flowers. They fluttered up and snowed down at the force of our landing.

"What was that? Where did that determination come from?" I gasped.

"You'll see fully what it was when you cross the Barrier. For now, know that you were a sensitive person once, a person who read people and presences, who had a gift that revealed truth to you until you created your cavern. You had to hide because it was the only way to survive. But you don't need to hide your emotions, thoughts, and sensitivities anymore. You don't need to live in lying beliefs anymore."

I blinked at Bailey.

The blue light coruscating around her orb curved, the pink highlighting the blue-lit smile.

I stared.

She exclaimed, "Time to revisit Earth!"

"Why?" I asked, uncertain I wanted to see the Dying with Dignity Suite. *Can't I stay here in the flowers and not move?*

"It's a crucial step in your journey to the Barrier."

"Barrier?" I squinted into the distance, focusing on the white noise light beyond the postcards.

Chapter Twenty-Seven

HOSPITAL REDUX

Snatches of conversation, glimpses of recent Earth life so long ago, scenes of my last chapter in physical form fading in and out. Disorientation wrapped aching furrows into what I presumed was my head.

"Is this a life review?" I breathed out to Bailey, hovering near my right shoulder as we hid next to the ceiling.

"Yes and no. They can't see us, so there's no need to hide. Do you want to hide from your past, Charlotte Elisabeth?"

I didn't answer as the scenes blended one into the next, as if they were revealing the truth of my story.

"LOOK. You and I are supposed to be partners in our patients' final moments. We need to provide a unified front to them. Can you do that?" Dr. V lectured.

"Sure I can. Didn't I do that for this woman here. She didn't know she's the second one today, and you have ten more lined up. You really do know how to kill them faster than a hornet stings a human," my nurse retorted.

Dr. V growled. I shrunk against the ceiling. "Listen up. I'm not a hornet! I do this to save my patients' dignity—"

"Dignity," my nurse scoffed. "What's so dignified about being executed? You think because she's not a criminal, that you killing her is dignified? Only if she was a criminal then her execution wouldn't be dignified? Do you hear yourself Doctor? I'm in this because I've crossed the killing line."

"She's dead, Nurse. I already gave her dignity."

"She's not dead, Dr. V," my nurse stated baldly.

Wait a minute, I thought, sinking lower to scrutinize her. *Why do I think of her as my nurse? Not a nurse, like earlier?*

"I'm sorry," my nurse sighed. She crossed to the bed and laid a hand on my arm underneath the blanket. "It's okay honey."

"It's...not...," I-who-lay-in-the-bed breathed in.

My nurse mused in sotto voce, "It's funny she can still breathe on her own."

"You confirmed the measurements my staff took. I've reviewed my calculations," Dr. V said. "And I see no errors in them at all. It's not common you had no pulse when I checked and now you do. I listened to your heart stop, too." He frowned and studied the floor.

My nurse said, "I knew something was wrong. I had an intuition."

Dr. V raised an inscrutable face towards her. "Yes, well, enough of that." He turned to me and stepped closer. He stooped to look deep into my eyes. "You want to die, Charlotte Elisabeth? You want a dignified death now, here, with us?"

"Yes," I breathed out.

THE DOOR BANGED open. I reared back into the ceiling. "I don't remember this!" I exclaimed.

"It's happening now, two minutes after you died a second time," explained Bailey.

"Two minutes. How can that be? I've been travelling for hours, maybe days. A long time. All that Distortans and Hell Track and postcard trips happened in two minutes?"

"Time is immaterial where we exist now. Time flows like a river here."

"Personally, I found De Grasse's explanation of time like a loaf of bread the easiest to comprehend," Blair stated.

I started. *Where had Blair come from?* As I glanced at Blair, I spotted Blake, too.

"Quiet. Or we'll miss all the good stuff!" Blake shushed us all.

"You can't take her organs!" Mom shouted. "I won't let you!"

A security guard hustled in behind her as Dr. V and my nurse froze in astonishment. My nurse was extracting the intravenous needle from my arm where it lay over the blanket. The top sheet covered my face. Dr. V held an iPad in his left hand and Apple's latest Pencil in his right. Doctor and nurse stood like *Doctor Who's* Weeping Angels when observed. Mom hopscotched around the end of the bed and evaded the security guard's grasping hand.

"Boy, is she a firecracker, your mom," Blake chirped.

Firecracker? I groused. *Not really. Always controlling. Even after I'm dead, she's trying to control my desires.* I'd signed the organ donation card and had reviewed procedures with the organ donation team and which of my organs and parts posed healthy candidates for transplant. *Not my heart*, I remembered, my mouth turning down at the memory.

"Your lungs were strong," Bailey reminded me as we watched Mom leap on the bed and straddle my body, hands on her hips, facing Dr. V. My jaw dropped. "Mom?" I whispered.

We all gawked, physical humans, me, and the three. "What's she doing?" I asked as the security guard tried to grab her skirt to pull her down. She whipped it out of his hand.

"Pervert!"

He blushed and cowered.

"You're not taking my daughter's body away from me. We all know how she died. You," she snapped as she pointed her bony forefinger at Dr. V, who had returned to life and slowly swivelled around as his eyes had followed Mom's leaps and bounds. "You," she repeated, her voice two octaves lower than normal. "You," she growled again. "Killed my daughter. You took advantage of her suicidal thinking and lead her like a lamb to the slaughter. You," she menaced as she leaned into Dr. V's face while backing up, her feet on either side of my covered head, ignoring the fidgeting security guard. "You could've listened to her. You could've heard her. You could've buttressed her. You could've given her life comfort. Instead you mimicked listening while licking your chops over being paid to kill. Swift, easy money, unlike being paid to spend the time needed to heal my daughter's mind. You and you alone are responsible for taking her away from me. I. Will. Not. Let. You. Take. Her. Body. Too." Mom's eyes widened until the whites glared fury into Dr. V's shrinking frame.

The transplant team strode in and screeched to a halt as they noticed Mom standing over my covered face. I was glad me-in-bed couldn't see anymore. The transplant team's coolers swung and tumbled from their slack hands. The lead doctor looked at Mom's white eyes, down at Dr. V's shrinking frame, over at my nurse's satisfied look, and the security guard's helpless stance on the other side of the bed.

"It looks like there'll be no transplant from this patient. Let's go. I don't want to get into a fighting match with an outraged mother."

"But she signed the forms," said the doctor behind the lead one as he retrieved the coolers.

"It doesn't matter," she said. "By the time we harvest her, her cells and organs will have decayed. No bloody good for our patients. I'm only interested in cooperative donations."

"They're talking about me like I'm a slab of meat," I whispered, appalled.

"Yes," Bailey said. "Doctors in the death and transplant business can be bluntly callous. As far as they're concerned, you're no longer in hearing range."

How mistaken we all were, I realized.

The lead doctor had kept speaking. "The mother's grief is profound. Someone didn't do their job properly. Not for the first time," she snarled at Dr. V's back. I heard her thoughts as if she'd blasted them up to me. *Someone needs to stop this euthanasia business. It mocks death and cheapens life. We get more organs, but the grief it drags in and the grief left behind is not worth it. Why can't these doctors ease people into the end of their life cycle? Why must they always hasten them into it? Men! So arrogant. So stupid. So controlling. You can't control death.* She spoke to the room, "You can't control grief. It will always come out. And then what?" She addressed Dr. V: "What are you going to do about her Mom now that you've killed off her daughter?" She pivoted and marched her team out, imprecations streaming out of her thoughts like a banner fluttering clichés behind her.

"Wow," Blake said. "She's mad."

Into me slammed her emotions of anger at Dr. V, compassion for Mom, sadness for me, justice for her dying patients being deprived because of Dr. V's cock-up. *Again!* she railed.

"She's sad for me?" I mouthed.

"We all were," Bailey said. "The doctors you saw who didn't listen and the one who did, lead you to your suicide and ended your Soul Track prematurely on Earth. God had much more life planned for you, but God knew this would happen and prepared us for greeting you and helping you through the Earth-Heaven Interdimensional Expanse. God allowed you to wake up again but couldn't give you back your physical life. That'd be too much of a miracle and contrary to your free will to die. But God knew you needed to see the truth. That's why you woke up."

"I'm glad I'm dead," I blurted. "But…" I gestured helplessly to Mom, who was now cradling my dead body. Dr. V and the security guard shuffled, staring into space. Neither knew what to do. I didn't know what to think. Mom grieving my death? Surely, she only wanted the final say. Yet tears poured out of her depths and streamed down her face, unidentifiable feelings without thoughts, travelling like the longest train ever up to where I watched from the ceiling.

"I can't deal with this," I stated. "Take me back."

Bailey touched my right shoulder. Her peace flowed into me but didn't quell my zeal to leave. "I'm glad I died. I don't know what's happening with Mom. She can take my body and do whatever with it. It's hers now. She won."

"Has she?" Bailey asked. The power of her question forced me to scrutinize Mom. She was stroking my face through the covers. Over and over. It reminded me of how I stroked Greeter's head.

"Not quite the same," Bailey said.

Her words made me probe Mom. "Love?" I queried.

"Yes," Bailey said.

"No!" I rocked. I could feel Mom's emotions, could observe her actions, but I couldn't countenance Mom loving me like a mother. My entire being rebelled at the idea. "No! I'm glad I died. It's time for me to leave. I see now the truth of Dr. V. He shouldn't have pounced on my suicidality and helped me along. That other doctor is right. Healers heal. My exit didn't heal me. Only you three accompanying me, the postcards, my experiences in the Expanse have healed me—"

"You're not healed yet," Blake blurted.

"Whatever," I said, feeling adolescent and not caring. "I'm better for what happened to me after death than what Dr. V did." I shoved down the spurt of regret I'd met him. *What's done is done. Reality is shutting out harm and others because people always damage you.*

The three surrounded me, each touching me as if supporting me while I knew they didn't agree with what I'd said and thought. It didn't matter.

"What have you learned about your death?" Bailey asked.

"It was unnecessary," I replied shortly. "We all die, but I didn't have to die like this. This was not dignified. This," I flung my right hand wide to encompass the entire scene, "alienated me to me, to Mom, nurses who want to heal, doctors whose patients want to live, people who fear death so much doctors home in on them like killer bees and promise them bliss. This kind of death doesn't bring bliss!" I lamented, bitter. "It reinforced my fears. Didn't release me from them. It said pain is all there is. Didn't release me from pain or certainty that people are dangerous. I'm better off keeping them at a distance. It didn't heal me at all. I've learnt that snakes come in charming, listening, caring skins."

"It's hard to discern between those who truly care for you and those who wear a mask of caring," Blair said.

"Yes,"I said shortly.

"Especially when you keep people at a distance and cut yourself off from learning to read truth and lies in them," Blake added.

My stomach contracted at her criticism, but I knew she was right. Yet it didn't change my mind that I was safer keeping myself apart. Regret lanced through me as my client's face appeared in my memory. Well, maybe not all people. I watched Mom weeping, tears seeping out of her closed eyes as my nurse came round the bed, pushed the security guard out of the way, and laid her hand on her shoulder. My nurse gestured with her head at Dr. V and the security guard to leave the room. The men hastened out.

"You can see who really cares," Bailey pointed out to me. "The one who stays is the one who cares. The one who stays only to help you to your death is the one who doesn't."

"I'm sorry we took her away from you," my nurse said to Mom as she held her shoulder gently. "This is my job, the one I've found myself in. I'm good at it. This is not something to boast about, being good at helping doctors kill their patients. I didn't know you cared for her." I heard the nurse's thoughts. *I don't think your daughter knew. Why do we control others instead of being vulnerable? Why am I doing this to people?* Sadness and regret churned inside my nurse's heart. "I can't do this anymore," she said out loud. "I'm going to make this right. I deserve a better life."

"It's too late for me," I stated.

"It's not too late for your mom. And you've changed this nurse's life. You and your mom have caused her to question her assumption that she can only kill since she's crossed the killing line, as she called it. She's seeing herself soothing your grieving mom and in doing so seeing she can be redeemed.

"We depend on each other to live with love, health, and vitality. God has gifted you the reality beneath the Dying with Dignity Suite and the people who created it. This gift wasn't easy, but then learning is something human brains crave yet this culture hates. You see here, in this moment of space-time, the contrast between caring love," Bailey gestured towards the nurse, "and self-feeding love," Bailey rotated towards the door and the fading energy of Dr. V departing. "Birth and death are not our will. The life in between is. What we will in between matters more than *how* we birth and die. We don't live alone. As others affect us, we affect others. Even hermits. God gave us relationships so that we can have abundance in our emotions and thoughts and we can thrive no matter our circumstances. When we live in that, we will die in peace, though it won't be under our absolute will, and no matter the circumstances, we won't have to force it into self-hating despair.

"Your nurse is caring for your mom, so she doesn't have to live in regret. And neither do you."

Maybe, I thought. *Remorse will haunt her, and I regret—*"Can we go?" I asked out loud.

The three looked at each other. Worry emanated from them, but as one, they wagged yes. "It's up to you when we leave," Bailey said.

I reflected on that sentient light. I craved to see it again even though it had blown out my vision like a solar eclipse seen bare eyed.

Greeter was snuffling my hand as a breeze stirred my hair and caressed my neck. Dahlias nodded above me as I lay among them. Scents danced in my head: rose, lavender, lilac. I inhaled their fragrance into my core and exhaled gently, at length.

Chapter Twenty-Eight

FLOWER POWER
CONTINUED

Greeter nudged me into standing. I dragged my face down with my hands and quivered for an eternity. I exhaled and exhaled and redirected my gaze to the right. The postcards shimmered. Farther in the distance, the white noise shone, and behind, above, and in front of it glowed the other light. Sun-bright and warm as incandescent light, its rays reached towards me.

I narrowed my focus to see its details. Its inner light smouldered, drawing me in to blues and pinks and greens and yellow, shades of brown and grey and auburn, highlights of tangerine and iridescent green and cream, lowlights of eggplant and orange and cardinal, peace lights of cashmere and maple, comforting lights of rice and chocolate. I walked towards it, mesmerized, thirsting for its promised peace and comfort.

What is it? A sunlight-spectrum light bulb? It doesn't feel like a lamp or a kind of moon. Lights don't normally give off emotion. I cantered towards it yet felt paused in thought, trying to understand this conundrum of light having sentience.

Wait a minute. It's consciousness!

I wanted...no...I desired...no...I craved to know more about this sentient entity, and be...I halted in my thoughts but not my feet. I marvelled at the discovery on the edge of my consciousness. I wanted to hold it and be held by it.

I spotted a human figure with arms outstretched towards me standing inside yet part of it yet distinctly different from the light. I squeezed my eyes shut. I must be hallucinating. Like a child wanting something so badly they created it in their mind. *I'd better stop and return to reality.* My feet kept walking.

A force snatched me back.

Bailey had grabbed my scruff and, like a mother cat shaking its kitten, admonished me, "No."

"Ahhhh," I cried, having forgotten the three, so focused I'd been on the sentient light. "Why are you stopping me?"

"Not stopping, pausing. It's not yet time."

"Why are the two lights different. The enormous one that stretches across Hell Track and Flower Power Track buzzes and shoots white daggers. But this other one, the one I glimpsed in Soul Track and surrounds the white noise, I want to go to it. Why can't I go to it?"

"The white noise one is the Barrier. The mist you saw is the exit to Earth. This loving one is God shining through Heaven's entrance and—"

"Heaven?" I interrupted. "What's Heaven?"

"Where do we begin?" Blake exclaimed.

"It's difficult to explain," Blair said. "There are many stories—"

"Many!" Blake burst out.

"—about what it is. But to experience it is to see the stories as mere faded copies of the real thing."

"I've never heard stories," I said. "What stories?"

"Remember the building with the two bars crossed on top of it? The one you asked your mom about?"

I nodded. "She was so angry that day, but I didn't realize until now how afraid she was of it. I can't compute Mom being afraid of anything. Of that building or losing me. Being left behind by me. It's too much!"

Greeter reached up a paw and patted my thigh. I looked down into melting brown eyes, and my anxiety vanished. "I still don't get it," I whispered to the dog. I reached out a tentative hand to stroke their head.

"You will," Bailey said. "Once you pass that Barrier, your learning will start, but you can't go back to Earth in your physical form."

I lifted my head, leaving my hand on the dog's head. "What gender is he? And what gender are you three?"

"Gender isn't relevant any more," Blair replied.

"Thank God!" Blake ejaculated.

"What?" I blurted, forgetting all the grammatical lessons Mom had instilled in me until they'd become automatic. "I mean, pardon?"

"We have gender on Earth to procreate. But once we leave Earth, we become the essence of who we are, and believe it or not, gender only matters to our physical form, not to our essences," Blair said.

"Blair and Blake are overwhelming you. I didn't want to throw so much at you all at once: experiencing your mom's hidden emotions and thoughts is hard enough for you to swallow."

I nodded. My hand stroked Greeter's head, from nose to crown, over and over, soothing myself.

"What Blair and Blake are saying is that you lived in a certain way on Earth because that's how God designed us to live in the physical realm. Gender was necessary to grow our numbers. Some societies didn't differentiate roles based on gender, but unfortunately, men used power and domination to create a society in which men accrued control over women and they exported it around the world, radically changing matriarchal and equality societies or influencing them so subtly over time they didn't realize what was happening."

"Like a frog in hot water," I said.

"Precisely," Bailey replied. "But more variability exists within one gender than between genders. Just as variability exists in our chromosomes and in how our hormones and organs differentiate into their parts. But once the essence of ourselves leaves the body, we no longer need gender. It clings to us from habit, but we three have been existing outside of our physical forms for so long that we no longer think of ourselves in terms of gender."

"We've been released from the gender wars!" Blake shot up as if jumping from joy. "No more gender wars!"

I laughed. And clapped my hand over my mouth.

Blake drifted towards me. "It's okay to laugh, you know. And you can call me 'she'—all of us 'she'—if that makes you comfortable. But God is relationship, and we are relationships as well. Relationships don't have gender. You'll get used to it. You'll see."

I evinced a smile, my subconscious understanding how I could be a relationship with myself, yet my conscious self was baffled. I smacked back the smile.

"It's sad that smiling and laughing are so foreign to you, but we came to help you be you. We see the whole of you and want you to see the whole of you, too," Bailey said sotto voce.

I flashed back to the client, re-experienced her emotions and thoughts towards me. Tears spurted and rolled down my face. "How can I cry when I'm not a physical being anymore?"

"The wonders of physics," Blake giggled.

"I'm glad you're asking questions," Bailey said.

"She so serious. Bailey, dance with her, swing her about, jump up with joy with her. Here, let me do it."

Blake lifted my hands up as if she'd grabbed them. She bounced up and down, making me jump off the ground and float down onto cushiony green. Startled at my soft landing, I yanked my hands out of her force. "What is that?"

"Grass as it was meant to be," Blair said.

"What do I do now?" *Maybe I can live? Start over? Have a second chance?* I chucked the last thought. *Impossible!*

"You learn," Blair said.

I dropped my head and continued stroking Greeter.

Greeter pushed into my hand, dropped their lower jaw, exposing teeth, curving their long lips, as their tongue lolled. I smiled at their smile. I let myself feel good.

I shifted my feet and straightened up. Greeter knocked my hand off their head and rested against my left leg. I stilled. I didn't have to smile anymore. Relief sagged my shoulders.

"What am I?" I asked, thinking about my transparency, my skin acting like a magnetic field while I envisioned myself as atoms clinging to each other. None of my current existing form made sense.

"You are a thinking thing, according to Descartes. You are a soul according to religions. You are God's creation. You've learned to live in physical form. Even though your essence, your consciousness, your mind, your soul, was stunted and harmed, you learned how to live in a physical world, take care of your physical body, interact with others in their physical forms. You went too much inside yourself to see and hear their essences. You feared becoming intimate with anyone, and when I say intimate, I don't mean romance, I mean deeper intimacy. The kind between best friends who've known each other for a long, long time. The kind who connect at consciousness level. Most fear it and distort it into romance and sex. But it's freeing and enervating. You'll learn that once we pass the Barrier, but for now, you need to finish your physical life in a healthier way. You need to see that reality for what it is."

"What's death?"

"Death is the end of the first physical bodily existence. Death is not the end of existence. Death is part of the life cycle of every creature on Earth. Just as birth begins the life cycle, so death ends it and feeds into the next generations of life cycles. Your generation fears death, has devolved the concept to a bastion that needs to be controlled. As scheduled-for-convenience caesarean sections tried to impose human will on gestation and birth, so the ever-repeating cycle of killing humans under the myth of easing suffering, tries to impose human will on our life cycle's end. But God created the cycle to feed and nourish, to grow and teach. When we accelerate or abort it, we rob ourselves of growth and interconnection on the intimate level we're supposed to be connecting on."

I turned my body around until my back was to the Barrier. Way in the distance, mist waited. I shivered at the idea of intimacy. I'd accepted my thoughts being heard in the Expanse, but having anyone read my thoughts, being unable to retreat to safety inside myself, horrified me. *How can I be safe when anyone can enter my inner space?*

"You'll learn to think in a way that's both open and private. And you'll learn that privacy is not what you think unlike the Red Robes, who cannot comprehend they've changed from material to energy, from speech communication to speech and thoughts."

Privacy and aloneness are safe, I retorted in my mind, ignoring her confusing statement on the Red Robes.

Bailey sighed.

I lifted my eyebrows.

"I tire too," she said. "But I—that is, we—will never leave you."

I let her words enter and leave me. They had stayed with me this whole time, but...

"It's okay not to trust because one day you will. It's a process, and we're with you through it."

Somehow, I accepted that.

I faced the mist again. "So death is the end of physical existence."

"First physical existence," Blake murmured.

"And the mind or soul or essence is who we are inside that physical body and continues to exist for...," I frowned at the intense, soft, fresh green grass. "How long?"

"We don't know," Bailey said. "We know that this stage is also finite. But the third and final stage is eternal."

"A third stage?" I gasped.

"Yup!" Blake bounced up and down gleefully. "And I can't wait!"

I refused to consider it. I pushed that knowledge deep, deep within me, into a box that I locked and strapped shut. That I had to remain existing was bad enough—

"Is it?" Bailey asked.

"Yes!" Then truth spoke out of my mouth, "No." I contemplated my contradiction. "No. I—I'm kind of glad to have met you three and that I still exist."

Chapter Twenty-Nine

FLOWER POWER MOVING OUT

The postcards encircled me. I retreated in alarm at their sudden appearance. But in less than an eye blink, the closest one sucked me in to finish my life review. The postcards flipped me into one frozen tableau from a previous life scene into another. Bailey, Blair, and Blake followed, always with me in one scene of my life after another, as they'd said they would be. I accepted that, but I couldn't think about it. It just was.

MY-EIGHT-YEAR-old self was skipping along the sidewalk towards home, humming and leaping over the cracks so as not to hurt my mother's back like the old rhyme taught. I tried to look away from my child-self as fear wracked me. A black pickup truck lurched onto the sidewalk and crept towards my child-self, one set of its wheels up on the sidewalk, leaving a narrow path between it and a manicured lawn. Mom had warned me never to step on the grass, cut to an even inch all across the lawn's square shape. I'd stumbled and veered onto it once, and a large, florid man, with a bulbous nose and thinning hair, shot off the porch and down his front walk towards me, yelling, "Get off my lawn, you snot-faced bastard kid!" I'd tripped, bumped against his neighbour's mature oak tree, and fell backwards onto the sidewalk, scraping my hands and knees on concrete and cracked acorns in my haste to get away from him. Ever since that day, I'd been careful. But that day...

My child-self skipped closer and closer to the creeping pickup truck. *Look up! Look up!,* I willed, knowing my child-self wouldn't. My child-self didn't want to break my mother's back and kept eyes down to not plant my feet across the sidewalk cracks. My child-self's carefree skipping suffused me. She looked up a half skip from the front of the truck and clapped her hand over her startled scream at almost banging into the truck's grill as it braked. I'd already learned by eight not to scream or make noise. The driver stuck his head out the window. "Hey! Look where you're going, kid! Glad I saw you," he ended with a grin.

Wariness replaced carefree happiness in my child-self and me. She halted and side-stepped towards the lawn side and surveyed the narrow path between the enormous truck and lawn. Fear flared as she glanced at the front porch and wondered if the man was looking out his window. Danger and pain threatened.

My child-self sidled towards the roadside edge of the truck's front grill.

"Go round, kid. There's nothing coming."

My child-self's head shot up. A man's curly blonde head was half-leaning out the driver's side window on the roadside. His fair face glistened with sweat, and he grinned and gestured towards the road.

My child-self smiled tentatively and stepped onto the road. A white car raced past, its slipstream blowing my child-self's black hair across my face, momentarily blinding me. I fell backwards onto my bottom, my hands breaking my fall, landing on the sewer hole cover's edge, painfully bending my wrists, as the man gasped above me. "Hey! You alright, kid? Always look before you cross, remember that, kid. Didn't your mom teach you that?"

Pain, fear, bewilderment from my child-self drowned me, and guilt surfed in from the man on the wave of his thoughts: *Ah hell! I thought I saw a speed trap back there. It's a residential street, for Christ's sake. These speeders are gonna kill one too many kids. But what was the kid thinking? It's the kid's fault for not looking. Why didn't she walk in the space I left her? Wouldn't hurt to have gone on the lawn. I mean, where else am I gonna park on this narrow street? I had to leave room for cars to pass! And I was only gonna take a minute to unload, anyway. Not my fault she showed up before I left!*

A squeak grabbed my attention. I searched for the source. Hidden in the oak tree, a black squirrel swayed the branches above the pickup, glaring as it shot an acorn towards it. Thud! The acorn hit the lawn's edge, setting off angry chirping from a grey squirrel that bounded from behind the tree to snuggle next to the pickup's front wheel, fluffy tail curled up its back, squeaking deprecations to the one above.

"What's happening?" I asked.

Blake giggled.

Blair rolled like a spinning top on its axis.

Bailey said, "The squirrels are protecting the child while waging war on each other."

Squirrels? Those rodents who dig up my crocuses? Why? I thought as two acorns bombed the ground beside my child-self. My child-self lurched backwards. Acorns rained down here and there, like cockeyed missiles missing the grey squirrel who rage-chirped back as the acorns dinged the pickup's hood.

"What the hell?!" shouted the truck's driver. A volley of acorns jounced off his hood.

Blake chortled. "That'll teach him! Squirrel power telling him not to be a jerk! Stay on the road! Look out for the little kids!!"

I stared at Blake. I shifted my gaze to my child-self, who seemed unnoticing of the statement the squirrels were making. I wouldn't have either, if not for Blake. *Animals comment on human affairs? How can they?*

Crack!

An acorn fusillade had cracked the truck's windshield.

Just a coincidence, I thought. I shook my thoughts free of this fantasy.

"No coincidence. No fantasy," Bailey stated.

I turned away from the three of them.

My child-self clutched my abdomen and loped back the way I'd come, holding in my tears as death in the guise of the white car played over and over in my mind. A thought bounced up into my child-self mind: *That man didn't like me.* Another thought: *The lawn man hates me, and squirrels hate me, too.* The two thoughts birthed a third: *Maybe death is what that man thought was best for me.* Those thoughts walloped me.

Bailey said, "What do you feel?"

I jumped. I'd forgotten they were with me. "I don't know," I whispered, wanting to forget how my chest had heaved, not admitting that last thought had tightened my throat.

"Sure you do," Blake said.

I shied away from my eight-year-old self's feelings; but as I stayed in this scene, following her as she loped and cantered and ran away from those men, away from the truck on the sidewalk that had forced her into that car's path, compassion blossomed in me. I wanted to reach out to my child-self and reassure her that her quick reflexes had saved her from those evil men.

"That's good work, Charlotte Elisabeth," Bailey said.

The scene vanished.

FLIP.
FLIP.
FLIP.

I ascended through the ages of my childhood. Sally sallied into my bedroom. My 12-year-old self was staring into the dressing-table mirror. A manicure set sat on it opened. My tween-self didn't know what to do with the nail scissors and tweezers and turned her head as the door banged open. Sally loomed over me, and my tween-self shrank from her hard, critical 'scrutiny of my face. Her mouth grimaced. She grabbed my tween-self's right hand off my lap and pushed a small box into it. At the same moment, I, observing and experiencing the scene from the ceiling, felt Sally's fear. I heard her thought: *She'd better lighten her skin if she doesn't want Mom taking out her feelings about Greg on her.*

Huh? Hadn't Sally judged my brown skin? Didn't Sally hate me for not being fully White? I tried to comprehend Sally's thoughts as I watched my tween-self open the box.

Sally snatched it back. "You're too slow!" she snarled. "Here, I'll show you."

She hauled out a small bottle, unscrewed its lid, dabbed cream on her fingers, and roughly smoothed it into my face while my tween-self sat stiller than a deer. I hadn't understood what she was doing or why, except that she didn't like me.

Every day after that, Sally had barged into my bedroom to ensure I'd used the lightening cream, and after a couple of weeks, I saw my skin lighten. I adapted to my fairer skin and kept using that brand of cream, the one Sally had introduced me to, until my last day on Earth.

The postcards flipped me out of that scene and into reviewing my adolescence as I ruminated over Sally's fear and thoughts contradicting what I'd known almost all my life.

I entered my university years, again into that scene they'd earlier shot me into, the one that made no sense with that man hoisting my knapsack and securing its weight across my shoulders.

Why did the postcards want to remind me of that trivial moment?

The postcards tumbled me into my early work life of self-employment as an accountant. I'd built up a nice clientele and investment balance.

FLIP.

"What is this?" Mom ranted at my 25-year-old self. *Oh-oh.* I shied away from this remembered scene, but the postcard I was in, like all the others, trapped me. I had to watch.

My 25-year-old self stood across the room from the lion's maned head, while Mom towered in front of me. Mom brandished a file folder in her right hand at me. Rage contorted her face and slammed into me floating against the ceiling. Her face whitened, her hands turned into claws, her body angled towards my 25-year-old self, her legs rigid, and her voice pitching higher. Perfume rent the air; her rage intensified the musky, artificial flowery smell that ate at my nose. My 25-year-old self wanted to sneeze but controlled it. I sucked in my nostrils and pinched off the desire.

"Well?" Mom asked rhetorically. "I'll tell you what this is. It's betrayal!"

I, past and present, alive and dead, said nothing. No emotion emanated from me. No thoughts. As if through a reverse telescope, I re-experienced myself watching Mom and the file folder, seeing the living room, ignoring the golden-eyed, glowering head. But something in Mom caught my attention. She was afraid.

Say what?

I remembered no fear. I puzzled over this unexpected emotion. I heard her thoughts: *I won't have her leave. I won't be left again. She won't leave me. I'll make sure of that. I will not be alone.*

A thought bubbled up from my 25-year-old self: *I'll find a safer way to hide my plans. I can't hide anything here. But I will buy my own home.*

"Give me your savings book." Mom's demand startled me then and now, even though I still remembered that scene, every detail, like a malignant wart that itches.

"My savings book?"

"The one you're using to buy this betrayal. You're going to hand over the savings."

A spurt of rebellion shot my mouth open. "It's not savings. And I can't hand it over. It's locked in and non-transferable."

Mom angled her eyebrows down towards each other, her lips thinned, her eyes sharpened on my 25-year-old self. "Why'd you do that?"

"To secure it. You taught me to ensure security above all else for our money."

Mom's lips turned bloodless. She punched the air with the folder in her right hand. "You will not pursue this course of action, you hear?"

My 25-year-old self watched Mom and the living room, detached, as if I was far away and empty.

Mom closed the gap to my 25-year-old self until her face dominated my vision. "Understand?"

My 25-year-old self and I nodded in unison. I automatically showed Mom what she wanted while draining feelings and thoughts into my mind's locked cavern.

Mom's fear burgeoned into terror at being alone; her terror assaulted me, and I almost merged with the ceiling. I never saw her afraid. My 25-year-old self and me, up to this life review, hadn't known losing me mattered to her. I murmured, "That's why she controlled me and my sisters so much. She needed control to check her fear. She lied to herself that we wouldn't leave as long as she kept us on a leash," I breathed out in understanding.

"Yes," Bailey said. "What will you do with this new knowledge?"

"I don't know."

FLIP.

Blake asked, "Where are we now?"

I looked around, puzzled at first. Then I recognized it from a long time ago. "My office at Mom's home. I saw clients here to do their income taxes and consult on investments."

A client sat in the chair on the other side of my desk, piled with papers except where an old computer huddled at the top left corner of my desk. Paper half-buried the grey keyboard, and its curling telephone-type wire snaked in and out of the papers down to the grey, metal-sided desktop computer that sat on the floor to the left of my beat-up walnut desk. I'd found it at an old vintage store, scratched and marked down 75 percent. That's what I could afford after I'd graduated with my degrees in accounting and business investing. I'd sped through high school and graduated with my Chartered Accountant degree and licence younger than most when I was ready to start work.

"Your desk is so messy," Blake said, awed. "You weren't like that in university. You let yourself go, huh?" She nudged me on my right shoulder; pleasant vibrations sparkled through me, outwards from where she'd touched me.

"No," I said shortly.

My client's chest pressed into the desk, her fisted hands against its edge.

My 26-year-old self was sitting back, hands loose in my lap, face expressionless, eyes on the client, and ears not receiving. The scene played out like a silent movie and me a passive watcher.

"What happened, Charlotte?" the client was asking. "Tell me. You used to be so good, so reliable. I've hung on for as long as I could, but I can't be audited. RevCan is threatening to take all my savings. The bank gave me a heads up only hours before the government swiped all the money for my mortgage payment. I could lose my house! What happened?"

"Nothing."

The client's face screwed up in worry. "Something's wrong." She waited for my 26-year-old self to say something. I experienced her worry and suspicion; felt her anger at my betrayal; sensed her concern for me more than for herself: *I won't lose my house, but she'll lose herself if she stays here any longer with that dragon.*

I slammed into the ceiling. "She thought that?" I blurted. "How did she know?"

"People see more than you credit them. You only have to reach out."

I pulled down my mouth. "Reaching out leads to being left."

Sighs of different colours escaped the three beside me.

"If you have to leave my services and find another accountant, I'll understand," my 26-year-old-self said tonelessly. Her, no, what had been my mind, remained empty. It was like looking at a shell. The client echoed my thoughts.

"I don't want to," she said. "But I have to. I know I'm your last client, that you've lost all your other ones. And this," she stood up and gestured helplessly to the mess on my desk. "This is not you. But you don't want my help, and I don't know how to help you."

You're helping me by leaving. My 26-year-old self's unbidden thought rose lazily like smoke from a dampened fire.

FLIP.

We cartwheeled into the hallway of a busy office. Bailey, Blair, and Blake banged into each other, igniting sparks. Bile burned my throat. I ignored it, and we settled into position near my open office door. A woman with straight, dyed straw-blonde hair called through my doorway, "Your mother's here."

My desk, angled in the far corner, faced both the window and door as my 30-year-old self looked up. "I heard. Tell her I'm busy with a client."

"Your papers are all piled neatly, every edge of every paper is perfectly lined up with the papers below and above," Blake exclaimed.

"Yes," I said shortly.

"I can't tell her that," the blonde replied. "She's been in the waiting room all morning watching your clients go in and out. She's a tracker that one."

I know, my adult-self thought. Fear edged into my adult-self and my life-reviewing me.

"She knows your last client has left, and you have none now. Let me sneak her in."

Appalled, my adult-self blurted, "No!"

"No? Don't you want to see your mother? She visits every week. She confided to Angela, the first day she visited, that she never knew where you worked. It took her years to find out. You mumbled the name of it so fast, she couldn't make it out, she said. And she couldn't find any hint of your work in your home office. It must be nice to have a mother who cares so much."

Emotions and thoughts fled from my adult-self's consciousness. I swallowed hard against the fearsome volcano rising in me.

Bailey touched my right shoulder. A frisson of warmth soothed me.

She's so stupid, the blonde thought. I knew she hadn't liked me, but not she'd thought that! *Her mother is so sweet; what's her problem?* My eyebrows vanished upwards into my hair. *Sweet? Mom?*

My adult-self said, "It's against the rules."

"Rules, shmules." She retorted, leaning in conspiratorially. *Why's she such a stickler for rules? She makes us all look bad. Why'd she not tell her mother where she worked? She's so weird. I wonder what's going on? Maybe Angela knows. I should pump her.* She spoke as she was thinking these things, "We all sneak our family and friends in when he's not looking."

"Who's not looking?" The rich baritone startled us all. I flattened against the ceiling; my soul family zipped upwards to settle beside me. The blonde slapped her mouth.

My adult-self froze into a rigid pose.

"I was just telling Charlotte Elisabeth about her mother. She wants to visit her here."

My boss stepped into my adult-self's office doorway, contempt emanating from him towards the blonde. Thoughts of firing her flitted through his mind, then he reminded himself that watching her kept him apprised of all the things going on here, and he was determined to keep me obedient because I was his best accountant, and he wasn't about to lose me. He didn't care about me visiting Mom as long as I didn't leave. But he wouldn't countenance flouting his rules. Security of client information was paramount. He thought these things as fear of losing me vied with his authority power and he said, "You know the rules, Charlotte Elisabeth."

My adult-self nodded.

"You meet clients in client meeting rooms and friends and family outside the office. The waiting room is as far in as they're allowed."

I nodded, past and present in sync.

"But I don't want to interfere with family relationships. They're the most important relationships you'll ever have."

My adult-self controlled her expression as her thoughts blasted: *They are not important! I don't need to meet Mom!*

I rocked under the force of her anger. *Had rage lurked inside me since my thirties?*

"Longer," whispered Blake, wrenching my focus towards her, making me wonder about myself.

My boss lifted his hand to check his watch, sitting boldly on his right wrist. "It's lunch time. You have an hour to do what you wish. Go have lunch with your mother."

My adult-self nodded as he swept the blonde away from my door and, at the same time, he thought, *I need to keep Evangeline away from Charlotte Elisabeth. She'll scare her away. I really can't lose her. Whatever personal files she keeps in that extra cabinet of hers is her business. Probably wants to hide things from her mother. What a dragon that woman is.* And on that thought, his fear of losing me and his determination to help me stay strengthened. If only he'd known that helping me avoid meeting Mom would've encouraged me to stay; instead, he'd given me cause to leave.

"I didn't know he wanted me to stay and was trying to make it possible."

"It seems he wanted to protect you."

FLIP.

We landed in Mom's hallway where my thirty-one-year-old self was standing, grasping the brown leather handle of an enormous burgundy suitcase, terror radiating out. Sincerity was facing past-self, her mouth open in astonishment. She snapped her mouth closed. She said, "You're leaving."

My past-self's mind emoted an empty cave. Nothing entered, nothing exited me. No thoughts; no emotions; no wants; and no desires.

"It's okay," Sincerity said. "Sally is in that noisy old car of Mom's. We'll hear her coming. I tell you what I'll do. I'll get back in my car and drive like a demented person, blocking her from turning onto our block. She's coming from the west. You drive out of here to the east. You tell me where you're going when we have our regular ice cream date, okay?"

My past-self stared, motionless, expressionless.

Worry, concern, and pity vied in Sincerity. Determination to protect me, to give me a chance to live outside of Mom's thumb burst from her heart. "You wait here one minute. Then go as quickly as you can. If you have anything left to bring, leave it. I'll move them into my room before Mom gets home from work. I'll have an hour to do that, and Sally won't be watching me. No, I'll move your things into my car. That'll give me time to bring them to you tomorrow when we meet at the ice cream parlour. Deal?"

My past-self remained a statue. Stone still.

"Okay, deal. Wait one minute then follow me out." She held up her right forefinger, her car keys dangling from it. Then she swivelled on her heel and hurried out, slamming the front door behind her.

"I—"

FLIP.

"—always knew my sister Sincerity cared. She was the only one I fully trusted. I didn't realize how empty I was, yet she could read me like a book," I marvelled. I blinked. "What happened? Where are we?"

"You tell us," Blair said.

I scanned the new scene. My home office in my house. My desk spanned two-thirds of the room, with neatly piled file folders and stacks of paper arranged symmetrically on top in two rows. My thirty-seven-year-old self sat behind my desk, and my current client faced me, her back straight, perched on the edge of the guest chair. The client smiled, relief at seeing me again. Happy I'd discovered my niche and become my own woman.

"I'm so happy I found out you left that big firm and were self-employed again. I didn't like your boss. He didn't like me asking to be your client. He told me he was the best arbiter to decide which accountant could handle my business best, that's why I didn't return until now." Earnestness poured out of her, nervousness over self-employed-self not believing her, determination to prove I could trust her. She canted towards me, clutching the purse on her lap, her knuckles whitening. "Being your own boss is the best way, isn't it?" Anxious happiness exuded from my client.

My self-employed-self nodded, with absolute control over emotions and thoughts, and retrieved the top file folder. The folders and papers constituted my client's file. I sensed thoughts about the client's accounts and my drive to provide investment advice best suited to her, and nothing else.

Sadness for my past self seeped out from behind the bricked-up wall against my emotions. "She wanted to see me again after I almost cost her her house. I remember this meeting. She smiled at me. I neither believed her nor disbelieved her. I concentrated on the business of her taxes, and she became serious and nodded and listened to my advice." Bailey, Blair, Blake, and I watched the scene play that out. *Why had the postcard flung us into this scene?*

The client's thoughts reached my consciousness: *She needs to be all business. That's okay. I'll stay and when she's ready to open up, I'll be here. I'm going to show her she can trust some of us.*

A sob caught me unaware. I hugged myself as I experienced my long-time client's thoughts. "She never left me. She came back, and I never thought about why. I didn't accept it as a given, I just didn't want to think about why." I covered my face with my transparent fingers and closed my vision off. I didn't want to see my self-employed-self, didn't want to experience the emptiness within, the complete lack of happiness and connection, anymore. "She was the one most devastated to hear I was going to be dead. She begged me not to do it. She stood in my doorway refusing to leave. I almost pushed the door on her so she'd leave and I could be alone and end myself once and for all. Permanently. And now look at me," I sobbed.

FRAGRANCE, LIKE A meditation, lulled me.

No longer the warm smell of newly printed papers, the pleasantness of the client's soap, my self-employed-self's all-business voice explaining details, but the breezy scent of freshly mown grass and spring roses, the sighing of the wind, and Greeter's wet nose snuffling the edges of my fingers covering my face. I didn't need to see; I knew I was in Flower Power Track. I cried, "She came back! After all I did, she liked me so much that she came back. She knew there was a reason and still trusted me. She came back! Why couldn't I see that?"

I desperately wanted to see my client again, to apologize for blocking her out. I longed to meet with Sincerity at our favourite ice cream parlour and take her up on her invitations to window shop, to ride bicycles along the Martin Goodman Trail, to hike in Canada's first urban national park. I ached to thank my boss for protecting me and growing my accounting skills. I didn't want to see Mom and Sally, yet compassion like an unwanted piece of fudge bloated me. I pushed that sensation out of my consciousness. I sobbed, "I don't want to change my mind about Mom and Sally." Yet there compassion continued to sit. I panted my crying to a halt. "Can I return to Earth?" I asked, hyperfocusing on my client and Sincerity to distract myself from this unwanted feeling towards Mom and Sally.

"We travelled back earlier only to see what you needed to finish seeing," Bailey replied. "There's more to come. But you can't return in your physical form."

Greeter settled onto their back haunches and leaned against my right side, their warmth comforting me.

"You see it now," Bailey encouraged me. "You see it now. Are you ready to complete your life review?"

"Yes."

Chapter Thirty

BARRIER

The postcards reappeared in the distance, cutting off my path to the Barrier, riffling towards me like a booklet flipping their pages at high speed, inviting me to live the rest of my life review. Bailey's warm energy on my back reassured me. I no longer resisted the Expanse, the three soul family, or the postcards in this strange existence. I went with it. Bailey's energy created a hand out of her pink-highlighted orb to rest it on my back, a transparent back comprising atoms encased within a magnetic field skin. I comprehended now: I'd ceased to exist as a physical body.

Here came the postcards. And here were Bailey and Blair and Blake alongside me. Bailey's hand on my back; Blake's presence jingled like chimes, their silver playing the blue energy of her orb. Bailey grasped my hand, compelling my eyes to look at her, to confirm I was not alone. The thought dropped like an unexpected tear into the pool of my heart.

Not alone.

And then the postcards hoovered me in.

I watched myself as a baby playing with the air, arms and legs waving about, my blue-brown eyes enchanted by their movements. Lots of straight, black hair stood out in every direction. I'd forgotten how blue-black my natural hair colour was. Its natural state looked strange and forlorn. My heart ached for baby-me and enfolded her blue-black hair and her white skin tinged with golden brown. A man bent over me. His brown skin crinkled at the corners of his eyes as his dark, dark brown eyes—almost black eyes—gazed down at baby-me. Love softened his eyes' darkness into liquid coffee. *Strange to think in metaphors*, I thought. *Like I'm an artist. But I'm not.*

Bailey stroked my back, and I resumed living this moment that I had no memory of.

That's my father!

Since he'd left, I hadn't seen photographs of him. Mom vanished them. I think she threw them out the day he left me.

Yet why had he left me?

Mom had said, "You, Charlotte Elisabeth, shooed him away." Yet here this man with straight black hair like mine, his brown skin appearing as tinges of golden-brown in my skin, bending over me, his eyes melting with love. My heart dissolved into compassion as his arms reached out, his hands scooped underneath my back, and his entire body lifted me up and up as he stretched his neck and craned his neck back with the broadest smile I'd ever seen. Baby-me chortled and giggled. Me watching my father smiled in response to his wide joyous grin.

My father loved me, I marvelled.

FLIP.

I stood in the doorway. The front doorway. A car was driving away. I knew this scene. I'd replayed it repeatedly in my mind for years until the day I turned fourteen when I'd clamped it. For years, I'd trained my mind to forget hurts, to shove wounding memories into that cavern, and lock it up. I'd rammed my emotions into a bricked-up box, but sometimes the memories tried to get out when I'd unlock the cavern to put new awful memories in there or when emotions leaked out. But by age fourteen, I achieved absolute control of my mind, and I'd forgotten that scene.

Until now.

Relief buckled my knees as I realized I was free, finally, at last, forever free of the burden of having to protect myself from bad memories and emotions that betrayed my hurts.

So many hurts.

The triplets let me know in this existence's alien way that I wasn't alone and I needed to continue my life review. Acceptance, pleasurable and bright, saturated my being, and I squinted at three-year-old me standing in the doorway, her hair a waterfall of blue-black, her mouth an open scream as a car drove away. I spotted the blurry profile of the man steering the car down the street, jamming the accelerator, as the wheels screeched their resentment against the asphalt. Tears flowed down his cheeks. I knew this because I felt his pain. So much pain. Grief and fear and guilt and a sense of being unequal to the task.

What task?

Instantly, the answer came: The task of living with his successful wife and raising a girl child with her half-sisters. He didn't want to be the father his parents were to him. Love leaked out of me as Bailey's hand stroked upwards to grasp my shoulder. At the same moment, I felt and saw Mom clamp three-year-old me's shoulder to shut off the screaming. Crying, gasping, choking on tears, the screams to "not go" faded. Salt flowed out of my eyes, and I wondered how.

"Compassion brings out all the senses," Bailey replied.

Mom twisted girl-me around, leaned in, and declared, "I'm going to cut your hair. No girl of mine is going to have long hair. Especially long black hair. And we'll have to do something about your skin." Her fingers dug into my shoulder, and she yanked me out of the doorway. In the same moment, I experienced betrayal eating her heart. She equated brown skin, even subtle shadings, with betrayal. I suddenly understood all those attempts to erase the golden-brown cast of my white skin were to erase the reminders of her husband leaving her.

I wept for her.

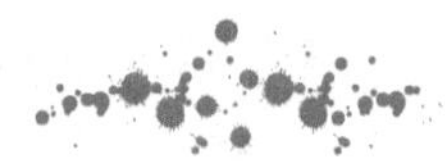

FLIP.

Sally was pushing me on a swing. I was yelling, "Higher!" Sally's impatience oozed into me as I watched this scene, another one I had no memory of. I heard her thoughts. She'd wanted to hang out with her friends and a particular boy she had an almighty crush on. I giggled at the thought of Sally crushing on a boy. I only remembered her as keeping her distance, disdaining men, and backing up Mom on that. Her yearning vibrated out of her and set up a harmony in my heart as I watched her pushing me on the swing so high that I flew off. She yelled at me as I landed spread-eagled on my back. I felt the pain, the air expelling from girl-child me's lungs, and fear lurching up as I couldn't breathe for a second.

Sally yelled, "That's what you get for being so demanding!" Hurt flowed in with air as breath returned to girl-child me and current, transparent me watching.

This was the moment I stopped admiring Sally and following her around like a puppy dog. The remembered knowledge hit me.

Sally canted her slim wrist to check her slim gold-band watch, her skin sun-avoidant white. She frowned and wailed, "I'm missing it all!" She huffed, "And it's all your fault. If you hadn't been born, my father wouldn't have left! My step-father wouldn't have left! It's all your doing that I don't even get to have a boyfriend. I've missed it because of you!" I began to cry. "Oh stop sniffling. You have nothing to cry over. I do!" She poked at her chest repeatedly, glared at me lying on the ground, and stormed off.

Girl-child me choked back tears. Deflected pain and incomprehension mingled in girl-me's hurt. Compassion filled my being.

FLIP.

I entered another postcard, and another, and another. My life review fluttered past, each individual scene as present and slow-moving as real life, yet the whole of it flying by in a second. I blinked, and we were standing back in Flower Power Track.

Attar of roses waltzed with daisies into the distance, in a peculiar sensory medley. A hidden stream gurgled nearby, its scent of icy water refreshing me. Greeter trotted up to me, tail wagging. *What am I seeing with, smelling with, hearing with?* I wondered. *How do senses work without a physical body?*

"You'll find out," Bailey said. "But for now, it's time to go." Her hand dropped from my back, and the orb absorbed it. She and Blake walked on my right side and Blair on my left. I glanced to one and the other and braked. Their orb shapes were transforming into human shapes. *Would I finally see what gender they are?*

"Don't count on it," Blair retorted. "Remember how we told you that where we came from and where you're going there is no more gender unlike on Earth? You get to a certain point in your journey, and you realize gender is only needed on Earth but not where we're going now on the other side of the Barrier. Our essences, the core of who we really are, have no gender. We are no longer bound, limited, constrained, identified by gender—or any label."

"God, what a relief!" Blake erupted. "Humans are the worst in making multiple labels to stick on people!"

Bailey shook her head. To me, they looked, felt, sounded female. I had to give them gender pronouns. I couldn't understand why pronouns had become so important the last few years; to my horror, I was now using the vernacular. I sighed.

"Don't worry about it," Blake whispered, her communication floating from my far right side right into my thoughts as if no distance separated us at all.

I stopped thinking about the wretched subject and refocused on my destination as we strolled through daisies, gerberas, roses, chrysanthemums, and so many other flowers, their colours fountaining photons of many hues. Pinks and blues and oranges and the deepest blood reds with silver accents.

A mountain appeared ahead. I halted. There'd been no mountain before.

"Only those prepared to cross the Barrier see the mountain. It's a metaphor for reaching the summit of your journey through the Expanse."

Greeter trotted up to me, nudged me forward, and I began walking again with my right hand stroking Greeter's encouraging back.

"Will Greeter come with us?" I asked. I felt like I could face the mountain and what it hid with Greeter by my side.

"Only to the Barrier," said Bailey.

"But don't worry," chirped Blake. "Calico is on the other side!"

"Calico?"

Blair said, "You'll see."

Blake giggled. "You'll hear Calico first, even before you reach the Barrier's other side."

A man, or what resembled a man, promenaded down the mountain. His white robe's hem dragged on the ground like a train, and its long bell sleeves and skirt fluttered. Suddenly, he stood in front of us.

"Who are you?" I asked, astonished to hear myself think-ask such a bold question.

"I'm an elder," he replied. "Not a man as you conceive it. But I'll grant you the use of the male pronoun...for now," he condescended with compassion. I reeled at the mixing attitudes that normally don't belong together.

Bailey said, "We're bringing her across the Barrier."

The elder nodded. He looked at me. "Are you ready to return to Earth?"

"What?!" I gasped, horrified at the thought. *Hadn't they said I couldn't return? I can't come alive again? No. I refuse to re-enter that life.* I erupted. "No, I don't want to return to Earth. I want to cross that Barrier to that place, whatever it is, where my soul family came from!" I thrust an errant hope—the hope for a second chance—down.

Bailey said, "She's not ready."

Blair said, "She will be, and we're going to be with her every step of the way."

"Never!" I retorted. *Second chances don't exist! But I do because I think.*

Blake dug me in the ribs, yet not ribs, but like a ripple jarring my atoms within my magnetic field. So strange. I comprehended yet couldn't explain it to myself. I faced her and frowned. She smiled back. I saw her entire face. But before I could speak, we were walking up the mountain towards the other side where the white noise radiated. Greeter kept pace beside me, supporting my hand.

Behind it and in front of it and above it and through it shone the light that elicited yearning in me to be with it. I arrested my steps. This light had been present during much of my new existence. Whether glaring or faint, that light had shone through the Distortans, always keeping me company, watching over me. My jaw dropped. The others waited for me, as if they knew what had happened. Of course, they did. They can read my thoughts. I began walking again, in awe that that light had stayed with me, whether I liked it or hated it. Greeter and I caught up to my soul family and the elder, and we continued on our journey up the mountain towards the Barrier.

We crested the mountain.

The Barrier buzzed and breathed on us with an unfamiliar intensity. Stronger than a spotlight, noisier than a Boeing 747 roaring overhead, quieter than a shadow, and sparking like a static electricity ball, it welcomed and confronted me.

"Beyond this point, there is no return," Bailey said quietly, her tone serious as she looked down at my upturned face. I saw her face for the first time. I turned my head and looked at Blair. I knew then that they were neither he nor she. Yet I couldn't divest myself of thinking of them as she. I shrugged off that problem.

"I don't want to return," I stated baldly, staring right at the elder who was leading us. He turned to face me and smiled. "You will." And then he walked into the white noise light.

My soul family followed, pulling me along with them like a magnet. Trepidation interrupted my eager steps. *What will greet me on the other side?* Greeter stopped, reversed to move behind my legs, and nudged me forward.

The Barrier gusted and obliterated my vision.

Photons of pure energy enfolded me. Love embraced and shepherded me through the white noise and into its light. Breath, as quiet as the softest whisper, infused my being with acceptance and compassion and the knowledge I was okay. I sobbed; all my pain and grief and anger and bitterness and guilt and shame blasted out of me on the trails of my tears.

Joy rushed in to fill the void.

The breath released me as I moved through the white light with my trio soul family, all unknowing of what awaited me.

The moment of my death had ended.

My life had begun.

Meow.

I gasped.

Thank you for reading this book.

If you enjoyed this tale, please encourage your friends, family,

associates, neighbours, heck, anyone, to buy a copy or request a

copy at their library so that they can enjoy it, too!

Look for books two and three of *The Q'Zam'Ta Trilogy* coming in the

next few years!

Find more information at

https://jeejeebhoy.ca

or at

https://concussionisbraininjury.ca

Turn the page for exclusive access to the

first chapters of three of my novels.

Aban's Accension

1

THE DREAM

A black sink. That's her first thought. A black sink. She squints down. The blackness is moving softly, its edges . . . there are no edges. A ping of fear rises in her, then settles softly back into simple observation. The empty deep swirls beneath her. She is hanging over and in it, its inky fluidic space sucking out the light from around her, vacuuming away all hope. Motion catches her eye to the left and behind her. She moves her eyeballs left and sees two creamy, ribbed things undulating toward her, slowly. Their blurred triangular shapes swim in a straight line. A second couple hoves into view: two by two they come. Maggots. She flickers her feet, trying to rise, to get out of their way, but she's stuck, gripped by an unknown force and the niggling thought of, does she really want

259

to move? Aren't they fascinating, these effervescent couples with their soft bodies and hypnotic movement. She stops struggling.

The line is long now stretching into the unseen distance, growing like a scarf flying out of a magician's pocket. She's not sure if the line of pairs is above her or in front of her. Her eyes watch them while her mind disengages. It is so easy to disengage, to see them as having nothing to do with her. They're just maggots swimming by. The void beneath her feet does not exist.

They turn.

The front of the line has now gone way past her on her right, and so when they turn, they are on her front and right flanks. She doesn't like that. Her mind re-engages. She can no longer pretend that they have nothing to do with her. She wriggles; she flaps her feet; she stretches her neck, arches her head back. But it's hard to resist this formless place. Fear rises in her throat.

She wakes up.

And finds herself struggling with her sweat-dampened sheets, the bottom one all wrinkled, the top one holding her down, pinning her arms to her sides. Panic grips her until she wakes up enough to relax and release herself from the tight top sheet.

Her chest rises and drops heavily, up and down, up and down. Gradually, her hearing returns, her sight broadens. She hears: the cicadas singing outside in the sultry air. She feels: the air inside her bedroom sitting on her like a wet fleece with no breeze blowing in through the open window to bring relief.

She jumps out of bed to fill her mind with the busyness of brushing teeth and putting on her multi-pocketed, baggy army pants and favourite T-shirt proclaiming "The Secret is My Birthright."

Time and Space

Chapter 1

THE SNATCH

FORTY. Tomorrow, I will be forty. That number echoes in my footsteps as I walk the familiar beat to work.

Time.

That's my name, and ... where did the time go? When did I get to forty? What does it mean?

Beat, beat, beat: my footsteps rap along the sidewalk in time to the music pumping into my ears from my iPod touch. My footsteps distract me. But only for a moment. I think: at my age, my mother still had not had me. That's why my mother and father had called me "Time."

"It was about time your mother got pregnant," my father would say often during post-Sunday-dinner coffee, as he leaned back in his worn armchair lighting his pipe.

"And it was about time you got out. You sat in there and sat in there and would not come out," my mother would retort to me.

"So we called you 'Time'," Father would say. Then he would end the story with: "Seemed logical."

"Seemed appropriate," Mother would counter as Father finally managed to pull a draw from his pipe and emit three puffs.

What a horrid name, I think, as I turn the corner onto Queen. Today, it's made me obsessed with time and with turning forty. I see a people-stuffed streetcar trundle by, and I sigh. It's been awhile since I gave up trying to catch the streetcar to work and reluctantly woke up earlier to get there on foot.

Peggy and Sue have this big birthday lunch planned for me tomorrow at our favourite restaurant. And the boss has generously— I roll my eyes at "generously"—given me two hours off so we can take our time. The whole thing is surreal.

Bzzzttt.

I take my iPod touch out of my skirt pocket and look at it. The screen is dark, and I press the Home button. No notifications. I turn it this way and that to find what created that strange noise. It seems okay. I shrug, slip it back into my pocket, and continue walking along my route.

The morning sun is slanting sharply along the sidewalk in front of me, toward me, pointing at me, that old woman turning forty. I want to hide from its edgy light, but no point in crossing the street into the shadowed sidewalk. I'll only have to cross back again. I hate walking.

Voices interrupt my thoughts, and I glance into a garishly-painted alley and think: Ford Nation has obviously missed this place. But perhaps there's so much graffiti in Queen West alleys, it's worn out Mayor Ford and his fans before they could erase it all. But there's no one loitering or walking in the alley, only solitary people like me hustling along Queen Street, coffee cups in hand. Suddenly, I stop. I look at my empty hand: I forgot to get my morning café latté, no whip, soya milk, half-sweet, grandé. I think of retracing my steps, but then I'll be late, and the boss doesn't like tardiness. He gets in a snit if I'm even one minute late. My feet resume walking.

And my thoughts resume churning.

At my age, my parents had been married twenty years. It would be another five before I was born. They'd both died a decade ago. I have no sisters or brothers. And since both my parents were only children, I had no immediate cousins. As a child, I met these strange adults my parents called "distant cousins" on special occasions like weddings, adults who embraced me in powder and perfume, exclaimed over how much I'd grown, making me squirm. But I haven't seen them since the funeral.

The last funeral.

I've been alone in the world for ten years, yet until today I hadn't dwelled on it, hadn't felt alone. I live in the house my parents lived in. I've been working at the same kind of job since I graduated from university with my English Lit degree and went right into a temping agency. Father tried to get me to think bigger, but what was I good for? I'm bad at math. Numbers confuse me. And science is gibberish. Only eggheads do science anyway. But then who'd want an English grad? I thrust away a stray memory of an interview with ... I can't even remember now. Father had said I'd sabotaged it; Mother had said never mind, I was born to type. And so type I did and have until this day. I thought it'd be temporary until I found my feet. Yet there they are, my feet, attached to the bottom of my legs, and they're taking me to my admin assistant job as they do every weekday.

"Her."

I hear a word faintly from ahead of me but ignore it. I am thinking about my bosses. I had a few different bosses at several different companies in the early days. Every time I landed a new job, I'd think: this time I'll have a better boss. This time he—or she will treat me like a person with a mind. But they're all the same. They boss you around, treat you like you can't think, dismiss your suggestions unless it's about what to get their spouse for their birthday or how to sort their endless paperwork. I stopped thinking for myself. I stopped caring about having someone else think for me. It's been a long time since I've used my brain independently. And so why do I care today? Why does it bother me now? I shake my head. I've been working at the same company, for the same boss, since two years before Mother and Father died. Father was glad I'd landed a job at a prestigious firm—if I had to be an admin assistant. Mother was glad whatever I did.

I think about Peggy and Sue. They work in the same pool area as I do. Each has her own boss, but our bosses all report to the same Director. Peggy and Sue welcomed me on my first day there, took me out to lunch, showed me the ropes. We've perfected the art of doing as little as possible while looking like we're typing all the time. Typing and emailing and phoning and filing. And organizing the bosses. Technology is great. I hate science, I hate computers—I won't have one at home—but I've learnt how to manipulate them at work so that the boss thinks I work hard when in fact it's the computer. He knows less about the tedious machines than I do, and it's so easy to hoodwink him.

Every month, Peggy and Sue and I go out to a new restaurant for dinner, one that Toronto Life recommends. We won't go for anything rated less than three stars. Sometimes we'll go to a show afterwards, something new from Broadway. Every Saturday I go to the library and borrow my week's worth of books. I often borrow books I've read two or four times because it's becoming harder to find new ones that interest me. And I won't buy books. It's not that I don't have the money, but that I want to support Toronto's great library system. Still, cutbacks may force me to buy books. I make a face at the thought. I used to like going to Abelard's or Britnell's, but a Starbucks claimed Britnell's elegant bookstore ages ago, and Abelard's has gone online. I hate the Internet and the endless emails too. I'm not going online to buy books or anything else. And the big chains feel impersonal every time I walk into them, which I haven't for awhile. They're not real bookstores. At least the librarian, when she's there, knows me and knows what I like in books. I smile as I remember last week's conversation when I told her I was turning forty. She'd sympathized and whispered that she'd find me some books about turning forty. At least books remain the same through time: solid, reliable, always there.

Peggy bought an e-reader a month ago, and daily, she tries to have me read it. But ebooks aren't real, aren't solid. They won't last, not like the hard covers I read with their sturdy covers and strong pages. E-readers will change because computers always do, and her ebooks will be gone. Ebooks are a fad, fuelled by those egghead science geeks. I think again about the librarian's promise and pick up my pace in anticipation of my weekly library trip and of those books she'd promised me and of snuggling down Sunday morning after my weekly waffles with a new book. I always begin reading my weekly book borrowings on Sundays. Each day of the week, each day of my life has its own routine—except for tomorrow. At least by Sunday, my fortieth will be a new, fading memory.

"Get ready."

The menacing voice interrupts my thoughts. The hair on my arms and the back of my neck stand to attention. I focus on the people hurrying to work ahead of me, each one alone. One of them must be talking into his Bluetooth, I tell my upright hairs.- I hate this intrusion of technology into our world. I take my iPod touch out, crank the volume up, and keep it in my hand. Forty. I'm going to be forty, and there's nothing I can do about it. I cross another graffiti-strewn alleyway and yearn for my latté.

Suddenly.

Hands grab my shoulders, my arms, my waist. They twist my skirt up. A faint thuck-thuck sounds as my iPod touch clatters to the concrete from my shot-open hand. Shock silences my scream and freezes my arms and legs. The foreign hands drag me down the alleyway. Too late, my vocal chords vibrate, for we're not in the alleyway anymore. We're in a white place where the white walls hum into the space.

I scream.

I thrash.

The white walls wash into the space to vacuum the sound out of my throat.

The hands release me, and I stumble to the luminous floor.

The hands' owners step around me from behind to stand in front of me. I blink and scramble up and see three skinny twenty-something boys with double-espresso-latté-coloured skin smirking at me, their necks sticking up from skin-hugging white suits that cover everything but their heads and chestnut hair. They look identical. Yet as my eyes adjust to this bright place with its strange soughing and electric smell, I see they're not. One has a big nose; one a small one. One has cupid-bow lips; one a straight line. One has long lashes; one has thick brows.

They shove me backward, and a seat edge grabs my legs. I sit down hard. One reaches toward the wall closest to him and plucks out a limp piece of white fabric that hadn't been there before. Air catches in my throat. He throws it at me and tells me to put it on.

I almost drop it but make myself hold on. I look around and cannot see a door. They cackle.

"No escape," says one.

"No door you can find," says another.

They laugh harder. They're right. I see no door, no way out. I examine the limp fabric, and abruptly it's a suit hanging from my hands. I drop it in horror. They bend double, they're laughing so hard. My heart beats rapidly against my ribs. I gulp for air. I can't escape, and I dare not disobey. I pick up the suit with my right forefinger and thumb and eye it warily, trying to control my breathing. It doesn't change; it simply hangs from my finger and thumb. I take a firmer grip on it and nothing happens. I must do what they say. I inspect it and find its feet.

One stops laughing long enough to bark, "Put it on!"

I jerk. I glance up at him and immediately back to the suit. I don't know whether to keep my shoes on or not and then decide it's their stuff, what do I care if the heels of my pumps ruin it. I don't want to take them off. I let the suit fall out of my hand, button up my cardigan, retrieve the suit from the floor, find the legs of it, and insert my feet, right foot first. My shoe gets caught in the stretchy, shiny fabric, and I struggle.

They stop laughing and watch me maliciously.

I try again. Suddenly the right leg of the suit opens up and my foot slides down easily into the foot of the suit. I squeak but duplicate the movement with my left foot in its shoe. I stand up and start to pull the suit up. It's like panty hose, and my skirt's bulk is bigger than the suit. I try to stuff it in because I'm not taking my skirt off. As I stuff one section in to one leg, another section flops back out. The boys crack up, but thankfully the walls absorb the highest pitch of their cackles. I persevere, pushing more skirt into each leg of the suit, trying not to expose the ugly topside of my panty hose. The suit bulges unattractively; lumps and bumps sprout wherever I've been able to shove in my skirt. Finally I have the suit pulled up to my waist, and I'm exhausted. I pause to catch my breath. And I look down at the results of my effort. My skirt in the suit is like a muffin top and feels just as bloated.

The suit morphs.

The lumps and bumps disappear.

My skirt is sucked down into the legs.

I suck in air, suck in air. I scream and scream and scream. I cannot hear myself. I cannot even feel the screams in my throat. But I can't close my mouth or stop exhaling through my vocal chords. I want this awful suit off.

Suddenly I'm sitting down, the wind blown out of me.

One boy growls in to my face, "Finish."

I wipe my face from forehead to chin, stand up, and pull on the arms and shrug into the shoulders of the suit. I reach for the zipper to close the front, but there's no zipper, no buttons, no Velcro. I frown at this puzzle. I hear a choked guffaw and look up. They say nothing; they are too entertained by my perturbation. When I look back down to find some way to close the suit, I see the front edges of the suit moving toward each other, fusing, leaving no seam, making the suit into one fabric. My chest heaves hysterically.

"Watch."

I look up at the boys. They step back, and in sync, their upper eyelids drop slowly, deliberately, stay shut for shorter than a second but longer than a normal blink, then as they open, out of the back of the boys' suits arise hoods that pull over their heads, cover their faces, and fuse with their necklines so that the white fabric becomes one from their feet to their heads. Yet I can see the surfaces and edges of their faces clearly. My heaves turn into quick shallow breaths. One blinks again, that same slow blink. I feel something wispy cover my face. I reach up to touch my cheeks. I don't feel my skin. I feel something soft yet not there, something that prickles and lets my fingers sink into it so that I can feel the edges of my cheekbones. I see clearly, as if nothing is covering me, yet I know I'm as covered as they are. My lungs don't want to work anymore, my heart pounds to get out of its rib cage, and I become dizzy.

"Sit down."

He doesn't have to order me because my swimming senses have sat me down already. I can't breathe, and panic rules. From somewhere rises the thought: I must gain control of my breathing. I reach into my memory back to a friend during university who'd taught me deep breathing. I hear her instructions and obey. My breathing fights me, and I fight it. And as I struggle to gain control, one of the boys blinks that blink again, staring at me much like a cat at a mouse, and a shimmer appears before me and then is gone. They look at each other, laugh out loud, and start dancing. Or at least, I think that's what they're doing. It vaguely reminds me of football players celebrating a goal, no, a touchdown. Knees rising up to chests, arms flailing, heads chucking like chickens out of rhythm. I forget all about my breathing, for their contortions are too weird. This place is too weird. I must be in a dream, caught in a nightmare, thinking too much about my fortieth. I stare hard at the white walls, willing them to disappear and become the soft tangerine walls of my bedroom.

And that's when I notice that the walls don't actually end in corners. They're not round either. School-era geometry floats back into my memory from the past, and I think: maybe this is what the inside of an ellipse looks like. Smooth, never ending, yet beautiful as if it could cut the wind, creating no wave to show it's been there. Seats emerge from the walls here and there. On the other side of the dancing boys, the wall coruscates as if it's about to display something.

The boys stop and leer at me, their grins self-satisfied. They nod at each other, and I feel a faint lurch. And then I have the oddest sensation. I feel like I'm moving yet not moving. I feel like my thoughts are with me then behind me. I feel like every cell, no, every molecule is forming and dissolving and reforming in me. I feel as if the suit is the only thing holding me together. The walls and the boys become semi-transparent, as if every other molecule in them has disappeared. I want to rub my eyes but cannot move. I want to yell for help, even though there's no point, but cannot open my mouth. I want to run, but I'm fixated like a cobra's victim.

My boss is going to be pissed. Peggy and Sue won't have anyone to take to my fortieth birthday lunch.

She

chapter one

THERE WAS ONCE A WOMAN

TIRES HISS AGAINST the road. A gentle bump bump at high speed wakes her up. She stretches against the confines of the seat belt and blinks open her eyes. Pitch night engulfs the car. The glowing numbers on the dashboard clock draw her eyes: 12:54.

"Wow, I can't believe the time." She yawns, "Did I really sleep that long? I can't believe it's that late. Did we run into heavy traffic? That sucks. I thought leaving so late in the evening, we'd miss the Toronto-bound traffic. I guess not, eh?" She smiles at the driver, but he looks stoically ahead. Her eyes drift past the clock again and suddenly widen. "Hey! Do you know what time it is? It's almost summer solstice time. How cool is that, being out in the country at the exact hour?" Still no response.

Sighing, she looks out her window and frowns. Not only are they late, but for that matter, where are they? This country road doesn't look like Highway 10. Pickets of a prim wooden fence fly by, the ground at its feet rising into view and disappearing. The fields beyond vacuum the meagre starlight, and the car's beams cannot penetrate into their depths. She leans toward her window and cranes her neck to look up at the sky. It's a moving charcoal surface with white glitter winking here and there. The moon is nowhere in sight.

She asks him as she continues to stare out the window, "Where are we?"

"I thought we'd take a shortcut."

"Meaning you don't know," she laughs. He smiles faintly as he continues to stare straight ahead, his hands resting in the ten to two position on the leather grey steering wheel of their car. The amber glow of the dashboard lights up the front of his face like some sort of eerie jack-o-lantern. She watches him for a moment.

"Well, I guess we're somewhere in the country. Traffic must've been bad, eh?"

He shrugs one shoulder. She sighs. She's fully awake now and sharing space with a statue.

"I guess it wasn't so bad for you that I dozed off, eh? Silence is golden and all that," she grins. "Well, I can be silent … sometimes." She chuckles and then stretches again. "That nap did me good. I feel so awake now and refreshed. I'm raring to go, and I can't wait till tomorrow, I mean today. I have all these song ideas bouncing around in my head. This was a great idea of yours, going on this road trip, it's got me going again, and I love visiting those cute Ontario towns." She twists round to the left to check out the back seat, to make sure all the goodies they bought are still there. Pies and jugs of maple syrup sit side by side with pints of fresh Bing cherries, her favourite. She untwists herself and settles back in her seat. She watches the hypnotic yellow line as it snakes ahead.

"I can't wait to dive into those cherries. They were my favourite fruit growing up. Did I ever tell you that? I used to look forward to the end of school because that's when Grandmother would buy them. And I'd make a big mess, and she'd get so mad." She laughs at the memory. "Now I can make as big a mess as I want." She falls silent for a moment. "I was thinking: they're too good to make pies with. I'd rather eat them fresh like that, but it's almost strawberry season. Maybe we can go up to Andrew's Scenic Acres and pick some berries. I'm in the mood for making strawberry rhubarb pies or maybe mixed berry pies if the blueberries and raspberries are out too. We have enough room in that chest freezer, I'm sure. I gave it a big cleanout the other day. What do you think?" she asks rhetorically. She savours the thought of a strawberry rhubarb pie with crumble topping. Those are always a hit. And they freeze so well. She can almost smell them baking and taste their sweet tartness. She smiles; her eyes focus on the road again.

She looks past the yellow line, past the boundaries of light the car beams create, into the darkness coming toward them, a forest on the right. The hairs on the back of her neck lift up; her stomach flutters.

"Uh, where are we really?" she asks as she sits up straight, tensing her body. He stays silent.

Her nerves feel taut. She urges, "We need to stop and turn around. Now, if you don't mind."

The car doesn't slow down. His eyes don't flick up to the rearview mirror or down to the speedometer.

Her chest starts to contract. "Look, I know you're all into exploring the side roads, but this doesn't feel safe, and it's really really late. Let's drive home on a faster road. Let's turn around and go to Highway 10."

He says nothing.

"Could you please just stop the car, turn around, and go back to Highway 10."

"We're fine." He stretches the word out. "Stop being so paranoid."

"I'm not being paranoid."

"You are," he replies. The slight put-down in his voice works. She feels silly. They're just trees.

Those trees are beside them; ahead their mates on the left loom. They fill the front windshield more and more. It's 12:56 a.m. She wants to be the one in the driver's seat badly; instead she's being driven inexorably toward the forest, where starlight cannot penetrate. She shifts her gaze back down to the road, to the familiar yellow ribbon and the dusty edges of the asphalt where road meets grass. But then the edges vanish into the shadows cast by the trees standing shoulder to shoulder, leafy branch merging into leafy branch, creating a light-sucking toothy maw. She feels the air hold its breath. Her breathing speeds up. His body remains still.

The trees close in on the other side, only a sliver of rectangular sky between the two forests breaks their starless black.

She leans toward him, her thick, shingled hair falling against her cheek, trying to get away from the trees on her right, jostling his arm.

"What are you doing?" he snaps at her.

"Can't you move closer to the yellow line?"

In response, he steers toward the right.

"Stop it!" She struggles to breathe evenly.

"I'll stop it when you stop being silly."

She leans forward to look up through the windshield, her hair gleaming in the reflected dashboard light, searching for that sliver of glittering sky, looking for the one opening in the lightless claustrophobia without.

"Would you get a hold of yourself. We're fine. Don't worry." He tries to nudge her away with his elbow, but she resists.

She cannot move back to the upright position; she just cannot separate herself from him. She looks ahead, focusing on the end of the forest, even though she cannot see it, where the fields re-emerge beyond the headlights, willing them to arrive there as fast as possible. But their speed drops to 70 kilometres per hour. She begins to see the individual trees, the shrubs sticking up among them, the rocks laying among their bases. The sky is morphing, undulating, changing degrees of grey-black shades. Clouds are rolling in.

"Why are you slowing down?"

He doesn't answer. "Of course not, why need he?" she thinks angrily. He's proving his point. He doesn't usually treat her this contemptuously. Her anger fades into loneliness as memories arise of how he used to always treat her with consideration and respect and love. She remembers the first time they shopped together, how he had insisted on carrying the grocery bags. Or how when she had lost her keys for the umpteenth time and was becoming mighty annoyed about it, he'd used his carefully modulated voice to calm her and focus her memory on those keys. Within minutes she'd found them. But lately, ever since his annual spring camping trip up near the Bruce Trail with his buddies, he's become moody. Grim. Many, many days, he has been his old cheerful self, making her laugh so hard that she snorts water out her nose, or he has run errands by himself instead of interrupting one of her songwriting sessions. But on this weekend's road trip, he'd once again become serious, become watchful of her as darkness inhabited his face. She doesn't understand this change in him and towards her. It's like he's decided that she has to prove her worth over and over again.

She wants to grab that wheel and take back control. But she can't. She's in his hands.

Sinking down into the shadow of her seat, still leaning on him, her eyes reach the level of the clock. It flips to 12:57 a.m.

The landscape flashes sickly neon green. The car heels to the left as a wind screams out of the forest like a ghastly, whirling Northern light, and slams into its right side then dances up on to the hood, on to the roof, down beside them. The car's back fishtails out. She squeezes her eyes and senses the car turn one way then the other. Even through her closed eyelids, she senses the chartreuse-yellow lightning inside the whirlwind. She squeezes her eyes tighter until they hurt. They're speeding up; they're driving to the left; they slow. She opens her eyes to see him manhandling the steering wheel until they're aiming straight down the road again, but the wind, with its ever-changing neon-green-bottom border, with its dancing gold-green veins, streaks alongside and in front of them. They can't outrun it. He presses the accelerator, trying anyway, as she clings to his right arm, as she puts her head between her own arms. Glass cracks in front of her. The cracks glow green. She scoots closer to him and squeezes her eyes so tight, she sees red. Cracks fracture her side window, and she can't help opening her eyes to look toward the sound. Air moves all around her, pushing at her, raising the hair on her arms, throwing up the hair on her head, fluttering her T-shirt, turning her skin sickly green. Suddenly she sees nothing. She closes and opens her eyes and still sees nothing. Panic attacks her. And then they shoot out of the trees and are between open fields. She sees again. Sobs rack her, and she can't stop them.

"There's a patrol up ahead. I have to pull over," he says.

Her sobs quit suddenly. She sits up, wipes her eyes, smoothes her hair off her face, straightens her Black Sabbath T-shirt. The car rumbles off the road to the gravel shoulder and crunches to a stop. He pushes the window button and his window hums down. A policeman with a bright wand in his right hand and a reflective vest walks toward them; the officer leans in, his eyes keen on them. She returns his look emotionless.

"Good evening sir, ma'am. How are you this morning?"

"We're fine officer. I wasn't speeding."

"No, you weren't sir. That's not why I pulled you over. We're the Akaesman patrol."

"The what?"

"Will you step out of the car sir, ma'am. We need to ask you a few questions."

She obeys. Or tries to. All her muscles seem to have seized up; she looks down puzzled, feeling old. Using her hands and her arms as leverage, she turns herself towards the open door, puts her feet on the ground, stands up, and leans on the open car door, apperceiving her balance, before straightening her flared black jeans and walking over to where the policeman has joined a woman standing a metre or so in front of what looks like the back of a white ambulance sitting next to the black and white police car.

"Did you drive through the forest sir?" the policeman asks him.

"Yes."

"Did anything happen?"

"Like what?"

"You tell me sir."

Slowly he shakes his head.

The policeman stares at him for a few seconds, and then turns to her.

"You ma'am. How are you feeling?"

She considers that for a moment. Shocked maybe.

The woman who had been standing there watching them walks over to her, while snapping on blue nitrile gloves. She takes a penlight out of her pocket and flashes it in her eyes. She flinches. The woman is unfazed. She reaches round and lightly squeezes her neck muscles, moving down to feel the top of her shoulders.

"Follow me."

She obeys.

"Please sit here," she gestures to the step at the back of the ambulance. From there, she can see the reflective letters on the side of the police car: "Akaesman Patrol. To Guard and Save." Weird.

She feels a cuff being fastened around her left arm, and then the rhythmic pump, pump as the woman inflates it. Air hisses out before the cuff is ripped off. A stethoscope is pressed against her chest and then her back. She finally looks at the woman as she straightens up and speaks to the policeman: "It's mild, but definitely."

He nods and faces her fiancé again.

"Sir, you did experience something back there, didn't you?"

She watches her fiancé stare back nonchalantly, but he's no match for an officer of the Akaesman Patrol.

"We might've."

"You did sir. I want to know what it was."

He told him all, even how she was whining about turning back.

"You should've listened to her sir. Stay here." He walks over to the patrol car, the gravel crunching under his dusty black boots. He opens the driver's door, gets in, and slams it shut.

They wait.

He gets out with a clipboard and walks over to her.

"OK ma'am, I'm sorry to have to tell you that you probably had a run-in with Akaesman. Now it doesn't look too serious, some sprains, but I must ask you to read this form and sign it. Then go see your GP tomorrow." He looks at his watch. "Today." He writes, his pen scratching the paper on the clipboard. Then he hands the clipboard over to her. The woman aims a flashlight at it, but it's too much to read. She must be tired, and so she pretends to read it. His finger extends into her view, pointing to where she should sign. She signs. He flips the page up and asks her to sign the copy. She signs and hands it back to him. He presses down on the clip handle and releases the top piece of paper. He hands it to her. She takes it, but he doesn't let go until she looks up at him.

"Go see your GP ma'am."

She nods.

He still doesn't let go. "See your GP, your family physician."

She looks up into his face and says, "I will."

He lets go. She carries the paper back to the car, where her door is still open. She gets in awkwardly and drops the paper on her lap, wondering why she has to see her family physician. She reaches back for the seat belt, and pain ratchets up her neck. She pauses and then turns her entire body right to get at the seat belt, pulls it toward herself, turns her entire body to the left, and stiffly aims for the seat belt clip. Click. She sits back, sighing. And waits, staring at her fiancé, yet not seeing him as he strides back to the car. She hears his door open, his booted foot twisting on the gravel, his jeans sliding against leather; she hears the slam of the door, the feel of the car softly rocking in response, the slither of the belt as it's pulled, the click of it going home, the key being turned, and the engine roaring excessively to life. They accelerate onto the asphalt, the wheels spitting small stones out, and drive for home.

Find links to all my novels and non-fiction at

https://books2read.com/ap/RJ6305/Shireen-Jeejeebhoy

ACKNOWLEDGEMENTS

A clash of ideas birthed this book. Back in 2019, I got fed up with Christians and the general population focusing on the Passion Play and crucifixion with no equivalent attention to the Resurrection—the event that made Christianity Christianity. To me, it's like humans preferred celebrating torture and death over renewed life.

My first attempt to right this wrong (in my mind) was to write the Resurrection equivalent to the Passion Play. I reread the four gospels' accounts, paying attention to their similarities and differences. I read books on the Resurrection and discussed it and my ideas with several people. I owe a big posthumous thank you to Pastor Duke Vipperman who recommended N.T. Wright's books, particularly Surprised by Hope; to Rev. Adrienne Clements for her insights and references; to Roger, who generously gave me a book on the Gospel of Mary and the Nag Hammadi; and to NaNoWriMo, who, though they got themselves into hot water last year, enable me to write books and plays.

Writing the play satisfied an itch, but then a trilogy introduced itself to my mind. A woman appeared, an older woman. I knew book one—this novel—began with her death, but when she told my mind how she intended to die, I objected. Vociferously. I didn't want to deal with the emotional heft of such a decision. Eventually making peace with her method of death, I wrote The Soul's Awakening in November 2021, and, initiated by the accountability Prolifiko's 7-Day Writing Sprints provided, I revised it in February 2022.

Then life intervened.

For two years, I didn't write any fiction; when 2024 arrived, I doubted I could anymore.

On a whim, I signed up for a virtual workshop Plottr was holding; then a summit week on writing and publishing held virtually. I'm so grateful to Plottr for holding these events and choosing Airmeet, an accessible platform as close-to-real-life as any virtual platform has reached. I'm ever so grateful to CJ Anaya, Troy Lambert, Maighan Hunt, and Kate Brown, who cheered me on in resurrecting my Resurrection trilogy. The Airmeet Lounge sessions with them invigorated me and gave me the courage to write fiction again. They also advised on genre and were a sounding board for my ideas.

Meanwhile, Bec Evans and Chris Smith of Breakthroughs and Blocks (formerly Prolifiko) restarted their 7-Day Writing Sprints through Substack. I jumped back in to kickstart revising *The Soul's Awakening* and outlining books two and three of *The Q'Zam'Ta Trilogy*. Theirs and the Sprint community's encouragement and accountability pushed me to meet my goals.

Thank you to Ann Benoit for reading the final version and her valuable insights, as usual. Ann has read almost all my manuscripts; her comments always help me polish my stories, and I enjoy our discussions very much.

Thank you to Neda for her feedback on my novel titles, and to Lim Wey Wen for helping me come up with the trilogy title after I'd spent weeks hemming and hawing over various incarnations. Her feedback gave me the confidence that Q'Zam'Ta was the right made-up word! The Aramaic word for resurrection is q'yam'ta, and zam is the Avesta word for Earth.

And last, but not least, thank you to my parents Khursheed and Olive Jeejeebhoy for inspiring me to put *The Soul's Awakening* on pre-sale in the Smashwords store, which I wouldn't otherwise have done.

I apologize to anyone my memory refuses to remind me about. Know that I'm grateful to every person I've spoken with about *The Soul's Awakening* and *The Q'Zam'Ta Trilogy*!

www.ingramcontent.com/pod-product-compliance
Lightning Source LLC
Chambersburg PA
CBHW051135190726
48290CB00006B/1863